THE
GREATEST OF THESE

TRUTH! the series: Book One

T. Randall Jones

Lvolution Books
Charlotte, North Carolina

The Greatest of These is a work of fiction. Names, characters, places and incidents either are the product of the author's imagination or are used fictitiously. Any resemblance to actual persons, living or dead, events, or locales is entirely coincidental.

Acknowledgments

For all that I have done, or ever will do that is good,
to God be the glory!

To Trevor,
Because: Love is… patient…

To the men of PowerHouse Project:

(Still) You inspired this story…your PROMISE, and the hope I have for you and for all you will be…

I pray that as you read these words, you will feel my heart. I used to say, 'I don't understand'; and now that I realize I don't have to, I do.

You don't have to be a pastor, or an entertainer, or a model, or an artist, or anything else that the world considers special… I celebrate that which gives you the *COURAGE* to be any and *EVERY* thing your heart tells you to be. I encourage you to BELIEVE in your unique power…because *WHO YOU ARE* is *ENOUGH* to change the world.

Namaste

Tia

.

A word from the Author…

WARNING: A small portion of this book contains specific references to abuse and / or sexual violence that may be difficult to read. I sincerely apologize to anyone who is caught off guard, hurt or offended by these passages. I promise I would not include them if I didn't feel very strongly as an artist that they are relevant to the character development and plot. If you wish to avoid reading them, these passages are marked *** well in advance, and then ### immediately after (so you don't miss too much).

This book, as well as the other novels in *TRUTH! the series*, also contains detailed accounts of actual sex, tastefully written, I'm told; and no, I have not marked those passages (Ya Nasty...). We're all grownups; or at least we should be... But if you are not, PUT THIS BOOK DOWN!!!

Oh, and sometimes there's some cussin'. See above...

And finally, there are references to scripture, including one or two interpretations that one might find, depending on one's raising, offensive, inaccurate, or occasionally, just plain blasphemous. (Hmm, what to say?)

TRUTH! the series is a collection of stories about, but not exclusively for, the LGBTQ Faith community. I am a Believer and an artist. I am not a pastor, and do not claim to be either a theologian or biblical scholar. The opinions, beliefs, and views expressed in this series are those held by the specific characters, not necessarily the by author.

With all that said, I do indeed hope that the characters, relationships and themes in these books inspire discussion. And I encourage you to mark the pages and reference them in your interactions with your book club members, partners, church family, friends, acquaintances; and when and wherever appropriate, your children. If you find any part of this book, or the others, encouraging or uplifting, or I dare to dream, worthy of passing on to someone else, then my prayers have been answered. I've found my purpose! I feel profoundly connected to each and every person who reads these stories... and GETS IT!

Thank you and God Bless!

Tia

PS - No really, it's been ten years!

The Greatest of These came to me as a dream. It was so vivid, and the characters so indelible, that I had to write it down. The books that followed, *Just Walk* and *Phoenix* were largely the result of a need to resolve many of the conditions established in book one. Folks needed to be made whole.

As time went on and it appeared as though the world was catching on: Gay marriage is commonplace; Transgender men and women are a staple of network television, and it's a crime to openly discriminate in most sectors of civilized society. I thought my work was done; and to be quite honest, books four, five and six felt...self-serving. Surely, I'd said enough. We've got basketball superstars and their (equally successful) wives to stand up to transphobia. Right?

Not exactly, because for every Zaya, Joshua, Liam, Alex or Jazz, there are still ten bullies. Trans women are still being murdered. For every me and mine, there are at least twice as many 'good parents' who simply don't understand that... they don't have to! LOVE is its own singular requirement. And it's still missing in swaths and droves around the world. So my work is not done yet; and if you're reading this, neither is yours. So, let's get back to it, shall we?

-T

PROLOGUE

"What's the matter?" Gabrielle rushed backstage as soon as she received the text from Kevin. It read simply, 'dressing room! hurry!' "You're not supposed to be in here," she whispered.

"Ah, that's not what the sign on the door says." He pulled her roughly toward him. "I just need a minute. You know I hate these things," he lied, referring to the opening of his latest play. Kissing her bare shoulder, he tossed her bag and wrap onto the sofa.

"You love these things. Someone's going to come looking for you. Don't you go on in three minutes?" Gabby remained unaffected but thought, "I did not fly seven hundred miles to be your fluffer (again), KJ!"

"We've got plenty of time. I need you, Gabby... Please..."

"Perhaps you should come home more often." She looked into his eyes and saw the desperation. She knew he loved her, had always loved her and their son, Ethan. She never imagined living such a ridiculous life – his secret wife. It seemed so foolish. She loved him, she understood. He was an artist! The theatre was his life, and he'd made his way in it the old fashion way, he'd earned it; even if the method was less than conventional. For the past eight years, he'd been living the role of a lifetime: Talented, twenty-something, semi-closeted - but very gay, small town boy turned headliner, struggling to live a private life, in the Big Apple. Initially, it was just to get the part; then it was to keep his standing as male lead / principal dancer. But there was always a reason to keep the lie going. Besides, that kind of 'real life' drama came naturally to Kevin. He was almost as beautiful as he was talented, and never minded working it to get the next job. Still, there were limits. He'd bat his long lashes at a casting director, and sit through a boring round of drinks with producers to present his script. They all thought he was just faithful, "but anything could happen… gay men are very fickle, you know…" Whatever the objective, he never actually strayed and always went home to her, eventually.

Gabby knew she was just as responsible for the charade as Kevin was. Putting her vows before her better judgment, she accepted and supported him completely. Gabby believed in Kevin's talent and had recognized, even warned him of, the trap he was walking into. On the other hand, she had trouble saying, "no" to him, and knew that things would be that way as long as she played along. She was frankly a little afraid of what would happen to their relationship, their marriage…her lifestyle, if she called an end to the game. Would he leave her if she demanded they be a regular family? She knew he'd have to. He couldn't function in the regular world. He was all about drama – literally, and he kept her entertained. The question remained whether she could continue to live half a life as his 'best supporting actress'. She wasn't foolish enough to think she'd ever be co-star. However reckless, or just plain sad, their situation was all too familiar to Gabby. She'd watched her mother play only bit parts in her father's life and ministry for decades. She'd accepted it as just something some women had to put up with. Gabby kept telling herself that it was 'no major sacrifice, really'. Their life in North Carolina was fabulous; her trips to New York made her the envy of all her friends, and the sex, when they had it, was…never boring. She reached to get a condom from her purse.

"I don't need it. This performance, my beloved, is all about you." He slid to the floor, pulling her down with grace only a trained dancer could display.

Gabby chuckled, thinking, "Of course! Let's make this all about me, because that will surely send me outta here looking like I just had sex. God forbid we just phone-in a good ole fashioned quickie! You want me flushed, biting my lips and

2

messing up my makeup! Selfish bastard!"

What Gabby didn't know was that Kevin did realize he was already asking too much of his wife. While, subconsciously, he was using her to relieve his opening night anxiety, he was deliberately, (and she'd kill him when she figured this out), using her to get into character. He wasn't about to treat her like a ho in the process. He just took for granted that she'd be appreciative of the gesture – his attempt to jumpstart their rare weekend together with a little adventure. Besides, he was good at that. Not by coincidence, he was almost as skilled (technically anyway) a lover as he was an entertainer; and as an entertainer he was great at everything.

Nevertheless, Kevin had yet to convince his wife that what he had in mind was worth wrinkling her dress. So Gabby slid only halfway down the wall, settling into that position her trainer used to punish her when she admitted to eating junk food. She could stay like that for at least twenty minutes before her thighs burst into flames. She could cross her legs and read a book like that for ten. She focused on a spot on the wall and cursed the man, "it must have been a man!" who invented stilettos.

Kevin stared up at her from his position on the couch. Disheveled, wearing a cheap cotton suit and synthetic, clip on tie, he even made 'down on his luck, out of work inventor, on the brink of success, but about to give up and drink himself to death' look hot and still convincing as a character! Gabby tried not to look at him and instead focused her energies on her pep-talk-to-self. "Damn him. Be strong, Gabby. It's just Kevin. You can do it. You can get up from this wall and walk back to your seat like nothing ever happened, your dignity intact. You do not have to be his…, his…whatever he wants you to be right now! Yes, I know it's been six weeks; but there's a principle at stake here! You wait for him all the time! He can wait for you through three acts and a shower!

3

That's less time than it took to do your hair! You can get your fix later, when he comes to you, in your suite at the Westin. He is not that irresistible. You can do this!"

"Come here." Yes, he was; and no, she could not.

Gabrielle, the Baptist preacher's daughter resigned herself to submit to her husband; and Gabby the educated, modern woman started to move, albeit slowly, remaining annoyed, uncooperative, and uncharacteristically belligerent. "You do know your dick is hanging out, don't you?"

He laughed out loud at her vulgarity. "Shut up and come here. Please?" Gabby continued her resistance and for a moment, Kevin actually thought he'd need to seek motivation elsewhere. The clock was ticking. Reading his thoughts, or perhaps a more visible indication of his waning enthusiasm, Gabby shifted ever so slightly, relaxing just enough that he could slide his hand up her skirt. "I see you're playing the victim today. That's okay; I don't need your help. Don't know why you're actin' like you don't love it; you don't have any panties on!" This revelation made her giggle and finally, showing her own bit of balance and grace, completely surrender her protest.

While his mouth was busy pleasing Gabby, Kevin's hands were busy pleasing himself, and Gabby wondered momentarily why he needed her help to masturbate. "It is after all, by definition, a solo sport."

"Kevin!" she gasped and tried not to scream. Quickly, before it was too late, she moved to return the favor. It was too late, and she was not surprised that he'd finished at precisely the same moment she did. She would surely die of shock if he ever did anything traditional, like kiss her, or allow her to reciprocate.

"Nope! Gotta go! My public awaits!" He lifted her off of him and onto the leather couch with one smooth motion. With another, he was on his feet and standing in front of the sink. He washed up quickly and splashed cold water on his face.

"Ahhh! Now I can face the world!" He held out his hand, she took it and he pulled her from the couch close to him. "Thank you. Will you wait up for me?"

She winked at him, hoping to conceal the empty feeling in the pit of her stomach. "You know I will; but do you mind if I stay and see the show?"

He smiled at her patience and devotion. "You know I'd be devastated if you didn't. Who did you bring?"

"Claire and Joy"

"Please tell them I said 'thanks for coming'". I'm looking forward to next weekend."

"Liar!"

"Uh, uh, uh, I am an actor!" He struck a pose and then relaxed. His face softened and she saw a hint of sadness, then the smile she adored. He kissed her softly and turned to the stage to wait for his cue. She watched him enter the scene as she had many times before, to thunderous applause.

"Break a leg." She whispered, when he was too far away to hear. She returned to his dressing room to compose herself. Looking in the mirror, she asked out loud, "how the hell did we get here?"

1

INTRODUCING: KEVIN JEROME RIVERS

New York City – 1986

"Tickets! I got tickets!" The scalper called out to passersby as they approached the theater door. Papa Bill loved giving those guys a hard time. He'd lived in Harlem most of his life and, if you asked him, everybody had a hustle. He winked at his grandson as he stopped walking to talk to the young man. "Do you fine folks need tickets, sir? Got three right behind the orchestra."

"This show's been sold out for months, where'd you get seats like these?" Bill was certain they must be stolen or fake.

"Um… I got 'em from a guy, you know, who works backstage."

Papa Bill shook his head. "No, I don't know any 'guy who works backstage'. How much you want for them?"

Kevin's grandmother interrupted her husband's interrogation. "Bill, leave that boy alone. Son, we already have tickets, but thank you."

"Enjoy the show, ma'am." The young man backed away, looking like he'd just been released from prison early.

Bill shook his head and laughed. "Baby, you know that fool stole those tickets! Why didn't you let me get 'em?"

"Because you don't know that."

"I'm just trying to teach my grandson a lesson. KJ, how do you think I know he was lying?"

Kevin shrugged his shoulders. "I don't know…because stage hands don't get orchestra seats?"

"Hey! That's pretty good!" Bill rubbed his grandson's head. "But you're wrong. I knew he was lyin' cuz his lips were moving!" Bill laughed at his own joke. Kevin and

Gladys laughed at Bill's silly expression.

Nana rolled her eyes and squeezed Kevin's hand. "KJ Honey, don't listen to that silly man. It's not our place to judge people or their motives."

"But he was lying, Gladys; and you know aint nothin' worse than a lie." Kevin shifted his attention back to his grandmother. He knew they weren't mad, so it didn't bother him to see them argue like this. It was kind of fun to watch. Papa Bill would always act like he was mad, and Nana was always right.

"Baby", Nana stopped and looked her grandson in the eyes to make sure he was paying attention. This time your grandfather is right. To tell a lie is just about the worst thing you can do. Lies hurt people, and you don't ever want to do that. But as bad as lying to someone is, Kevin Jerome, there is something worse." Gladys paused to see if he would come up with the answer. Kevin didn't know, so he just starred wide-eyed at his Nana. "The only thing worse than telling a lie is living one; because then you're not just lying to other people, but you're lying to yourself. Do you understand what I'm saying?"

Kevin thought this would be a very bad time to lie and say 'yes'. "No, ma'am, I don't really. How can I lie to myself?"

"The lie is in how you live, Baby. I know it doesn't make sense now, but it will one day. Grownups have to make choices about how they live that affect everyone around them. The wrong choice for you, when you know in your heart it's wrong, is wrong for everyone around you. Mm, mm, mm. A world of pain."

"Well, I'll never do that, Nana. I promise." Kevin still didn't understand. He just knew he wasn't about to disappoint is grandmother. He'd figure the rest out later.

Bill had been reading the playbill, waiting for the curtain to go up. He was still pretending to be annoyed about the scalper. "Would you two stop all that yappin'? The real worst thing you can do is make me miss a word of this show I paid all this money to see."

Gladys tapped her husband's hand and he reached for hers and held it tenderly. He put is free arm around his grandson, as they settled in to enjoy their annual musical.

Kevin thought his grandmother's second husband must be the best grandfather in the world. He'd spent every summer with his mother's parents in Harlem for as long as he could remember, and it was always so much fun. He especially liked that they took him to see at least one Broadway musical every summer. This showing of *The Wiz* would be his sixth trip and he couldn't wait. He loved the dancing and the singing, and got especially excited to see kids his own age up there on stage. Kevin thought that must have been the coolest thing in the world, to dance and sing on stage... and make people laugh! He was going to do that one day. He'd already started getting ready by taking tap lessons. It all started when they went to see The *Tap Dance Kid* the summer before. He'd barely stopped dancing long enough to eat or sleep since.

"What did you think of the show, baby?" Nana asked KJ already knowing the answer. He hadn't stopped grinning or tapping his feet since he left the theater. It was getting on her nerves, but she would endure anything for her only grandson; she saw so little of him.

"It was so cool! I'm gonna do that one day! I'm gonna be the best tap dancer ever! Look, Papa Bill!" The boy would not stop shouting as he flailed his arms wildly and jerked his body for emphasis the way he'd seen Alfonso Ribeiro do. He didn't care that his sneakers didn't make much noise on the hardwood floor or that the sound they did make wasn't particularly rhythmic. And neither did his grandparents. They lovingly encouraged him to be whatever he dreamed he could be, as long as he did it with passion.

Kevin's parents were just as supportive, and even more demanding. He knew nothing bothered his father more than to see someone do something halfway, especially if they had a real talent for it. Kevin learned that lesson early, as well. Soon after starting tap lessons, he'd seen boys coming into ballet class as he was leaving his lesson. When asked why he wasn't in that class too, he was cocky. "I don't need to take ballet lessons. Miss Black said I might be the best natural tap dancer she's seen in years! I'm gonna be on Broadway one day!"

His father heard the comment and was not pleased. "So you think you already know everything you need know to be a good dancer, as good as you need to be to dance for a living or be in a musical? Do you know that you have to compete against hundreds of people for one role, and that's for a small production? Your chances of becoming a Broadway star are slim, even if you do one thing better than anyone else. If you're great at everything, it's still as much about timing, discipline, and politics. Just because you want to be an entertainer doesn't mean you don't need to work hard; and if you're dancing because you think it will make your life easy, it ends here."

Kevin stuttered and hoped to himself that the 'it ends here' his dad was referring to was tap dancing, not his life. Anyway, he didn't mean it that way, or so he thought. "I-I'm just saying, Daddy. I'm a tap dancer. Why do I need to do anything else?"

Aaron Rivers was a patient man. He adored his son and would not allow him to just 'get by' with what came naturally to him. "A real dancer wants to be good at everything, KJ, and a real man doesn't take the easy way out. You can never stop learning, son. I don't care what your dream is or how good you think you are. Do I make myself clear?"

"Yes, Sir." Kevin was embarrassed. He heard people at church say what a 'good and humble man' his father was. It made him proud to hear his mom talk about how hard he worked, even though he wasn't a singer or dancer like his mom. He knew people respected him and he wanted to be like him. Kevin was smart and caught on fast, even to life's more subtle lessons. Before they could pull out of the parking lot, he asked his dad if they could go back inside and sign up for whatever classes fit their schedule. From that point on, he studied tap, ballet, contemporary, and African dance.

Kevin's dad never gave him bad advice, even if it took years to manifest. Sure he starred in a local production of *The Tapdance Kid*; but tap was just the beginning. He also danced the leads in *The Nutcracker, Beauty and The Beast,* and *Cinderella.* And as luck, and good genes would have it, he could sing, too. To no one's surprise but his own, he received rave reviews for his high school's productions of *Grease* and *Little Shop of Horrors*. By the time he graduated from high school, he could honestly say he could do it all; and he did it all well.

Kevin would never say it out loud; not after that whole 'I'm a tap dancer' fiasco, anyway, but he knew he'd get into Julliard. Applying was just a formality; and he only applied because it's what everyone expected him to do. He was still weighing his options. His girlfriend, Gabrielle, wanted him to go to Stanford with her. His best friend, Michael, even tried to encourage him to 'go pro and enter the draft' – skip college altogether and start auditioning for major productions on Broadway. That's where his mom stepped in.

"You're going to Julliard or you're going to Stanford, but you are going to college. I personally think Stanford University, although a fine institution, is a stupid choice for a triple-threat with a free ride to a world renown performing arts academy; but again it is your choice."

"Yeah, right." Kevin rolled his eyes and mumbled under his breath.

Tresa stopped in her tracks and slowly turned to face Kevin, abandoning the laundry she was putting away. "Oh, you've decided to pick what's behind door number three and be bludgeoned to death! Who do you think you're talking to?"

"I'm sorry, Mama; but you know it's not my choice. You've been grooming me for Broadway since I was six. Why can't I just go? I'm ready." Kevin wouldn't dare admit it to Michael, but Michael's plan for him actually was his first choice. Sure, he loved Gabby, and he was excited about Julliard, but he'd been taking classes for the last eleven years. He figured he'd paid his dues in school as well, taking honors classes and getting better than average grades. What harm was there in starting his career now while he was still young? He could go to college later. He was already good enough to get work in New York.

"So was I, baby, and I didn't get far. I was just as talented as you are–well, almost." Tresa bowed mockingly to her son. "And when my career didn't take off, I didn't have anything to fall back on. That is one mistake you will not be allowed to make. You will complete your education."

"Okay, plan 'B'." Kevin was determined to live a life of his choosing. "Of course, I will. I'm just saying maybe it wouldn't be such a bad idea to go to Cali. I could go to a traditional four-year school and still dance."

"I'm not stupid, KJ. You want to go to California because that's where Gabrielle is going. There is no way you can go to college, perform, and lay up under that fast little girl. You've never done anything just a little. What makes you think you can suddenly split yourself three ways?"

"Mom! I thought you liked Gabby!" His mother's characterization of his longtime girlfriend shocked him but made him laugh a little.

"I love Gabby, but she's the bishop's and the bishop's wife's problem, not mine."

"Gabby is not a problem, Mama."

"You're right. I'm sorry, sweetie. Gabrielle is no problem at all…and she'll be even less of one when she's a continent

11

away!" Tresa smiled at her handsome son and touched his cheek. "Oh, did I mention that your partial scholarship to Stanford doesn't include housing, and your father and I won't be paying for it?"

"Now see, you know you was wrong for that. Why didn't you just say that, Mama?"

"I thought you liked our little mother-son summits. Oh, I mailed your scholarship acceptance to Julliard yesterday. You're welcome."

"Thank you, Mommy." Kevin threw himself back on his bed. Tresa walked away. When Kevin assumed she was a safe enough distance away he mumbled. "Control freak."

"Heard that." She sang as she pitched a softball-sized roll of his father's socks back into the room.

"S'posed to." He lied in the same tone as the ball smacked him in the head.

"That's funny. Mommy said something like that to me about getting away from you! They are ca-ray-zee! It was their idea for us to date in the first place." Gabrielle sat on Kevin's bed and flipped through a theatre magazine the way she had a thousand times in the eleven years they'd been neighbors.

Kevin was moving around in his bathroom and talking to her through the door. "I know. Remember how your dad would always make you come and say, 'hi' to me at church? And don't let either one of us wanna go out with someone else! You'd think we'd started smoking crack! Crazy."

"I thought Daddy was going to have a stroke when you said you might not go to the prom. You'd have thought he was going! …No, really, I think they just want us to spend some time apart; see if we're really meant to be together before we settle down. I can handle a little test of time and distance. You skerd?"

"Oh, I aint scared." Kevin returned from the bathroom and placed a rolled towel on the bed and sat on the middle of the bed facing Gabby.

"So where are they tonight? What's going on at the church?"

"Revival, you heathen. They've only been talking about it for a month. Do you listen to anything in church?"

"Yup. The music." Kevin snatched the magazine from Gabby and tossed it on the floor.

"Ooh! I'm tellin' my Daddy!"

"Tell him what? That I took my magazine from you while you were in my bedroom when you were supposed to be home studying with Crystal? Okay. You can tell him that."

"No, Stupid. That you don't listen to his sermons!"

"Gabby, nobody listens to your daddy's sermons!" Kevin loved to tease Gabby about her father, The Bishop Robert Nichols. Truthfully, he didn't really like him; and he really didn't listen to his sermons. Kevin never seemed to know what the man was talking about; and when he did get it, it didn't seem relevant. Church seemed more about making people feel bad about themselves than about getting closer to God or being good to people. If it weren't for the mime team and men's ensemble, he would find a way not to go to church at all; but he knew his parents wouldn't allow that.

"I'm still tellin'."

"No you're not." Kevin closed the blinds in his room.

"Okay, I'm not; but don't think it's cuz I like you or nuttin."

"Girl stop playin'. You know, and I know, and everybody else knows you love me."

"Lord help me, I do!" They laughed and Kevin gave her a quick kiss on the lips.

"I love you, too, Gabrielle. So what time is this revival thing supposed to be over?" Kevin fumbled with the buttons on Gabby's blouse.

"Eleven – twelve... And you know the bishop, first lady and deacons will be the last people to leave..." Gabby had already pulled Kevin's t-shirt off and had begun working on his jeans.

"Um huh... I love church."

"Heathen..."

"Shut... up..."

Being a freshman at The Julliard School was a humbling experience, to say the least. Sure, Kevin was the most talented student in his high school for the performing arts in Georgia; but he soon discovered that Georgia wasn't exactly a cultural Mecca. For the first time in his life he wondered if he really was good enough to fulfill his dreams of superstardom. As big a wakeup call as the first few days were, it only took him a moment to figure out that the only thing that separated him from Julliard's best was another level of training, dedication and hard work. So, he poured everything he had into becoming a star. He even stayed in New York to attend Summer programs for three straight summers.

The distance proved to be more of a strain on his relationship with Gabby than either of them anticipated. Not so much that they officially broke up, they just seemed to slowly drift apart. Neither of them came home except for Thanksgiving and Christmas breaks. That time was dedicated more to their families, and they were lucky if they had more than a few hours together. If either of them thought that was odd, they didn't say. By senior year, even their phone calls were sporadic. Kevin, always a little self-absorbed, even in the best of conditions, did nothing but attend classes and study the theater. He had plans for his career that stretched far beyond performing. He'd given little thought to what Gabby might be doing, or even whether he missed her. He'd always had it in the back of his head that they would be together when they were through with college, one way or another. That was just the plan.

2

HOMOTOPIA

New York, New York – 1997

Every lead actor, playwright, producer, director, and choreographer since The Company's inception in 1972 had gone on to win a Tony, and from there, superstardom. The Company was Hitsville USA to the American Black theater world. As with any elite group, regardless of your talent, it was harder to break into than any top university or Fortune 500 company. Since it's founding in the early 70's, The Company's leadership practiced a form of gay affirmative action, whereby every candidate had to meet their 'special qualifications'. Simply put, if you weren't gay, you weren't getting in.

'Breeders', as some of the nastier chosen ones liked to refer to heterosexuals, never stopped trying. On the morning of every audition, you could be sure that there were at least a dozen straight boys and/or girls standing in line a full hour before 'the kidz' were even out of bed, praying the best of them literally broke a leg on their way to the stage. In twenty-five years, it had yet to happen; so consequently, there had never been a straight lead actor or principal dancer in one of The Company's one hundred productions.

Kevin couldn't bring himself to wish any ill will toward anyone. That's bad karma; besides, it clearly didn't work. Instead, he hoped that, at least about this most recent bit of breaking news, his roommate, Michael Lawson, wasn't delusional. Michael had rushed home earlier in the week to inform Kevin that he had it on good advice that the casting rules were changing, and he'd have no problems, if he simply showed up and mentioned Mike's name. Gary, the director would do the right thing.

"Just tell him I said 'hello'."

"Why would that matter? How do you know him?" Kevin looked at Mike sideways.

"Naw, it's not like that, man. I aint gay! …I just know he'll do the right thing if you tell him you know me." Kevin didn't say anything, just starred at Mike like he was an alien, and waited. "We were at a party. I got wasted. It was no big deal, really. Trust me, you're in."

Kevin did not trust his long time friend. Sure, he loved him like a brother, because they grew up together; but they had very different ideas about how to get by in the world. Kevin, for instance, chose to work hard and study his craft. He'd been dancing, singing and acting since he was six, took private lessons to ensure his acceptance to Julliard; and had since accepted more 'small parts' than probably all of his lesser accomplished classmates combined. He had every confidence in his talent and a great deal of Faith that his diligence would pay off, as long as he didn't compromise his principals. Yes, he was born and raised in a small town in rural Georgia; but it wasn't yesterday, and it wasn't by wolves.

Michael, on the other hand, was just plain lazy. Kevin figured it was because he was used to getting by on his looks. Sure, he was attractive in a lovechild of Jessica Biel and Taye Diggs kinda way, and women, and some men, seemed to throw themselves at him; but Kevin thought, as his Nana would say, his 'aura was ugly'. Then he wondered why he'd spent so much time contemplating the 'aura' of another man, anyway.

Kevin walked center stage and waited for his cue. He was ready. He preferred to prepare his own material rather than read the script for an audition. So when the advertisement said, 'bring your best' he knew exactly what he'd do. He felt a strange connection to Cheryl West's monologues from

Before It Hits Home. The scene he chose was supposed to end with him walking off playing a saxophone; but since he didn't have one, and couldn't play it if he did, he exited instead singing Donnie Hathaway's *A Song for You.* Even with his back turned, you could hear the purity and velvety tones in his rich tenor voice. When he was done, Gary, the director asked him to stick around for some questions.

"So, that was some pretty impressive stuff you were laying down out there, Kevin. Where did you train?"

"Atlanta High School for the Performing Arts." Gary nodded knowingly and waited. "And Julliard." It always made him uncomfortable to admit that. They had his resume, and he didn't like to brag.

"How's your boyfriend going to feel about you spending so much time with an all gay cast? Is he pretty secure? Despite what you might think, we can't do a whole lotta drama while we're working and touring."

"Oh, well Mike's not my boyfriend. I'm not gay." The words were out of his mouth before he could pull them back.

Gary smiled and nodded, thinking, "that explains a lot." "Tell me something, Kevin. Why do you think a man would suck another man's penis to get a job for you?"

"What are you talking about?"

"Your boy came to see me the other day, said you'd be coming in to read for the part and he'd give me whatever I wanted, if I'd give you a shot. I didn't want anything, and told him that, if you were good enough, you didn't need his help. He assured me you were, and said he still wanted to thank me for my time."

Kevin felt sick. "Excuse me..." He managed to make it to a bathroom and threw up in the first available stall. He felt a little better once the cool September air hit his face, but just well enough to get home. He didn't even remember boarding the train.

Mike came to the door wearing only a towel, his arms outstretched, and a big goofy grin on his otherwise perfect face. He'd expected Kevin to show up and thank him for the hook-up right about then. Kevin thanked him by punching him in his face. Mike fell to the floor just inside the house. "What the hell is wrong with you, man?" Michael rubbed his chin.

"I should be asking you that!" Kevin shook his hand from the pain. He'd never actually hit anyone before. "Why the hell do you think I'd need you to screw some director to get me a part?"

"It isn't like that, man! It was a way in. I'm tired of those faggots thinking they runnin' shit. I was thinking we could infiltrate the mf's and blow the shit up from the inside!" Michael did some shadow boxing, fanned his long muscular arms out wildly and finished with what looked like jazz-hands, all from his position on the floor.

Kevin couldn't help but laugh. "You have lost your mind."

"Oh, like you hadn't thought of it before."

"Trust me, I hadn't" Kevin lied. As he stepped over Mike, he noticed his towel had come off and he had an erection. "And why are you always naked? Put some clothes on!"

Kevin slammed the door to his bedroom, fell face down onto his bed and screamed into his pillow. For a second he wondered if it wasn't too late to curse every gay triple-threat in the city. He'd known when he decided to pursue his passion, success wouldn't come easy, but this was ridiculous. He'd been going on auditions for a solid year, and still couldn't get anywhere. Sure there were small roles in the chorus and the occasional spot as an understudy. But he had come out of Julliard with all the promise in the world. Everyone believed that he was going to be the next Black Broadway Star. What everyone forgot, or failed to mention to him, was that The Company controlled Black Broadway and they DID NOT hire straight leads. It wasn't even a secret, and there was nothing that he could do about it. There was no ACLU for straight performing artists. No one cared that they couldn't find work. In fact, in a lot of cases, even their parents were hoping they'd fail and move onto something normal and secure.

Kevin glanced at his degree on the wall and considered whether his minor in Liberal Arts and his near perfect SAT scores would be enough to get him into graduate school. "Hell, no." He wasn't ready to give up yet.

Gary returned to the theater to join his friend and colleague Nikki Vanderpip, The Company's president and executive producer of the show they were casting.

"Well, he was certainly amazing, wasn't he?" Nikki nudged Gary. "Yum-my! Almost makes me wish I still liked men. Oh wait, that wouldn't matter…"

"Actually, you might have a shot. He's straight." Gary waited.

"Shut up!" Nikki smacked Gary with Kevin's headshot.

"No, you shut up. Apparently, he's some kind of anomaly."

"Clearly. No straight man can do all that." Nikki did a shimmy and a twirl, awkwardly attempting to simulate Kevin's dancing.

"Well, if he's gay, he doesn't know it" Gary looked crestfallen.

"Well then. Moving on." Nikki tossed Kevin's headshot on the reject pile.

"Just wait a minute, Nik. I'm the director and I think I would like to give this kid a chance."

"I see you simultaneously grew a pair of balls and had your mind erased during your fifteen minute session with 'the Great Straight Wonder'! No! The rules haven't changed,

Gary. I'm still President and Executive Director, and President and ED trump artistic director every time. I have the final say. Send in what's his name... Roger's latest pet."

"He can barely read, let alone act."

"You're exaggerating, honey." Nikki giggled.

"Okay maybe a little." Gary chuckled. "Fine. He's good; but Kevin is better."

"Yes, of course, now run away to a world where that matters. Next!"

Gary shuffled off to his office in the building adjacent to the theater. "Bitch." He wondered to himself what happened to his career and life that the work no longer mattered. When did he become the kind of man who would sit idly by while such an injustice was happening? He was an artist not an activist. Of course he cared about equality and the rights of ALL people; but, this time... it had to be different. He recalled The Company at the beginning, in the early 70s. Back then it was still hard for Black actors to find work on Broadway. Some of the best talent stopped trying and headed west to Hollywood. Sure, there were shows with all Black casts, and then there was off, off, off Broadway; but there simply wasn't enough work to go around. And even shared passion for the theater couldn't keep racism and classism from creeping in. White producers and directors still favored White artists. At the same time, great works like The River Niger were inspiring a whole new generation of Black artists who wanted to do more than dance and sing. And so began the New Harlem Renaissance, as writers, aspiring directors and producers once again began gathering to support and inspire each other. What made this new revolution special was, this time, they knew about the business, not just the art. It was Nikki's mentor, Chris, who first suggested the six artists and three business students who lived together on 125th Street organize and form their own production company. It took them little more than five years to purchase their own venue and become the self-contained, completely self-sufficient monster they were by the time Nikki started working as a production assistant. Nikki remembered how hard it was; and when Chris died of cancer, she promised she would run The Company and preserve its vision and mission, to promote and serve African American gay, lesbian and transgender artists. Being multi-racial herself made it easier for Nikki to ignore the race of an otherwise qualified performer, but her experience as an outcast lesbian made it impossible to overlook the ironic hypocrisy that still existed in the theater. Not a day went by that Gary wasn't reminded of that.

Gary called Nikki the morning after Kevin's interview. "I'm bringing in Kevin Rivers to play 'Troy Wilson'. Mark can be his understudy."

"Has his orientation changed since yesterday, Gary? Look, I know you think I'm being a bitch, but The Company was formed specifically to give gay and lesbian artists and performers the leg-up. You know better than anyone that a role in a major production here is the equivalent to a paid internship. Better, in fact, because it guarantees their success. Marginalized groups have been doing it for years. It's not a crime, and I won't apologize for it. As good as you think this kid is, he's not more important than the vision and mission of this organization. Our hiring a straight lead would be like the NAACP hiring Rush Limbaugh."

"Okay, who's exaggerating now?"

"You know what I mean, Gary!"

"Yeah, you want to give a football scholarship to a third string quarterback and leave the next Heisman hopeful in the locker room, because you don't like the way he walks! It's wrong, and I'm not going to let you do it. Have you even thought about this policy of yours? The vast majority of male performing artists in New York are gay! The playing field is level. Sure, it's phenomenal that we now control six blocks of prime real estate in Manhattan, but seriously, is it really relevant to continue fighting this particular battle?"

"The playing field is not level. Stop being obtuse! You know as well as, hell, better than, anyone that this place provides a springboard for launching careers well beyond starring roles. Name one director or producer working on Broadway who didn't start out as an actor. We don't just produce musicals, Gary, we produce *producers*; and it is at the business end of the business that our kids need the help. Can they dance, sing and act better than any straight kid on the block? Abso-friggin-lutely! But that's where the respect ends. How many times did you hear 'sure, you're talented, maybe even beautiful, but not smart enough to direct', for no other reason than you're gay? Gay equals pretty. pretty equals not smart enough. So, gay equals not smart enough! I didn't make the rule; but everyone knows it is a rule, and frankly, I like the rule. Besides, there's no way a gay man walks into an audition for this company and says he's straight, when he knows doing so will cost him the gig... unless he really is. Since when are you such a fan of the heteros?"

"Have you considered the possibility that he might be gay and just not know it yet?"

"Have they started admitting creepy little boys to medical school based solely on their ability to dissect fetal pigs?"

Gary squinted at the phone. "Did you just have a stroke? What the hell are you talking about?"

"Exactly. If he doesn't know; then he can't fully appreciate the value of this opportunity. It doesn't count. He isn't part of the marginalized, under-appreciated minority. He'll be fine on his own. Why are you pushing this so hard?"

"Because I created the character; and met him for the first time yesterday when Kevin Rivers walked across that stage! I need this to be one of those times when the stupid rule doesn't matter, Nikki."

23

"Waah, waah! You make me sick with your crying and your principals and your 'hire the best actor for the job' crap! Where were you when I was fired from my paralegal job because someone found out I was a lesbian? Stupid rule or not, it's one that levels the playing field, even if it is only in our tiny piece of Manhattan."

"Would you rather be stuck in some law office today, Nikki? I have a feeling, if this kid doesn't get a break soon, the theater world will lose him to corporate America. And that would be a real crime."

"Damn it, Gary!"

Gary waited, confident that he'd sufficiently made his point.

"Okay, Norma Rae, I'll ask you again: Has his orientation changed since yesterday?"

"I'll bet you the new S Class it has."

"I'm going green. I want that new hydro thing Toyota's making now."

"I think you mean 'hybrid'"

"Whatever. You're going to have to buy me one."

"Dyke."

"Your mama."

"Thanks, Love." Gary smiled into the phone.

"See you in the morning." Nikki smiled back.

Kevin had been having the oddest dream. It was ... pleasant, comforting. What was odd though was that he kept hearing a man's voice. It was the voice, in fact, that seemed to wash over him like waves. In the dream, he was traveling toward the voice that seemed to be coming from behind a door. When he opened the door, the man who'd been calling him smiled and opened his arms. He awoke just before he reached the beautiful man with the voice. The sound of his ringing cell phone startled him. He caught it just before it went to voicemail. "Hello."

"Good morning, Kevin. This is Gary Sheppard. How are you?"

"I – I'm good, Mr. Sheppard. How are you?" Kevin sat straight up in his bed.

"Well, first of all, it's just Gary; and as of right now, how I am, professionally anyway, is somewhat up to you."

"I don't understand."

"I wouldn't expect you to. Kevin, I want you to star in my production of *No Greater Sin*."

There was silence on both ends as Gary waited for Kevin's response and Kevin held his breath. "Does that surprise you?"

"Yes and no."

"Explain."

"Yes, because I know that The Company only hires gay leads. I only auditioned because my idiot roommate told me he had an in."

"And no?"

"Well, no because I think I'm good enough. I really want this role, Mr., uh, I mean Gary."

"Good answer. And for the record, there is nothing anyone could have done to get you in if you weren't the extraordinary talent I believe you to be. But there is a catch, Kevin."

"Yes, sir?" Kevin braced himself for something really bad.

"You can't tell anyone you're straight. In fact, it would be in your best interest, and mine, if you start researching your next role as an openly gay man immediately. We'll be spending a lot of time together, so I'll explain more later. In the meantime, know two things: You don't owe anyone for getting you this role; you did that on your own. But if you betray my professional confidence, I will scratch your eyes out, you'll never work in New York again, and I'll have to buy an angry lesbian a Toyota. And then you will owe me forty thousand dollars. Do I make myself clear?"

Kevin pulled the phone away from his ear to look at it. "Yes, sir. Thank you, Mr. Sheppard."

"It's Gary, and you're welcome. See you at 7:00 am tomorrow."

Kevin silently jumped up and down on his bed and did the goofiest victory dance ever. He didn't tell his roommate about the call because he didn't want him to think he had anything to do with it. Instead, he threw on some sweats and practically ran the twelve blocks to his grandparent's apartment. Papa Bill wasn't going to believe this, because Papa Bill didn't believe anything.

3

ABUNDANTLY GIFTED

Kyle Tsegaye Tye was born to fight. His weapon of choice: words. His first words were poetry. Poetry soon became song. The only child born to native Ethiopian and Jamaican parents in what's been called 'the Most Homophobic Place on Earth', his parents noticed early that, while there was no mistaking Kyle's special anointing, his gifts would be more greatly appreciated, and protected elsewhere. The beautiful boy with the heart of a lion and voice of an angel did not immediately understand why his parents always talked about moving to Canada. He didn't want to go. He liked his school and his friends. He had cousins nearby. He was especially not anxious to leave his church. He sang in the children's choir, but also got to help with the adult choir. Kyle had perfect pitch and taught himself to play the piano by age seven. The adult choir director couldn't really play and direct at the same time, so Kyle would often step in to do one or the other. Sure, the adults, especially the young men, laughed at first and complained that he was taking up their time… but then they heard him play!

Still, just before he would enter middle school, his parents said, 'it's time to go'. Kyle was devastated. "I won't have any friends there. Where will we go to church? Why can't I just stay with Grand Mother?"

Kyle's mother didn't have the heart to tell him 'Grand Mother', as she insisted she be called, was a big part of the problem. Instead she did what she always had and lovingly focused her attention on her son. "I'm sorry, baby, but it's what must be done. I know ya don tink so now, but ya tank me fa it one day. Now please git to packin ya tings."

"Yes, ma'am." Kyle would not dare show anything but

complete obedience to his mother; but underneath, he was hurt and confused. He'd heard Grand Mother whispering to one of his aunties, when they thought he was asleep, about how they knew the family was moving because of him. Kyle spoke English, Jamaican Patois and a little of his father's Ethiopian Semitic, but he still could not figure out why his older male cousins would snicker when they called him 'Kyle-Boi'. Having given it more thought, he realized he wasn't going to miss them much.

The summer before he started fourth grade, his family made the long move to Toronto. Kyle was an especially sensitive child and saw right away that the move was harder on his mother. Canada was, after all, an entirely different country, and it really did feel like a different world. His father was a regional manager for a large hotel chain and spent most of his time away from the family opening new hotels, so he was seldom home for more than a month or so. When he was home, Kaleb Tye was loving and supportive, but without her close-knit family nearby, Naomi was lonely. Kyle adored his mother and made it his job to entertain her and see that she was happy. Kyle knew anything they did together would be fun, and he loved to learn. It was his idea that the two of them learn to speak French. When Kyle came home with books and tapes he'd borrowed from the library and told her his plan, she just shook her head, laughed and gave him a big hug. "Where did ya come from, my angel?"

"I came from the library, Mama." Kyle smiled and wriggled away. "Did you know that French is the official language of Quebec?"

"I did not. Did ya know we live in Toronto which is 495 miles from Quebec?" Naomi winked at her son.

"Well, I wasn't sure how far, but I knew it was far. Still, we're closer to Quebec than we are to France. A lot of people in Canada speak French. If we learn another language we'll have more people that we can talk to." Naomi watched her son in amazement. He truly did think differently than …everyone she'd ever met.

"Okay. What will we talk ta them about… in French?"

This was gonna be good.

"God."

"Of course. God. Anyting else?"

"And Jesus and God's love for us, and how God loved us so much that He sent Jesus to die for us so that no one who believed in Him, Jesus, would perish."

"Hallelujah! Amen! You are absolutely right. We must learn to speak French. Let's do it."

By the time Kyle was twelve, he began to understand his calling, and why the family left Jamaica. They left because he was different. He had an unusual love of books and music, especially gospel music. He liked going to church, but he preferred to study the bible alone. He spent hours in the library and would come home with various translations of the bible and other religious books. Kyle was concerned about what was happening in the world and watched the world news as if it were required viewing. His mother actually encouraged Kyle to do things other boys his age did, like read comic books or watch regular television. But he didn't have time to read for fun and he was afraid that he might miss something if he didn't watch the news. He needed to know what was happening to people, even if it broke his heart.

In 1986, a popular Jamaican reggae artist was on trial for brutally beating a known gay man, nearly to death. All of the evidence pointed to the rapper and his entourage, but all of the defendants were quickly acquitted of all charges. The world news announcer stated with a modicum of concern that "the verdict reinforced the deadly climate in 'the Most Homophobic Place on Earth'," making it clear that it was open season on gays and lesbians in Jamaica.

Kyle ached for the young man who'd never receive justice

on Earth for his assault; but more for his home country and the world at large. He prayed for the rapper who was so hate-filled that his music spewed such violent anti-gay rhetoric. He prayed for the young gay men and women who were forced by peer pressure or self-loathing to listen to the popular music set to powerful dance rhythms. Kyle imagined their pain, the reality that expressing any distain for the latest releases of such superstars would be tantamount to suicide. He prayed for the souls of the producers and radio executives who built the monsters on the radio by not simply saying, 'No. You can't say that to people!' As far as Kyle was concerned, the blood of innocent people was on their hands as surely as if they'd held the bats or worn the steel-toed boots themselves.

Kyle knew that the world outside of his safe Canadian provincial home was cold and mean; still, he loved people and tried to find his place in the world. Although he was friendly, he was also a shy, introverted child. He had friends at church and in school but preferred to keep to himself. He was well over six feet tall, with his mother's muscular build and skin the color of Hershey's dark chocolate. He received more attention from girls than he was comfortable with. While he was naturally athletic, he didn't like team sports. He craved discipline and structure and found martial arts to be the perfect fit. He was third degree black belt in tae kwon do by age fifteen. No one messed with him; but people did talk.

Kyle paid very little attention to the whispers from his peers. He'd looked up the word 'queer' in the dictionary and decided that he was perfectly comfortable being 'strange' or 'unusual'. He knew people didn't mean it as a compliment, that they meant 'homosexual'. He even understood by then that most people believed homosexuals were wrong, sinful, abominations who would burn in hell. He didn't believe any of that. He knew God loved him. And although he probably would have figured it out on his own, Kyle knew God loved him mostly because his mother loved him. He'd seen that with his own eyes.

On a visit to Grand Mother's house in Jamaica, Kyle overheard the mean old woman berating his mother. "Me know ya left me 'ere fa dat sissified little boi ya gave birth ta, and i't'aint made one bit a difference! He's as queer as they come. Ya need ta be takin' im somewheres ta get him fixed right, before the people get him, if ya love him."

"I do love him." Naomi's usually thick Jamaican accent became virtually undetectable as her subconscious rejected the woman and country that threatened her child. "That's why I would never even think of changing him. He's my baby and he's perfect the way the Good Lord made him. It's the world that needs changing, not my Angel Kyle. He's going to teach the world something one day!"

"And what on earth do you tink that little soft chile knows anyting 'bout ta teach the world, girl?"

"Love. My son has a heart as big and beautiful as the Christ Himself! I never met a soul so loving and kind, so eager to make people feel good - about themselves, and about God! I wouldn't change him if I knew how to, because there is nothing wrong with my baby."

"Hmph. If ya so damn proud of da boi, why ya hall tail and run outta 'ere wit him da way ya did five years ago?"

"Because the world, Jamaica , isn't ready for him, yet; and I would not have him hide his light for anyone! These people do not understand, and they don't know any better than to try to destroy what they do not understand!"

"What's there ta understand? He's wrong. Ya won't be able to save him, Naomi, not even all the way in Canada, when he starts ta actin' like the little queer boi he is. Faggots were not meant to walk this earth wit da rest of us. Ya know that, girl! I raised ya to know better than ta try to protect someting evil."

Naomi's mother's words broke her heart, but she wouldn't give the woman the satisfaction of seeing it. Instead, she stood calmly and closed her eyes before she spoke. "My son, Kyle Tsegaye Tye, is a beautiful creation of God. The same God that made you, Mother, lovingly made him. He was made for a purpose; and that purpose is good. That purpose is divine. My husband and I could not be more proud of who he is and what he is; and we consider it an honor and a blessing to be chosen to watch over him. When I left here five years ago, I promised I would return to visit because you are here. You are my mother and I love you; but I will not return to your home or your country ever again." Naomi slowly turned and walked toward the door. Before she left her childhood home for the last time, she stopped and turned toward her mother again. "You hurt me, Mother. You have made me feel loved my whole life. I wonder if you would have loved me if I'd been born different, like my son. My son and I will continue to pray for you."

When Naomi stepped outside the door she saw Kyle. She didn't ask him if he'd heard what they said, she just smiled at him reassuringly. "Il est temps de partir, bébé."

"Oui, maman."

They rode to the airport in silence. Kyle prayed silently for his mother, for her mother and for their homeland. Neither Kyle nor Naomi would return to Jamaica for many years. Instead they watched, and waited, from a distance and for different reasons. Naomi waited for change to come to Jamaica and to her mother. Kyle waited for the right time to help change the world.

In the meantime, he trudged through his adolescence. By high school, the whispers had become full-blown rumors. Now strikingly handsome, an honor student, and the surest bet to have your teenage daughter home by curfew, Kyle became his community's escort of choice. Doing small favors for the mother's of shy girls soon earned him real popularity with his more socially conscious classmates. Showing up to a dance with Kyle Tye on your arm made you look almost as good as he did. It wasn't long before even senior girls were competing for his attention. Boys fell into three categories: those who were jealous, but knew better than to mess with him, those who wanted to be him, and those who wanted to … date him. He just wasn't interested; but since no one, male or female could claim to have gotten anywhere with him, he remained a mystery.

Kyle graduated from high school at age sixteen and entered New York University – Steinhardt. At nineteen he enrolled in New York Theological Seminary. The freedom of campus life had little effect on him. He had friends but he didn't party. He studied, he sang and he wrote music and books. If he had any interest outside of music and ministry, he kept it to himself. Gary Sheppard, who was finishing his final year at NYTS when Kyle started, tried to pull the younger man out of his shell.

"I don't understand. You are the oddest gay man I know."

"What makes you think I'm gay?" Kyle asked with a smile. He'd long since stopped being offended.

"Um, you look like…that; you could have any woman or man on this, or any other campus, and you live like a monk."

"That doesn't mean anything. I could just be waiting for the right woman."

"Or man… Whatever, man. I don't know why I know. I just know. Tell me I'm wrong."

"You're not wrong."

"Thank you. But, why all the mystery? Why don't you date?"

"It's not a conscious choice. I just haven't met anyone I'm interested in."

"So you're gonna die a virgin?"

"Better than dying from something I contracted having meaningless sex."

"You make an excellent point."

"Besides, there's more to life than sex."

"Really? What would that be?"

"Love."

"And again, how do you expect to find this love if you don't date?"

"God's got that all worked out."

"And God told you this?"

"God did, indeed."

"Okay, I'm in. What did God tell you about this love?"

Kyle smiled and folded his arms. "I'll know him when I see him."

4

I'LL KNOW HIM...

For Kyle, 'knowing him' also involved knowing himself and knowing what he didn't want. He really wasn't a monk. He did have feelings, desires...passion. He'd even fallen in love once, well almost. Richard Richmond was the choir director of the church in which Kyle was associate pastor, just after seminary. An aspiring gospel artist, himself, Richard had a rich, soulful tenor voice and a smile that made Kyle...smile. For more than a year, they tried to ignore their mutual attraction. Richard was ten years older, recently divorced and as far as anyone knew, straight. Even if he were gay, it wouldn't have worked. Kyle knew who he was. It wasn't even a reality he needed to 'accept'. He was a proud gay man. He was thankful for the gifts God had given him, which he directly attributed to his 'different-ness'. Kyle walked in the world gracefully and gratefully embracing everything that God made him: compassionate, courageous, creative, maternal, protective, sensitive, discerning, masculine and feminine, loving... His sense of self was a direct result of his faith, which could be summed up very simply: 'love God, love yourself, love others as you love yourself.' He knew he could only be with someone as spiritually grounded and personally secure as he was himself. So, things with Richard were complicated when they finally acknowledged their feelings for one another.

Kyle sat at the piano playing a song he'd written for the choir. "Wow...beautiful..." Richard whispered, staring at Kyle.

"Thanks, I think I wrote it for you...to sing."

Richard took a deep breath, walked around the piano and sat on the bench next to Kyle. "Thank you, but I wasn't talking about the song. ...Kyle, why do you spend so much time here... after everyone else is gone? I know you've got more equipment at home than we do here at church."

Kyle wasn't nervous at all. His dazzling smile was natural and easy as he closed his eyes and continued to play. "I like churches. And the company's... not bad..." He opened his eyes and looked directly at Richard.

Richard put his hand on the piano and tried to play the chords to Kyle's song. Kyle slid off of the bench so Richard could sit where he needed to be, stood behind him and leaned over him to play the right notes. Richard inhaled Kyle's hair as it brushed his face. "Oh my. Kyle..." Richard leaned back against Kyle's torso. "...I'm not gay."

"Clearly." Kyle leaned over Richard's head and looked pointedly at his lap.

"I-I mean. I like you. You know I do. But it's not like that. This is wrong. We shouldn't." Richard turned around and stood. Kyle stood in front of him. His expression was sweet, kind.

"What's 'wrong'? That you love spending time with me? That I'd rather be here with you than almost anywhere else? That I'm younger than you?"

"No, don't do that. You know what I'm talking about. Don't make me say it. Can't we just..." Richard put his hand on Kyle's. "...Let's get out of here."

Kyle grabbed his keys, locked up the building and followed Richard home. As they walked the stairs to Richard's apartment, Richard looked around as if checking to see if they'd been followed. Once inside, Richard grabbed Kyle, shoved him against the door, and kissed him. Kyle thought it was too fast, too hard and too wet; but it was his first kiss, so hopefully it would get better. Perhaps he needed to take control of the situation. Kyle grabbed Richard's hands as they switched positions. Kyle held Richard's hands above his head, kissing his neck and working his way up to his mouth. He kissed him slowly, not using his tongue until Richard invited him to with a sigh that ended in a high-pitched moan. "That's better," Kyle thought as he settled into the kiss and released Richard's hand. He slipped his own free hand under Richard's shirt, rubbing his stomach and chest. Richard slid his hand down Kyle's body and gasped. Kyle was rock-hard and hung. Richard rubbed Kyle through his pants and Kyle bit his lip and breathed heavy, trying to contain himself. Before things got out of control, he took Richard's hand again and pulled it back up to the wall.

"What?" Richard asked breathlessly.

"Are you sure you're not gay?" Kyle smiled.

"You know what I mean, Kyle... c'mon."

"I really don't, Richard. See, I am gay. I really like you. That felt really, really good to me; not 'wrong' at all. You apparently enjoyed it, too; and I assume you like me, otherwise, I wouldn't be here. So when you say, 'I'm not gay', I really don't know what you mean."

"Why do we have to label this? Can't we just be friends who enjoy each other's company?"

"Of course we can." Kyle picked up the keys he'd dropped on the floor and stood in front of the door, waiting for Richard to move. "Oh, you mean now? You want to 'enjoy my company', now...as long as we don't call it anything? Richard, move please."

"Kyle...I don't want you to go. I want to..."

"You want to what? You want to use me to make yourself feel good, while you simultaneously pretend that you're something I'm not, something you think is better and not wrong?"

"No! It's not like that at all. I'm just not gay. I just have these feelings... Sometimes I want something a little... different; but I don't want to be with a man. I couldn't be your boyfriend or anything like that, that's all."

"Oh! Well, that's different. Let's just continue to work and minister together, spend all our free time together, and when no one is looking, sneak away to your little closet here and 'enjoy each other's company'." Kyle starred at Richard.

"Kyle…!" Richard laughed nervously. "Please don't go. I want you!"

"No, you don't." Kyle wasn't smiling anymore. "You want... something else." Kyle lowered his eyes without moving anything else. "I want and need more than that. I am more than that."

"I know you are, Kyle. You're beautiful and you're so smart, and you're so sexy I can barely look at you."

"Thanks. I'll see you in church, Richard. By the way, it's not my business whether or not you think you're gay, but…"

Richard interrupted him. "I can't be. I'm not. I only feel this way because…something happened to me."

"Something like what?" Kyle was more curious than concerned. He'd heard this before.

"My uncle used to do things to me."

"And you think that made you gay?"

"I'm not gay; but yes, I only have these urges because of what he did to me."

"So you think being gay is some mutation caused by incestuous abuse. And you're NOT gay, but you feel some need to act out these 'urges' that have been inflicted upon you…with me…a GAY MAN?"

"I'm not saying I'm better than you, Kyle. We're just different."

"Yeah, you're right. We are different. So, what happens to the person who falls in love with you when you decide you don't want to be wrong anymore?" Richard didn't answer and didn't move. "I thought so."

As if nothing had happened, Richard started to unbutton his pants.

"Okay, I'm leaving now." Kyle walked toward Richard and stood in front of him. "Please don't make me move you."

When Richard didn't move, Kyle picked him up caveman style and dropped him on the first available couch.

"Mm, and so strong…" Richard probably didn't mean to mock Kyle, but in that moment, he looked like a monster. Kyle stood over the man he'd had a crush on for the better part of a year and wanted to shake him. Why did it have to be so hard? What had happened to this lovely man that he didn't see the beauty in who God made him to be? Kyle turned and walked toward the door, but stopped and went back just before leaving. He sat in a chair across from Richard with his elbows on his knees and his hands clasped.

"Richard, what's happened between us before today wasn't my imagination; and it wasn't because some nasty old man couldn't keep his hands off of an innocent child. I believe you when you say you like me, that you enjoy my company, and when you say you want me. All of those things are easy for me to believe because I have felt exactly the same way about you for a very long time. But, Richard, I am a gay man. I don't believe I am bad or wrong or anything other than what God made me. I can't say who you are or what your truth is, but I pray that you'll find it. If you're not gay, fine; but please stop saying that the only reason you want me is because something horrible happened to you. Please, don't say that to anyone else ever again. I don't want this to sound condescending. I don't mean for it to be; but you should get some help. Tell someone what happened to you. Let them help you sort out the connection between the abuse and your 'urges'. Abuse couldn't have created your attraction to me any more than it could cause your musical ability, your sense of humor or your kindness. God is the only being with the power to grant such gifts."

Richard sat on the couch looking at Kyle and finally reached for his hand when he stopped talking. "I'm sorry."

"So am I." Kyle pulled away slowly and stood to leave. He didn't stop this time.

Kyle took the long way home. He knew that in the quiet of his own home, he wouldn't be able to ignore his hurt, loneliness and disappointment. When he did get home, he didn't write or workout or pray as he normally would. He didn't even eat. He went to bed and tried to sleep off the sting. It was still there the next morning, and the morning after that. By the third day, he was hungry and cranky and tired of being sad, but still too hurt to pray. He knew he was being defiant, and when The Holy Spirit spoke to him, he got an attitude. "What?"

"I beg your pardon?"

"Forgive me. Yes, Lord."

"Whatever. Why the long face?"

"You're all knowing and all seeing. You tell me." Kyle was really mad.

"Oh stop it! You know he was not him!"

Kyle sighed. "Yeah, I guess I did. But…"

"But what? I promised you love beyond your wildest dreams – friendship and partnership, laughter and passion, honesty and trust, caring and compassion…Do you think I would give you those things in someone who is not yet whole? You were supposed to help that man, not bed him! And you did! He will be better because of his experience with you; and you are stronger. These trials are just a test."

"Thank you, Lord."

"Be at peace, Kyle. God is pleased with you."

Kyle returned to church a few days later and braced himself for the awkwardness. He and Richard hadn't spoken since their encounter. When Kyle didn't see him right away, he asked the pastor when he was coming.

"Oh, he's gone. He's going on tour with some group from Atlanta. Thursday night was his last rehearsal with us, at least until the tour is over. He told me he would tell you. You didn't know?" Elder Nation saw the hurt on Kyle's face and understood immediately. "Kyle, I'm sorry. You two spent so much time together; I just assumed you knew of his plans. He was only hired to work with the choir for the year. And we only needed him because we didn't want you to feel pressured to direct the choir and keep up with your AP duties while you were finishing school. But, you'd been around so much lately... I just assumed he'd told you."

"It's fine, really. Do you need anything?"

"Well, I thought Richie was going to ask you to direct the choir, at least for the next few months. I know LvC (Lvolution Church) is opening soon. Can you help us out just a little while longer, until we can get someone else in here? Kyle if you can't, I can pull someone from one of the ensembles..."

"No. I'd love to. It's no problem at all." Kyle went back to doing what he always had and poured his heart into his work. His work was serving the people of God.

New York City – 2004

"I don't understand why you don't just go to work for an existing church. You didn't need to get two masters degrees and a doctorate to start your own ministry." Kyle's father was questioning him more for his own amusement than out of any real concern. He believed his son to be a wise and anointed man of God, but he rarely felt like his father. Kyle felt the awkwardness of their relationship, too; but it was because he saw so little of his father, not because he didn't love and respect him.

"No, technically, I guess anyone could rent a space and put up a sign, but that's not what God told me to do." Kyle opened the door to the converted warehouse on 7th Avenue in Manhattan that would serve as the home of Lvolution Church.

"And what is with the name, again?" Kaleb Tye chuckled to himself.

Kyle remained patient. He was determined not to let his

father get under his skin. He recited the church's 'Who We Are' again for his father: "Lvolution Church is a wholly affirming, place of refuge, founded on the principals of Liberation Theology. Although we are founded on the teachings of Jesus Christ, believers of ALL faiths are welcome and encouraged to worship with us and share in our mission to minister to the world by joining the Love Revolution."

Kaleb smiled to himself as he walked around the spacious building Kyle had secured without asking for his help or going into personal debt. He knew that part of the reason Kyle didn't start his ministry sooner was because he needed to give it a solid foundation. Kyle knew he needed to reach 'the least of God's people'. Sure there were 'wealthy' men and women who needed God's love and salvation as much as anyone; but he was called to minister to the lesbian, gay, bisexual and transgender communities and to teach the world about who they were. He knew he needed to start reaching young gay men and women in particular immediately. They were still dying spiritually at an alarming rate. He realized it was happening all over the world, but in New York City... Kyle couldn't explain it. There was so much freedom of expression, so little fear. How could people be so liberated and still so bound? He'd been born with and understanding that freedom without salvation was a recipe for disaster. Saving a generation of young men and women from the misery of self-hate, promiscuity and fruitlessness was his calling. He trusted that God would provide everything he needed to fulfill that calling. What he needed immediately was for people to be free to come in and not be burdened by thoughts of mortgages and light bills for that space. He would do the work until help arrived. And help did arrive, in droves. By LvC's first-year anniversary, they had over two hundred active members, two Sunday services, and a lean, but efficient liturgical staff. Their primary mission was 'community service'. Of course, people always had their personal needs; but if you were a member of LvC, you knew you were to serve God by serving the needs of God's people.

Toronto, Canada – 2008

Kyle resisted the urge to throw something at his TV and instead looked for his remote to turn the channel, but not before cursing in one of the five languages he spoke other than English. He paused to listen out of morbid fascination to the interview on the third-rate cable program. An ultra-conservative television evangelist was interviewing a young man with stringy, shoulder-length locks, a well-known gospel artist. The list of things wrong with the picture on his screen was so long it made Kyle's head hurt. He sat on the hand-carved mahogany table in front of his television and glared at the screen.

"The problem is not the homosexual; it is the homosexual choir director...!"

"That's the dumbest thing I've ever heard!" Kyle yelled back at the TV. "God made homosexuals, same-gender-loving individuals, two-spirits, our feelings, desires, gifts, as lovingly and purposefully as He made yours. A gay choir director is the opposite of an anomaly; it's practically a liturgical necessity! To suggest that God would pour such gifts into something or someone 'He' does not love is not only inaccurate and arrogant, but it's blasphemous. God doesn't make waste!"

He muted the TV and closed his eyes. He knew what this was. He was being called to move, again. The Holy Spirit spoke to him about the man with the stringy locks calling his brothers and sisters 'a threat to the people of God'.

"Look! My children are still dying. That man needs your help! What are you waiting for? You have everything you

43

need. Do you think I gave you ALL that I have given you for you to sit on your hands? When you speak, people will listen. When you sing, hearts will open. You know better than this! I am not sending you out to judge who is right or wrong, only to say what you know: that My love is REAL and it is for ALL of GOD'S CHILDREN, not just for those who love a certain way. What are you afraid of?"

Kyle cried silently and thought for a long time before he answered. "I am afraid, not of dying; but of dying alone. Lord, you promised me that if I would pray, and fight, and sing and tell the world what I know...I've tried so hard; but I don't think they are hearing me, and I am still alone."

"Have you helped just one of my children to understand and accept God's love for them?"

"Yes, Lord, I have."

"Did it kill you?"

"No, Lord it did not." Kyle smiled through his tears at his heavenly parent's enduring patience and LOVE.

"Then keep walking, keep singing, keep praying, keep fasting. You are almost home."

Kyle wiped his face and opened his eyes. The devil's talk show had been replaced with The *Ellen Degeneres Show.* Kyle laughed and did a quick shout. God was fun-knee! He turned off the TV and went downstairs to the piano in the basement.

Kyle gave thanks for his life and for every day he lived knowing he was loved. He knew that he was different; but he was not 'special'. Everyone should walk in the same freedom and knowledge that they are loved; no person or group has the authority to say otherwise. And to do so in a song, in the name of God, was simply irresponsible! It was time to put an end to the bloodshed. Kyle prayed for the courage to press forward further into battle. He played his piano as he prayed; and his prayers became songs.

5

BRAVO!

New York City, March 2001

By the time Gabrielle Nichols arrived in New York, at the end of the first week of Kevin's Broadway debut, Kevin was a star. The reviews were unanimous, "Kevin Rivers is… BREATHTAKING…AWESOME…MARVELOUS… TOO MANY WONDERFUL THINGS: ALVIN AILEY AND SAVION GLOVER; DENZEL WASHINGTON AND … DENZEL WASHINGTON IF HE COULD SING; GREGORY HINES, JAMES EARL JONES AND JOE MORTON!!!"

Gabby left her front row, center seat the moment the curtain went down. Of course, she thought the play was spectacular, but she didn't need to stay for the encores; she needed to get to her car. She wanted to be waiting when he left the theater. Kevin wasn't expecting her, but she was sure he'd drop whatever else he was doing to see his life-long friend and girlfriend. She wasn't even concerned that they hadn't spoken in months. She knew he was working. Kevin was just focused like that.

Gabrielle checked her hair, makeup and breath in the back of her limo and exited the car to wait outside the stage door. Kevin was among the last of the cast members to exit, looking surprisingly refreshed. Of course, he was enjoying his success in the here and now, but he was also looking ahead. He was more excited about the opportunity to share his ideas for future work than bask in the glow of any personal onstage achievement. Everyone else was going to celebrate. Never much of a partier, he was on his way to Gary's apartment to unwind with Gary and the producers.

Gabby leaned against the rented limo and clapped. "Bravo!"

"Gabby?" Kevin was too shocked to consider whether he was happy to see her. "Oh my God! What are you doing here?" He slung his bag from one shoulder to the other and gave her a warm hug.

"I was transferred here. I work for Tillman and Pharr, the PR firm. Actually, I'm only in New York until the Charlotte office opens in a few months. I wanted to surprise you! Congratulations, Mr. Rivers! You're a star!"

"Thank you. Thank you." Kevin glanced over at Gary who was waiting outside his limo. "Excuse me for just a second, will you."

"Gary, I'm going to need to catch up with you in a little while." He motioned to Gabby who waved. "That's Gabrielle! I'm just going to grab a quick drink with her and get caught up. I'll be over in an hour or so."

"O-kay." Gary looked suspiciously at the beautiful woman smiling at him. He was not going to mess with her. He quickly reminded himself that Kevin wasn't actually gay; he was indeed just a fabulous actor. "Just try to be discreet, please."

"Of course. Relax. I'll be there soon. It's just drinks. We haven't seen each other in years." Gary looked again at Gabrielle and shook his head at his naïve friend.

"I'll see you tomorrow, Kevin." Kevin walked away laughing and hopped in the car.

Gabby directed the driver to take them to her hotel, which was fine with Kevin since he was, after all, instructed to be discreet. Once inside, Gabby poured champagne from a full size bottle, not the minibar. "To your success."

"To the theatre!" They lifted their glasses. "Wow, Gabby! What are you doing here?" Kevin shouted. As Gabby disappeared Kevin sat down on the couch in her well-appointed executive suite.

"Okay, we've done that already. I told you, I'm here on business. Aren't you happy to see me?" Gabby shouted from the bathroom.

"Of course I am, just surprised, that's all."

"I almost expected to find you slinking off to celebrate with that fine-ass Rebecca Martin. When the reviews said she was beautiful, I assumed they meant, 'with good lighting and makeup'. Then she came out and I thought, 'oh, I'm gonna have to cut her!'"

Kevin laughed. "I see you're still crazy. Leave that woman alone. She does not want me."

"How is that possible?" Gabrielle emerged from the bathroom having changed into a slinky black negligee and poured her second glass of champagne.

Kevin took a big gulp, still working on his first glass. "Wow. You've been working out."

"I told you, I need to stay competitive. That little heffa can probably bend herself in half." She sat close to him on the couch.

"At least that's the tale as her girlfriend tells it. She's very, very gay."

"Oh you're kidding! Why? She could probably have any man she wants."

"I don't know, but I'm pretty sure it's not a consolation thing. You do know there are attractive gay people, don't you?"

"Sure, men, but there are no 'real lesbians'; only dykes who hate men, because they were abused, or ugly women who can't get men." Kevin looked at Gabby like she had eight heads.

"Oh my God! You can't really believe that! Is that what five years in California taught you?"

"Uh, no. That's what my daddy taught me." Gabby said with a straight face.

"Wow. I bet he's still preaching, too." Kevin looked

47

away and mumbled.

"Yup. Every Sunday. But I did not come all this way to talk about my daddy or your co-star. I've missed you." Gabby straddled Kevin as he sat on the couch and nibbled his ear. Kevin instinctively placed his hands around her tiny waist. Then he thought out loud.

"I thought you came here to work?"

"Oh, you know what I mean." She started unbuttoning his shirt. Kevin did not object, but he didn't like to kiss. Instead, he kissed her throat and caressed her breasts through the thin layer of expensive silk. When she'd gotten his shirt off, he moved as if to lay her on the couch, but she stood and guided him to the bedroom. Kevin gave very little thought to the flickering candles and the turned down bed.

It was almost as if they'd never been apart. As a couple, they never were big on conversation. Sex was just what Kevin and Gabby did when they were together. In fact, they'd spent so much time together growing up that pleasing each other was almost instinctual. Neither of them seemed to notice that it took Kevin a moment to get excited about being with her. Had he really gone over four full years without actual intercourse? Well, if his intense and extended showering rituals didn't count, then yes. He was too busy to date and he wasn't interested in anything casual. Sure he had needs; but he found it safest to keep those in his head. In fact, that's where he went with Gabby, in his own head. That's probably how he managed to spend so much time down there. It wasn't so much that he enjoyed her taste and scent all that much, it was more like he could get lost in his thoughts, and because he was good at it, she was none the wiser. At least that's how it had always been.

"I need you, Kevin. Now." Gabby pulled at Kevin's free hand to get him to come to her.

"I don't have any condoms. Do you?"

"It's fine. I'm on the pill and I haven't been with

anyone. Have you?"

"No." Kevin told the truth. "Really? Wow." Always a little gullible, Kevin thought 'she has no reason to lie about that'. Almost immediately, he remembered why he preferred flying solo. He was overwhelmed by thoughts and images in his head that had little if nothing to do with Gabby. Not even sexual images…just stuff. He was distracted. As he went through the motions of making love to Gabby, he recited his lines from his earlier performance in his head. He made a mental note to pick up his dry cleaning when he visited his grandparents the next day. He redecorated the over the top, outdated design of their reunion suite, replacing the heavy drapes with an Asian-inspired shade and the standard hotel prints with some he'd seen in a friend's debut last month. Occasionally he let out an 'ooh' or an 'ah'. He even managed to muster a 'baby, I missed you so much…' Eventually, he switched gears to the thoughts that usually got him through and finally surrendered to them, finishing, as always, precisely when she did. As they lay there, Kevin realized he could probably go another couple of years on his own and be just fine.

"Bravo!" Gabrielle was applauding again, which made Kevin feel weird. "I really have missed you." Barely winded, she continued to reacquaint herself with her old friend, only until he was fully recovered, and mounted him again. Kevin could see she was experiencing more pain than pleasure but was working very hard to please him. She moved up and down purposefully, but carefully until, due more to friction than excitement, and with some help from a segment on NPR about gays in the military (and without an inkling as to why he cared), he was seventeen again.

As she slept quietly, Kevin lay awake looking at the ceiling. He really wanted to get up and go to Gary's, but he didn't dare. He would never dream of doing anything so impolite, to anyone, and certainly not to Gabrielle. Besides, he felt ungrateful not being satisfied. What man wouldn't kill to trade places with him? He was celebrating the biggest night of his professional career to date by making love to a beautiful woman he cared about. What could be better…?

…Kevin woke Gabby after an hour or so, kissing her breasts lightly on his way down. He slowly massaged her with his tongue and fingers until he thought she was ready. Then he positioned a stack of pillows on the bed. "Turn over." Gabby lay on her stomach with the stack of pillows positioned under her hips. Kevin continued, letting his fingers wander. When she did not complain, he continued, venturing into new territory. Gabby let out a slow, low moan, but did not speak. When he thought she was ready, Kevin entered her slowly in the traditional manner, then pulled out slowly and tapped lightly on her back door. Startled, Gabby tensed. Kevin squeezed her hips and reassured her, "If you relax, it won't hurt."

"If you don't do that, it won't hurt either!" Gabby had her head twisted almost completely around to her back like an owl.

Kevin thought, "Fine", but said nothing. Instead, he retreated to familiar territory, slipped inside, at least as far as he could, and finished 'on his own' again; that is, relying more on the thoughts in his head.

Gabby was speechless. She lay very still except for her own breathing. When she finally spoke, her tone was a mixture of anger and curiosity. "What the hell was that?"

"What do you mean?" Kevin decided playing innocent was probably the safest course.

"What do you mean 'what do you mean'? You just tried to shove your gargantuan …man-thing up my ass!"

Kevin chuckled. "You can say 'ass' but you can't say 'dick'?" He couldn't decide if he was more frustrated or amused at her prissiness. Either way, he was in no mood to argue.

"Who told you, you could do that to me?"

"Did you tell me I could not? Tell me you didn't like it."

"Oh, that is so not the point at all, and you know it! You don't just do that to someone without their permission, Kevin."

"Sex is sex, Gabby. What's the big deal?"

"It's just not something 'good girls' do."

"Gabrielle, you haven't been a 'good girl' since we were fifteen years old!" He chuckled, shaking his head.

"Hey!" She smacked him hard with a pillow.

"No. Sweetie, I'm sorry. I didn't mean it like that. But seriously, who are you trying to be good for? If you don't want anyone to know you nasty, don't tell them what you do, or allow to be done to you, in the privacy of your bedroom."

"Since when are you so liberated?"

Kevin didn't actually know, so he decided to ignore the question. "I'm sorry if I hurt you."

"It didn't hurt..."

"Do you want me to try again?" Kevin asked enthusiastically.

"I'm not going to say all that. Do you want to?" Gabby blushed.

"Uh, yes!" Kevin paused, considering how best to explain his uncharacteristically presumptuous behavior. "...Have you ever noticed that... say when you're on top... there's about six inches of extra space between us?" Kevin held his hand up to demonstrate the gap. "See, that six inches is me... well, the rest of me... out here in the cold, while the lucky first half is tucked away, all snug and warm... on the inside. So what I was thinkin' was, what I've read anyway, is that perhaps there is more... legroom... in the back."

What Kevin had actually read was that, that particular act, when properly executed, of course, could strengthen a couple's bond. He'd have mentioned that, but for one thing: the article specifically referred to male penetration by his male partner. In that moment, he didn't necessarily feel the need to bond emotionally with Gabby. Perhaps he wanted to submit? Whatever. He didn't want to submit to her. He just knew he needed more. He just wasn't certain what that was. Kevin couldn't explain his feelings about sex and intimacy to himself, let alone admit these things to Gabrielle; so, he... improvised. "Actually, biologically speaking it kinda makes sense, doesn't it?" He tilted his head and squinted a little, waiting to see if she was buying it.

"Whatever! That's just nasty! Besides, you can't make babies that way."

"Oh my God! Did you just say that? Hopefully, we're not trying to make any babies."

"Uh! Kevin!" Gabby looked wounded.

"What, Gabrielle? What do you want me to say? We haven't seen each other in over four years. You show up out of the blue with no other plans than to screw my brains out and I'm not supposed to do what feels good to me?"

"You never needed that before."

"It's not about 'need', Gabby. It's about sex. Sex is about what feels good. If you've decided that it's only for making babies, first of all, who the hell are you and what have you done with my girlfriend? And second, okay, we won't do it anymore."

"Any of it, or the part where you go up my butt?"

"Gabby!? ...Wow." Kevin honestly wasn't sure how to answer that. In that moment, he didn't see the point of having mediocre sex with Gabby just because it was what they had always done. He certainly would never force himself on her physically, and he wasn't selfish enough to force himself on her psychologically by giving her an ultimatum; so he got up and took a shower without saying anything else.

Gabby was the first to speak as he got dressed. "Maybe it was a bad idea to just jump in the way we did." She sat on the bed in a robe and sipped a fresh glass of champagne.

"You think? Seriously, Gabby, I'm really happy to see you. I've missed you." Kevin stretched the truth. "It's just been a really long time."

"I know. We've barely even spoken. I just wanted to surprise you. I've missed you too. I should have at least called you. Are you seeing anyone?"

"No. I told you, I've just been working."

"Can we have dinner tomorrow night and get caught up?"

"Of course. There isn't a show until next week, so I've got a few days off. I'll call you around six."

"Okay." Gabby got up and walked Kevin to the door. Kevin gave her a quick peck and headed toward the elevator. He looked at his watch. It was just after midnight. He called Gary to see that it wasn't too late to stop by. It wasn't at all; in fact the party was just getting started. The small group of studio executives greeted Kevin with cheers and ovations. He grabbed a bottle of sparkling water, helped himself to the buffet and listened as they discussed the upcoming plans for the company and his role in it. His night was finally going to end precisely as he hoped it would.

Kevin and Gabby continued to see each other a couple of times a week for a month or so. When Kevin told Gabby that Gary had him pretending to be gay to stay with The Company, she was surprisingly understanding.

"Don't get me wrong, I think it sucks that you have to lie, but we do what we have to, right? It's stupid, really; you're clearly not gay and clearly talented enough to make it, but again, if it's what you have to do..."

"It's really not such a big deal. I haven't been dating, so it's not like I'm lying to a person I'm sleeping with. That, I could not do." As a publicist, Gabby understood that image was everything and Broadway was one of the only places in the world where being gay might actually be to Kevin's benefit. Of course she didn't like the idea, but she figured at some point, 'we all tell bigger lies for less'. And Kevin's career had always been as important to her as it was to him.

"...Kevin, I have to tell you something, too." Gabby took a sip of her ice water with lemon.

"Gabrielle, there are only three ways this could go from here." Kevin glanced at her water and quickly counted the scenarios in his head: One: she's leaving New York; two: she's given him cooties, or three...

"I'm pregnant. Was that one of the three?" Gabby sounded defensive.

"Yes and the one that you basically assured me couldn't happen." Kevin didn't bother to ask what happened. He was solution oriented; and that seemed irrelevant now. He was well aware where babies came from, but they'd made it through four years of high school without any mishaps. He trusted her when she'd said it was not an issue. He'd kick himself later. "How far along are you?"

"About six weeks."

"How can you be so sure so soon?" He squinted at her.

"There are tests to tell as early as your first missed period; you've seen the commercials."

"I don't watch TV, Gabrielle. What do you want to do?"

"What do you mean, 'what do you want to do?'"

"Oh, I wish you wouldn't do that – repeat my questions back to me. I mean are you going to have the baby, and if so, what role would you like me to play?"

"You make it sound like your life is over, or worse, you're being cast in a bad play!" Gabby looked like she was about to cry.

"Gabby, I'm sure it's neither of those things. Do you want me to lie and say I'm thrilled? I can't. I'm also fully aware that we used to say this is what we would do. It's just that it's been a long time. I didn't know what my life was going to be like when we were kids. It's very different than I expected. I wouldn't know how to work a family into it..."

54

Kevin stared across the table at his childhood sweetheart. "...But I will figure it out, if I have to. You know that. Are we keeping the baby?"

Gabby smiled at 'we'. "Yes. I want to."

"Gabby, I'm going to lose everything I built here if I suddenly become Heathcliff Huxtable."

"Actually, that part may be okay. Remember when I got here and said I'd only be here for a few months? The Charlotte office is ready. I can go down there whenever I'm ready. The baby and I can live there and you could commute."

"From New York to Charlotte, West Virginia?"

"Actually, it's Charlotte, North Carolina. There is no Charlotte, West Virginia. I think you're thinking of Charleston, West Virginia."

"A geography lesson now? Really, Gabby?"

"I know! I know! Kevin, I want this baby, but not without you. We'll make it work. If you don't think we can make it work..."

"Just let me think, okay?" Kevin reached across the table and held her hand.

They left the restaurant and went home to their separate quarters. Kevin didn't talk to anyone. He just prayed and cursed and cried. He was not ready to be a husband or a father. He knew that there would always be a special place in his heart for Gabby. She was, after all, his first... everything; but since she'd come back, things just weren't the same. Growing up they had more in common: friends, their church, school, sex. All of that was gone. College kept them apart for four years. And the sex? Apparently, any sex you get in your teens is 'great sex'. Now it was just something to do. He needed more from a relationship - a spark, a spiritual connection. It wasn't there. But they did have something new to bond over. They were about to bring a life into the world; one he prayed would have her beauty and his... everything else. Sure, she was also smart and loving, and he was just as much fun to look at, but some of the things she said lately scared him. She was always quirky, but he never thought she was 'small' before. He didn't want his son or daughter to grow up 'small', like Gabby's father. If she was going to have a baby, Kevin was going to be there. He prayed that they loved each other enough. He knew he would love their baby. He wanted that child to have everything they did growing up: a happy, stable home with two loving parents. It was time to grow up. Kevin called Gabby early the next morning.

"Let's get married."

"What?"

"You heard me. I'm not doing any baby-mama drama. I can't. If you're having my child, we're getting married. I'll send you my show schedule so you can pick a date. Just let me know when. But, Gabby, I can't promise that I can come down there more often than one week a month."

"I think after not seeing you for four years, I can live with that."

"Please remember you said that."

"I love you, Kevin."

"I love you too, Gabrielle."

Kevin and Gabby were married in a small private ceremony presided over by her father. Gabby would have preferred a large, extravagant wedding, but her family insisted there was no time. They didn't want anyone to find out that the bishop's daughter had gotten pregnant out of wedlock; and Kevin's career was still at risk.

Ethan Jerome Rivers was born, four weeks early, on October 26, 2001. Kevin adored his son and loved being a father. He missed not seeing EJ every day, and when EJ was old enough they talked on the phone daily. Kevin also kept his promise to come home at least one week during the month; and Gabby came to every opening night for seven years. They did indeed 'make it work.

6

THAT AINT IT

Present Day

Kevin continued to stumble over his lines. Gary was getting annoyed. "What's the problem, Kevin?"

"Marcus wouldn't say this." Kevin shook the script he was holding at Gary.

"Well, what would he say?"

"I don't know, but certainly not 'what's the big deal? I like dick!'" (Gary suppressed a giggle.) "There's no way he'd say that to his wife, or anyone else for that matter. He's more complex than that. I don't think it's about sex at all. Who wrote this crap, anyway?" Kevin was the only person on the stage that could get away with bashing the script. In his seven years with The Company, he'd starred in four long-running, hit shows. He was a bonafide headliner, and hardly ever a diva; but he was known for rewriting a script in rehearsal.

Nikki Vanderpip threw an orange at Kevin's head. "I wrote it! Do you have a problem with me?" She stood with her arms crossed glaring at Kevin while trying not to laugh herself. Despite her initial resistance to his joining the company, she and Kevin had developed a healthy working relationship, if not friendship. But they did butt heads from the beginning artistically.

"Figures. You throw like a girl, too!" He ducked and giggled.

"What do you want him to say, Shakespeare?"

"I'm not sure. It all just feels artificial. He's more thoughtful than this. And sure, he's fun, and sexy, but he's not callous. He's not this okay with the possibility that he might gay. He hasn't gotten here, yet. I think it's closer to: he has the feelings; he knows they're real, but he doesn't know how to – or want to – act on them. He's got too much to lose. He doesn't want to hurt anyone, and he doesn't see yet that the truth is a lot more satisfying than the lie he's been living."

"So you're saying it's not the line-s, it's the character himself?" Nikki wanted to strangle him, but she knew he was right. Kevin was always right about the script.

"Um...Yes. I think it's the character, not the script that is poorly written and lacks depth and believability..."

Nikki pulled off one of her Jimmy Choos and hurled it at Kevin's head. When he caught it, she took off toward the stage.

Gary threw his copy of the script on the table as Nikki chased Kevin around on the stage. It was clearly trash now. "Let's break for lunch, everyone! Please be back by two o'clock." He called after Kevin who was fixing his shirt and walking toward the exit. "Where do you think you're going? You have script to re-write. Please go to my office and have Cory order lunch. We'll be there in ten minutes."

Nikki did a double take." What do you mean 'we'?"

"I mean 'we' – you and I - will be in my office to meet with Ke-vin to rework the script as soon as 'we' – you and I – talk about him behind his back while he orders lunch." Kevin just shook his head and walked away.

"Fine. What?" Nikki slipped her shoe back on.

"He's ready." Gary had a huge grin on his face.

"Ready for what?" Nikki squinted at Gary.

"He's ready to do more than act, dance and sing. You know he is."

"Well, it's about time! Do you know how hard it is to write bad dialogue on purpose?" Apparently, Nikki had deliberately written crap in the hopes that Kevin would run with it. She'd been watching him clean up bad writing for years. In fact, it was his sensitivity and intelligence that finally won her over. She'd been determined not to jump on the 'he's a great actor' bandwagon, without proof that he could do more than look pretty and recite lines like a trained bird.

When Nikki finally made it to Gary's office, Kevin expected The Company's executive director to throw something else at him. She did, a set of keys. "Take Riley's old office. Have the new pages ready by Monday, please." Gary and Kevin stared at each other and then back to Nikki. "Congratulations, Kevin. Good work." She winked and left as quickly as she'd come in.

Gary walked over and rubbed Kevin's shoulders. "See, I told you it was only a matter of time."

"What? Not to sound ungrateful, but it took me seven years to get assigned one rewrite. At this rate, I'll be sixty before I can direct."

"Hey!" Gary was offended. "I started almost exactly the way you did and I'm barely thirty-six. Things move a lot faster from here. Prove you can tell a story with compelling characters and you'll direct the first thing you write alone… I promise."

Kevin tossed his new office keys in the air. "This is pretty cool, huh?"

"Oh, I'm not surprised at all. I'm excited to see what comes out of you. Get to work. You know where I am if you need me."

Kevin left Gary's office and went to find his smaller interior office around the corner. It didn't have a window, but it had potential. Anxious to get started, but unable to work without plants, music or his laptop, he went home and hunkered down to rewrite the play about a married, thirty-ish, African American man struggling with his sexual identity. When he reached the part in the original script where 'Marcus' begins to question his feelings for a man, Kevin was blocked. He tried to consider who Marcus really was; to get inside his head. Sure he could write great dialogue, but still the character felt flat. What was his motivation, the heart behind the lines? Why did he really work sixty-hour workweeks and never go home? Why was it so hard to say the words? For two days, he came up with nothing and finally thought to himself, "I don't know who he is; but I know who he's not. I can't relate... Damn it, KJ, you're an actor! Why is this so hard?" He went to the bathroom and looked in the mirror and continued talking to himself. "Just think about a man. You're a man. It's not that hard." He closed his eyes and tried to consider his character – the character he was writing for:

"The feelings aren't new. They've always been there; he just hadn't met anyone to ignite them before now. It's different than his relationship with his wife. He can be himself: vulnerable, silly, impulsive, youthful, flirtatious, but still strong, masculine, sexual, aggressive. With his wife he feels responsible, but empty; with 'him' he feels carefree, open, whole. It's not about sex; but, with his wife, sexually he feels confined, limited. He hasn't been with a man, but he suspects he'd prefer the uninhibited, the passion. Sex with his wife feels like a duty. He wonders what it would be like to submit, to be held, and to please someone who has no limits or requirements. What if he could fall in love with someone who thinks and loves and makes love the way he thinks, the way he wants to love someone? Why doesn't he think he can have that with a woman? Why not his wife? He can't let her, any woman, see softness. That's not manly. That would ruin everything. Men aren't supposed to need tenderness and warmth. Sure, a wife should be supportive, understanding, helpful, a partner; but that's not what he has. He lives with a stranger he's known all his life. They know each other intimately, and they know each other's history; but their souls aren't connected. They love each other because they're good, loving people, but they don't like each other at all. Somewhere deep inside he believes there must be more to life than this. He's dismissed his attraction to men for years, most of his life. He has thought about what sex would be like, but he isn't going to live like that. He's not going to lie and cheat and sleep around. But could he really live the life of a gay man? Could he date, fall in love with, be in a relationship with a man? Society says, 'no'. He's tortured by the thought of being an outcast, of losing his family. Everyone he loves will leave. 'Real love' can't possibly be worth losing everything else."

Kevin opened his eyes. "No." He began shaking his head wildly. "No, no, no, no, no!" He looked at the clock. He needed to get to the theater. As he showered, he continued muttering to himself. "Nope. That's not it."

By the time Kevin made it to the theater, Gary was already there. "You look like shit. If I didn't know better, I'd think you were hung over – or still drunk. Are you high?"

"Of course not. This body", he did an effortless arabesque, "is a temple!"

"Whatever. Your temple has consumed more cheeseburgers and pork ribs than all Five Guys and Tony Roma combined. Seriously, what's the matter with you?"

Kevin started walking out of the theater toward Gary's office, leaving the rest of the cast to run through their lines undirected and without the male lead. Once inside, Kevin threw himself on the couch and screamed into a pillow.

"Okay, you're starting to scare me. Would you please tell me what's going on?"

"When did you know you were gay, Gary?"

"When I was five. All I wanted for my birthday was a 'Baby Crissy' doll, you know, the one whose hair grew... and a pink feather boa."

"That just means you've always been a girl. Do I have to be a girl?"

"No, I guess not. You can be masculine and still be gay. Thank God! Can you imagine a world full of bottoms with no tops? I wouldn't wanna live in a world like that." Gary's face looked grim.

"Can you focus, please?"

Gary pretended to shiver a little. "Okay, I'm back. What's going on, Kevin?"

"I've suddenly been having these thoughts."

"Well, it's about time." Gary teased.

"No, seriously. Do you know I have never dated another woman other than Gabrielle? Isn't that weird?"

"No. She's beautiful, and sweet, and smart; and if that thing she wore to the show last week is any indication, sexy as hell. And you grew up together, right? I'd say that makes you about the luckiest straight guy in the world."

"Oh, it's not luck. We'd been basically engaged since birth."

"Again, why is that a bad thing?"

"Because I think I might be gay." Kevin whispered just in case Gary's office was bugged.

"Um, you know we've already got everyone here pretty well convinced of that. You don't need to lie to me. ...Why are we whispering?"

"I'm not lying to you, Gary. I'm serious. I think I'm gay. I've been telling myself for years–my whole life really, that I'm not, that I couldn't be. The more I try to explain it away, the more I remember and the more I realize it's true."

"Okay. Slow down. There are a couple of tests. Who was your first crush? That's usually the first sign."

"Wait a minute, isn't the first sign the fact that I've been trying to convince myself that I'm straight?" Kevin frowned at Gary.

"Good point. Okay, second test, first crush..."

"That's easy, captain of the men's basketball team."

"Stop lying!" Gary burst out laughing.

"I'm not. His name was Shawn Mitchell. He was in my Chemistry and AP English classes. I used to daydream about pushing his lab partner down the stairs. Junior year, he did a presentation on, I don't know, *Great Expectations* or something, and let's just say, I had to stay in my seat so long after the bell rang I was late for my next class. Talk about 'beautiful, smart and sexy'! Why do you think I never played sports?"

"Because you've been dancing since you could walk?" Gary shrugged at his friend.

"Well, yeah, that and I couldn't let anyone find out that the sight of a half-naked man made my dick hard. Funny, little gay boys and Greco-Roman wrestling don't mix nearly as well as one might think."

Gary paused to consider the scenario. "Okay, you've been dancing since you were six. What about the boys in the ballet? Surely, they would have triggered something for you?"

"No, not really. I felt at home with them, but I wasn't attracted to them. But, I wasn't attracted to the girls, either. My fantasies have always been about quiet, muscular, masculine, nerdy men."

"Basically, your complete opposite."

"Shut up." Kevin gave Gary's characterization of him further thought and then nodded his head. "Yeah, that's pretty accurate, really."

"As intriguing as this all sounds, Kev, don't you think it sounds a little superficial?"

"Absolutely! That's why I'm freaking out. I won't be a statistic. I will not be another Black man on the d-l. I want whatever this is to go away. I will not live a life based solely on some primal desire to have some strong, dark, sensitive, well-endowed, deep-thinking, compassionate man devour me!"

Gary was laughing and fanning himself. "Are you sure, because that was an oddly specific description of something you don't want to happen to you?"

"I won't leave my wife and son to be an outcast."

"Who says you have to be an outcast? What if it's the best thing for everyone involved?"

"How could that possibly be the best thing, Gary?"

"Are you happy, Kevin? Don't think about it, just answer."

"No."

"Why do you think that is?"

"Because I've been living a lie, and not the one you made me live! I was lying when I got here. My whole life is a lie!"

"Not all of it. Your career is real. Your son is real. I hope our friendship is real."

"I'm sorry. You're right; but stop being a baby, you know what I mean."

"I'm just listening, Kevin. Maybe you're having an early mid-life crisis. How can you be sure you aren't just bored with Gabby?"

"Because she's the most beautiful woman in the world. Most of my life I've wanted to be her; but I've never had any real desire for her. I have never been emotionally attracted to any woman before. I'm barely attracted to her. I've just been acting out my part. She's my wife. We have sex. I get what I need from her and try to give her what she needs. Wow..." Kevin sat up and looked at Gary. "...I don't think I've ever made love before. Don't misunderstand. We've had a lot of sex; and it's pretty good, I think, but it's just that, sex. I've never been in love, Gary."

"Wow. Now that's deep. Do you think you could fall in love with a man, have a relationship with one?"

"I really don't know. I know I couldn't right now. I'm a mess."

"Smart move. There is nothing more frustrating than a newbie. Oh, wait, yes there is: a married, confused, newbie. But, why the suppression? You've been around gay men your whole life, at least your whole career. Your parents must know 'creative' people. Are they homophobic?"

"I don't know. I don't think so. Like you said, they must know plenty of gay people, but it's not like they introduced them to me as such. I've never heard them say anything negative. But they are both deacons in the church."

"Well, what church? Ya know, they're not all the same, especially now. Is it affirming?"

"No, it's Baptist. What's affirming? Is that like AME?"

"Oh boy. It's a really good thing you're pretty." Gary was shaking his head again. "An affirming church is one that affirms the whole person – gay, straight, lesbian, bisexual, transgender... The church I belong to, for instance, was founded by a gay man, on the belief that 'God loves everyone, regardless of his or her sexual orientation or gender identity'. A more radical approach is the belief that gay, lesbian, bisexual and transgender individuals are God's chosen ones."

"Okay, I don't know a whole lot about the Bible, but I know that thing you just said aint in there."

"In those exact words? No, you're right. But do you live your life strictly according to every letter of the Bible, or do you rely some on your own experience, what the Holy Spirit tells you?"

"I've never thought about it before. I've barely even been to church since I left home. I've been sending checks to my parent's church for years. I pray; but it's more a prayer of Thanksgiving than need. It's funny; I do feel disconnected from God. I just thought it was natural. Some people are religious, some aren't. Or perhaps it's something you grow out of. Michael used to be churchy; then he turned into a ho."

"Maybe it's something you grow into. There is a revival at my church tonight. You should come."

"Okay, but don't blame me if the walls cave in. I told you, it's been a while."

"I think we'll be okay. We just put a new roof on." Gary gave Kevin a brotherly hug and kept his arm around him as they walked down the hall. Kevin let his head fall on Gary's shoulder as Michael was walking by.

"Hey, Superstar! Mr. Director! Don't you two make a handsome couple?"

Gary rushed to set the record straight. "No. It's nothing like that, Mike. You ready for rehearsal?"

Michael still looked skeptical, especially since Kevin wasn't talking. "Oh, you know me. I'm always ready."

7

HEATHEN!

Kevin entered Metropolitan Community Church, New York just as revival was getting started. He immediately thought it looked more like backstage at one of his early auditions than a church. The people were young and old, Black, White, and Hispanic. What struck him was the come-as-you-are-ness of this place. He felt over dressed in his slacks, dress shirt and tie. He watched the lesbian couple in front of him holding hands as they settled into their seats. A few pews in front of them, a large, but surprisingly attractive, woman with an Adam's apple was hugging someone Kevin did not dare label as male or female. He couldn't tell if they were a really, really pretty boy or a tomboy. His mind raced as he tried to determine which possibility made him more excited. He went from confused to embarrassed when Gary introduced the young man as 'Stephen'. He had to remind himself he was in church, not Studio 54.

As if seeing all the beautiful people walking around in their own skin weren't over stimulation enough, what happened next literally made him run out of the sanctuary. The pastor approached the pulpit, wearing jeans and a button down shirt. "Brothers and sisters, I will not be before you long tonight. I am as excited about our guest speaker as most of you are. If you're not excited, it's because you don't know what's about to happen; you should come to church more often." Elder Tracy Nation paused as laughter sprinkled the room. "Okay, okay...I'll save that for later. Tonight, we will be hearing from my brother in Christ and dear friend, Pastor, Rev. Dr. Kyle Tye. Welcome!" The sanctuary erupted with applause for the local recording artist and founding pastor of a nearby church. Kevin just sat still trying not to look clueless. Surely, they were over-reacting. What was all the fuss about? Rev. Tye stood up as the cheering continued and Kevin thought to himself, "Oh. Oh, I see." Then he thought again. "You heathen. No, seriously, who is HE...? Heathen...!"

8

...WHEN I SEE HIM

Rev. Dr. Tye walked into the pulpit and retrieved the microphone from the mic stand, then stepped back down into the half circle that had been created in the middle of the sanctuary. He wore jeans, cowboy boots and a white embroidered tunic. Kevin thought it looked very similar to something he'd seen Gabby wear and then he thought, "That top never looked like that on Gabby. Heathen! Oh my God! I'm going to Hell!" Kevin struggled to contain himself so he could listen to what the man was saying. When the music started playing, he became anxious. "Oh, please tell me he doesn't sing. I'm gonna wet myself. Yup. Right here in this church, on this pew." Kevin looked around. No one else seemed to be having the same reaction. It was just him. He closed his eyes and tried to just listen.

♫They tell me that I'm wrong, Lord; that You'll never let me in, that who I am is not of You, I'm wrong and full of sin. But, when I close my eyes I feel the truth, I'm Yours and I am Good! My God, You made me, like nobody ever could...♫

Kevin tried to listen to the words and ignore the man who looked like a god and sang like an angel. When it was clear he wasn't going to be able to on his own, he excused himself to the men's room to splash some water on his face. When that didn't work, he walked out to the parking lot and, for what must have been the first time in his adult life, began praying, and pacing. "Dear Lord, please forgive me. I know I came here tonight looking for something... an answer, the beginning of an answer? I want to know You better, Lord. I know that the only way to know me is to know YOU and to understand who you intend for me to be. I know it's not as simple as walking into this place and seeing these people, seeing myself for the first time. I know I have to wait for you to answer, but God... You know you wrong, right? He's beautiful and he looks like Jesus (with dimples)... and he can sang! You could have found another way to tell me... You coulda just told me I was gay! You didn't have to do that, God!" Kevin continued pacing and chastising the Lord. "Wow! Really?! Na uh! For me? Oooooh weee. But I gotta reel it in, huh? Yes, Lord. Can I get some help, please? Thank you, God. Oh! And thank You, God!" Kevin continued to pace, opening his eyes long enough not to hit anything, until he thought he was ready to go inside and sit like a grown-up. When he returned to his seat, Gary looked him over quickly and smiled at him. He looked okay; better than okay...

Rev. Tye had stopped singing and he was preaching from what Kevin remembered as Acts 10. "To exclude... segregate... block anyone from a place at God's table is about the worst thing you can do as a believer. Who are we to say who is or is not one of God's children? If you meet a man on the street and, because he sees the God in you, calls you brother, but you frown at him and say he is not welcome in this place, because he's straight, dirty, or worse, Southern Baptist, (laughter sprinkled the room) you are doing that thing which Christ himself said we should never do. But Mark 9:37 says 'whoever embraces one of these children as I do embraces me, and far more than me, God who sent me.'...

...Church, it is not enough that we come here and sing some songs, hear a word that encourages us and leave knowing that we made each other feel loved. A church is just an armory! We're supposed to come in, get what we need and take it outside of these walls to where the real need is. Someone who was too afraid, sick, tired, depressed, broken, drunk, embroiled in addiction, promiscuity, self-hate...to come to church tonight is waiting right outside these walls to hear that God loves them! What will it take for you to step outside yourself and share God's unconditional Love? Let us pray…"

Kevin's eyes were already closed. He found it best not to look directly at Rev. Tye. Closing his eyes allowed him to actually hear what he was saying. Wow! As he prayed, Kevin considered for a moment whether he had ever felt separated from God's love himself and realized he had; but, not because of anything anyone else had done. He'd separated himself. He'd long since stopped seeking God's Love, acceptance, grace. He arrogantly walked around as though he was the man he was today by his own power. What was there to give back? He liked himself well enough, but was not so impressed that he saw the God in himself. No wonder he felt empty. Kevin blocked out the sound of praying around him and turned to kneel in front of the pew.   "Heavenly Father, thank you for your many blessings. Forgive me for my selfish ways; my arrogance, my fearfulness. Help me today to walk closer to You, Lord. Guide me. You know me. You know my heart. Give me the strength and courage to be the man you made me to be, whoever that is, God. I want to start today. Make me over. Make me over. Make me over. Restore my heart, so I may do Your will... These things I ask in Your Son's name. Amen."

Kevin took his time getting up. When he did, Gary was gone. Music was playing in the background and people were milling about. Before Kevin found Gary, he spotted Rev. Tye near the door speaking to the woman with the Adam's apple. Kevin tried not to stare, at either of them; but before he could look away, Rev. Tye caught his gaze and flashed the most amazing smile Kevin had ever seen. Kevin smiled back briefly and turned away from the door to continue to look for Gary. He found him near the choir stand speaking to the minister of music.

"Well, what'd you think?" Gary put is hand on Kevin's shoulder.

"I think I've stayed out of church for way too long. I'll have to come back." Just as he said it, Rev. Tye walked over.

"Hello, Gary. It's good to see you. How have you been?" They gave a quick man-hug.

"I'm really good, Kyle. I see you're still steppin' on toes." Kyle smiled and shook his head; his ponytail came to the middle of his back. Kevin tried not to stare. Gary noticed and tried not to introduce them. Then Kyle turned to Kevin and extended his hand.

"Hi. I'm Kyle."

"Oh, I'm sorry. Rev. Dr. Tye, this is…" Kyle interrupted Gary.

"Kevin Rivers. It's a pleasure to meet you. I really enjoy your work. I've seen *No Greater Sin* at least six times."

Kevin could feel his face getting hot. "That's quite a compliment coming from you, Reverend. My silly little productions seem like child's play compared to the work you do."

"No. Make no mistake, entertainment is important. There is more than one way to minister to people, Kevin."

Gary realized Kyle was still holding Kevin's hand and cleared his throat. Kevin didn't seem to mind "Again, thank you, Reverend. I must say, your sermon already has me feeling inspired to do more."

"Well as long as you know it's not my sermon. I'm just the messenger. It's just 'Kyle', by the way."

"Kyle. Okay. It's very nice to meet you."

"You too, Kevin."

Gary cleared his throat again. "Kevin, are you ready to go?"

Kevin was still looking at Kyle, who'd turned to speak with someone. He heard Gary's voice and shook his head as if to jolt himself back to reality.

"Um… sure… Just let me get my jacket." Kevin walked away. As he approached the door on his way out, he saw

Gary talking to Kyle again. As Kyle walked toward Kevin, Gary pointed to Kyle and signaled for Kevin to call him later. Kevin looked confused.

"Are you leaving?" Kyle smiled at Kevin.

"I think we were going to head out." He glanced passed Kyle and saw Gary walking out the door.

"Do you have plans? I was hoping you might like to grab a cup of coffee."

Kevin had never been asked out by a man before. He tried not to giggle. "Sure."

"Great. Let me grab my things and say, 'good night'."

"I'll be right over there." Kevin smiled back and pointed to the lobby of the church.

Kevin waited by the door and Kyle returned after only a minute or two with his jacket draped over his arm. "Okay. Do you mind walking? There's a place just a few blocks that way."

"No, it's nice out. A walk sounds good. I could use the fresh air."

"Are you troubled by something?" Kyle looked concerned.

"No, not at all. Actually, quite the opposite; I feel renewed."

"Ah, the sign of a successful revival." Kyle nodded.

"I wouldn't know, actually, I can't remember the last time I went to one."

"Really? Well, what'd you think?"

"I think this church and its members are a far cry from what I grew up with. I don't remember people leaving church looking and feeling quite so... energized."

"You clearly didn't grow up in an 'affirming church'."

"Ha! I just heard that term for the first time today!"

"Well, I'm glad you enjoyed yourself. It's important that your spirit is fed. I hope you'll go back." As they entered the coffee shop, Kyle held the door open for Kevin. That did make Kevin giggle just a little. "Sorry. Habit."

"What? Oh! No! It's fine, really. Wow. I feel silly."

"Why?"

"I'm not sure yet. Let me figure it out and I'll get back to you."

"I'm going to hold you to that." Kyle's voice made Kevin's stomach wiggle.

"Do I hear an accent?"

"Yes. I'm not sure which, though. My mother is Jamaican and my father is Ethiopian." Kyle chuckled. "And I am a dual Canadian / US citizen."

"Interesting. Where did you grow up?"

"Jamaica, until I was ten. Then we moved to Toronto."

"That's quite a move. Did your parents travel for a living?"

"Yes, my father, but that's not why we moved. My parents figured out I was gay before I did and didn't want me to be killed."

"W-wow."

"Yeah, 'wow' is right. Jamaica is no place for a gay child. Being homosexual is still a written crime there; but the police are almost the least of your problems. It's the people. It's actually worse in Ethiopia. My mother used to tell me God has quite a sense of irony, if not humor."

"Well, I've always believed everything happens for a reason." Kevin caressed his coffee cup. "I think I know what it is... that has me feeling silly. Have we met before?"

Kyle flashed that smile again. "Um...about an hour ago...at the church down the street..."

"No... I mean before then. Your voice sounds familiar."

"Oh! Okay. Whew. I thought perhaps you'd forgotten that quickly." Kyle pretended to wipe his brow. "Let's see. I am senior pastor of a church not far from here."

"Nope. That's not it."

"Well, I've recorded a couple of CDs but they haven't

74

gotten much circulation, yet."

"Oh, well that's only a matter of time."

"Thank you for that. I'm hopeful. I did some radio shows a few months ago. Maybe it was on the air."

"Well, I split my time between here and Charlotte, North Carolina."

"Well that must be it, then. I did a discussion on NPR on gay marriage and the church. I sat in a small studio for forty-five minutes with Satan himself, a Bishop Robert Nichols. I believe he's from Georgia; but I know the show aired in Charlotte."

Kevin spit out his coffee. "I'm sorry." He reached for a napkin. "I heard that program."

"Clearly."

"No. That's not what's freaking me out. Wooo! Next time you talk to your mom, tell her she aint nevah lied! God certainly does have a sense of humor!" Kyle looked anxious. "Bishop Nichols is my father-in-law."

"You mean by marriage to a sibling?"

"Oh, I wish, but, no. I'm an only child. I mean by marriage to me. I am married to his only daughter."

"Wow."

"'Wow' aint even close to what I was thinking. Will you excuse me for a moment, please, Kyle?"

"Of course. Can I get you another coffee, something to eat?"

"Yes, thanks. Anything you're having will be fine. I eat just about anything."

"Now that surprises me."

"I'll be right back." Kevin went to the men's room and tried not to talk to himself at the urinal. But when he looked in the mirror as he washed his hands, he had to. "Just don't panic. God always has a plan…"

By the time Kevin returned to the table, their food was there. Kyle ordered a foot-long Philly cheese steak and a club

75

sandwich. "I thought we could share. I can't say I have much of an appetite left, though."

"I'm sorry, did I do something wrong?"

"Aside from being married, no." Kyle tried not to sound too heavy, but he was visibly disappointed.

Kevin was determined not to panic, that included not letting Kyle panic. "Then why did you order the food?"

"I wasn't ready to say, 'good night'.

"Neither am I. Eat your sandwich, please." Kevin smiled at Kyle and saw his mood visibly lift. "You probably need details, don't you?"

"Unless you want to eat by yourself, yes."

"Oh, well that's no problem. I can eat. I can always eat." Kevin picked up a quarter of the club sandwich from the plate in front of Kyle and placed it on his.

"Start talking. No, wait." Kyle bowed his head to bless the food and held out his hand for Kevin. He prayed aloud and squeezed Kevin's hand before releasing it. "Okay. I'm listening."

Kevin took a bite of his sandwich, a sip of water and tried to speak slowly. He wanted to get everything out into the open. He didn't know what was about to happen, but he knew if nothing else, he wanted Kyle as a friend. "We've been together practically all our lives. My family moved next to theirs when I was six. The church I talk about is the Bishop's church."

"I'm sure he thinks that. Hopefully, it's God's church." Kevin could see the distain Kyle felt for his father-in-law. He found it comforting to see someone else respond similarly to the man he'd never liked or trusted. "I'm sorry. We shouldn't talk about him. Please, tell me about your family."

"Well, Gabby, Gabrielle has been one of my best friends my whole life. She's the only girl, woman, person, I've ever kissed…had sex with. She's actually kind of fantastic. I couldn't ask for, don't deserve, a better wife or mother to my son."

"What's missing?"

"Why do you assume something is missing?"

"Because it's a Friday night and you're here with me instead of on your way to be with her…"

"And on the day before my birthday, mind you. You're right; but I don't know what's missing."

"Are you gay?"

"I honestly don't know, Kyle. I've never been in love before. Don't you find it weird that I'm almost thirty and I've never been in love?"

"No. I'm thirty-one and neither have I. But you were motivated by something to get married. What do you think it was?"

Kevin answered easily. "Responsibility. Commitment. Family. I do love Gabby. It was expected, arranged that we'd be together. I simply never imagined that I would be settling. Really. If you meet her you'll understand. She is no one's consolation prize."

"Neither are you. Have you considered that you both deserve to be truly happy?"

"I haven't; but you're right. She does deserve better."

"You did it again."

"What's that?"

"Minimized your own value and needs. Do you think you deserve something more than the feelings you're describing?" Kyle stared at Kevin and it made his head swim.

"I feel responsible for this mess. I haven't even considered that anyone is going to be happy on the other side of it, least of all me."

"What do you think your options are?"

"Stay miserable or destroy everyone I love."

"You mean 'and', don't you?"

"Wow. You're tough. What are your degrees in, by the way?"

"Theology with an emphasis on Pastoral Counseling, Music, and Psychology."

"You could have warned me." Kevin smiled.

"Sorry. You didn't ask until now." Kyle played with a cold french-fry. Kevin was jealous of the poor dead piece of potato. "Did you answer the question?"

"I honestly don't remember the question."

"What are your options? Okay. Let me rephrase. What do you want to do?"

"Run away with you to an island paradise. Not Jamaica, of course…" Kyle laughed out loud. "Wow! Did I really just say that out loud?" Kevin blushed but he didn't look away.

"Yes." Kyle signaled for the server to bring the check. "We should get you home."

"I'm sorry. Is that thought so unappealing?" Kevin's nervous act was only partially an act.

"Uh, no, on the contrary. There's some work and some praying that needs to take place and I don't think we can accomplish much more sitting at this table." Kevin still looked puzzled. Kyle held up his blackberry. "Kevin, if you weren't married, I'd be online buying plane tickets." Kevin smiled until his cheeks hurt.

They exchanged numbers and Kyle put Kevin in a cab to Harlem. He walked the four or five blocks to his Manhattan apartment.

9

MAN-HUGS...

Kevin flew up the stairs, two at a time, and fired up his laptop. He remembered the radio broadcast Kyle mentioned and wanted to find it. It was originally on during a drive to Charlotte. Ethan was in the car with him. Just as it always had in church growing up, the sound of his father-in-law's voice made his skin crawl. He'd found the voice of the other man in the debate equally distracting, but for an entirely different reason.

"What's so funny, Dad?" EJ turned off his Ipod to question his father.

"Oh, nothing. I'm just listening to your granddad on the radio."

"What's he talking about?"

"Oh, nothing, really." Kevin was telling the truth. He thought the bishop was a narrow-minded, hypocritical, idiot. Of course, he'd never elude that fact to his son; so, he turned the station.

Kevin was thrilled to find the conversation in the NPR archives, almost a year after the original broadcast. Kevin grabbed a bottle of water and an apple from the kitchen and curled up on the couch with his laptop. He muttered to himself how stupid it was that it wasn't a video archive. He had this image in his head of the pompous, self-righteous bishop in all his assholy glory standing across from Kyle, the dreadlocked, giant, doctor of theology, music and psychology...with dimples. The first question went to the bishop.

Host: "Bishop Nichols, as pastor of a Baptist church here in Charlotte, what would you say is primary objection to granting equal marriage rights to same-sex couples?"

Bishop Nichols: "It's actually quite simple, the Bible clearly states in Romans and Leviticus that your homosexuality is an abomination and that anyone who practices it is outside the will of God. The only marriage sanctioned by God is that between one man and one woman for the procreation of children."

Host: "Dr. Tye?"

Kevin was still grinning at his screen.

Dr. Tye: "First of all, 'marriage', as opposed to 'holy union' is sanctioned by The State. The State has the power to grant licenses for people to marry in churches or wherever else they choose, by ordained clergy or by any other state-sanctioned entity, like a justice of the peace. The Church should have no role in State matters granting or withholding equal rights to all citizens. I was raised in Canada, so it's been a minute since my citizenship test, but I understand the U.S. still claims to operate under the original policy of separation of church and state?"

"The matter of Holy Union is for each individual couple to decide. No church has the authority to tell someone who they should or should not love and partner with. This program is not long enough to debate the incidences of scriptural reference to homosexuality in the Bible. On that we'll simply have to agree to disagree; but I can tell you that it does clearly say that ALL sex outside of a committed relationship is wrong. Denying a loving, committed couple the right to join in a holy union, and have that union recognized in the place where they live is to deny many their freedom of religious expression."

Host: "Okay, then; Bishop Nichol, you're shaking your head.

Bishop Nichols: "Ordinary people cannot begin to know the mind and heart of God. All these people walking around saying that 'God made homosexuals' are delusional. God made Adam and Eve. If gay people are allowed to marry, it will ruin marriage for everyone. Who would my daughter marry?"

Dr. Tye: (Chuckling) "I have been studying the Bible my entire life. Some might say that I have an extra-ordinary understanding of The Word of God; yet, I know I don't know it all. I can tell you that I will never fully understand the mind and heart of God. I do believe that the genuine affinity for and attraction to qualities in a person of the same gender is something some people, myself included, are born with. I believe to tell anyone that God didn't make them, just as they are, and God doesn't love them, is the greatest of all possible sins! And I would hope, Bishop Nichols, that you would encourage your daughter to marry someone whom she loves, who loves her in return. Your question suggests that you believe that if gay marriage were legal and acceptable in this country, that suddenly everyone would turn gay. That's like saying that if marijuana is ever made legal, everyone will start getting high. Actually it's more like my waking up tomorrow morning and suddenly being able to perform brain surgery. Sure it's legal, and looks like a really cool thing to be able to do, but that's not one of my gifts."

Bishop Nichols: "Sir, I will pray for your soul, that you see the error of your ways and that you discontinue the practice of leading people away from God's truth. Apparently, you've been mislead."

Host: "Gentlemen, we have time for just one call. Joshua, you're on the line."

Caller: "This question is for Rev. Tye: I'm a gay man. I've known it my whole life, and I love God and my church; but what do I say to people who come up to me and say that I can't be gay and be a Christian?"

Rev. Dr. Tye: "Joshua, I always found it helpful to remember John 3:16. That 'whosoever' does include you. If that isn't enough, then remember that, while people may try to judge you, your heart, even your faith walk, they cannot judge your experience. Only you know what God says to you about who you are. Let people try and judge you. Just know what my mother used to tell me,' They have neither heaven nor hell to put you in. That power belongs to God'."

10

...AND PHONE CALLS

As Kevin lay on the couch smiling to himself and thinking about the day and Kyle, the phone rang. Since it was after midnight, he answered expecting it to be a wrong number.

"Hello."

♫Happy birthday to you...♫ Kyle's voice was yummy.

"Mmmm. That's nice."

"Did I make it?"

"Depends on what you were trying to accomplish..." Kevin fanned himself and did the pee-pee dance, still managing to sound composed.

"I wanted to be the first person to wish you 'happy birthday'. Did I make it?"

"Yes. Thank you." Kevin smiled into the phone.

"So did I lose all my points calling you so soon?"

"Probably about as many as I will when I tell you that I came home and pulled up your NPR interview."

"Wow. It's a tie. We are the silliest men I know."

"Oh, com' on, now. You know Gary, he's pretty goofy."

"Yes, he is. Thanks for reminding me."

"How do you know each other, anyway?"

"We went to seminary together, actually. He was leaving as I was coming in, but we've remained friends."

"Wow! I forgot that about him. The world really is small, isn't it?"

"It is, and I am glad about it."

Long silence.

"So, are you still married?" Kyle sounded hopeful.

"Yeah..." Kevin's response was a wistful sigh.

"Okay, here's what we're gonna do..."

"I'm listening."

"We're going to be friends. We'll only see each other in church, and occasionally talk on the phone."

"Wow. That sounds serious. Why so serious?"

"I'm gonna give you a moment to think about that." Kyle whistled a generic tune while Kevin contemplated the situation.

When Kevin did speak, his tone was flat, as if he'd conceded defeat. "And when we do see each other, we'll only shake hands, or give a hardy 'man-hug'."

"Exactly." Kyle chuckled.

"Oh boy. So, where do we begin?" Kevin moved from the sofa to his bedroom and bounced on the bed like a little kid.

"Well, let's start with why you were at MCC tonight. I mean, I know they get straight people in there from time to time, but they're usually lost..." Kevin laughed. "Seriously, you mentioned you hadn't been in church in a while... Don't get me wrong, I know all about fate, I just want to know why you think you were there."

Kevin sighed deeply and stretched across the bed on his stomach. "I've been thinking about that a little tonight. I really feel like I've been ...floundering lately. I don't know when it started; maybe about a year ago; actually, pretty consistently my whole life, but I've always just pushed the thoughts aside. But then I started writing."

"That'll get you every time."

"Well, nobody told me. I've had all these characters in my head and I started thinking about 'motivation' and 'truth.' And I then I started thinking about my motivation and my truth. My life has always been easy. More and more lately, it feels like a struggle. Not the everyday things, but the big things, the part that's supposed to matter most. I've been telling myself for years that I love my life; but I don't. I love my work, and that has been enough that whatever else I thought I needed didn't matter. But the theater, as much as I love it, is not my life and it is not enough by itself anymore. So, I think to myself, 'you can start living your life now, right?'"

"Right."

"But my ungrateful butt doesn't really like my real life. I don't like living in an apartment in Harlem with my childhood best friend while my family is nine states away. But I don't …" Kevin was quiet for a long time.

"What is it?"

"I don't need to be with my wife every day. I don't miss her like that. I never have. I love my son. I miss him every day, but not so much that I want to live there. Isn't that awful?"

"Not if it's true. It probably feels bad to say it, because you're not used to selfishly talking about your needs. But, it's not so bad. What matters is how you handle yourself, and how you communicate to the people you say you care about."

"Man-hugs and phone calls."

"Yup. There's more."

"Is that a question or a statement?"

"Both. What aren't you saying?"

"I don't know. There's just a feeling." Kyle waited. "I don't really know."

"I think it's probably more like you know, but you're afraid to say it out loud. Kevin, anxiety doesn't exist in a vacuum, it comes from a place. Your feelings are real. You're smarter and more thoughtful than the person who 'can't put their finger on it'."

"Ya know, you psychoanalyzing me is cute and sexy today; but I'm thinking ten years from now, not so much…"

"Yeah well, it's still today. Spill it." Kyle's tone sent a wave through Kevin's body. It was kind and light but it told Kevin that he was, as Nana would say, 'not to be trifled with.'

Kevin let out a deep sigh. "I'm a man. Right?

"Right."

"I think I pull off 'manly' pretty well for a ballet dancer of medium complexion and stature, don't you think?"

"Absolutely." Kyle suppressed a chuckle.

"Did you know I was gay when we met?"

"Honestly, not immediately, and I have a pretty finely tuned gaydar. Every gay person develops one eventually; and of course, we all hope someone we're attracted to will give off some kind of signal, but to 'the world', on stage, no, I didn't get that from you. With that said, I was a little confused when you said you were straight, because last I heard, The Company didn't hire straight leads." The man knew his theater, too.

"Yeah…" Kevin took a deep breath. "When I auditioned in 2000, I was straight, so I thought; and I even knew about the rule. I only auditioned because I listened to my nut of a roommate who insisted it wouldn't matter. And I did tell Gary I was straight. But he called the next day and offered me the part on the condition that I not tell anyone that I was. It wasn't that big a deal, really. I didn't date anyone and Gabby knew from the beginning…"

"Did you ever consider the reason they have such a policy?" Kyle asked.

"I didn't. I was really just excited about the opportunity. I didn't lie my way in, technically. And if there were a gay actor better suited for the part, he would have gotten it."

"You're probably right…"

"What is it?" Kevin heard Kyle's tone change.

"It's not my place to judge you, Kevin."

"But you think I should have done things differently?"

"Not necessarily. I think I'm just wondering how far you would have gone to get the part. How easy was it for you to deceive people?"

"Well, I did as much, and only as much, to get that part as I had any other: I showed up on time and I danced, sang and acted my ass off. Then I talked with the director for five minutes and ran away like a little girl and hurled at the thought that my best friend might have prostituted himself on my behalf."

"Wow."

"Exactly."

"So even when your career depended on it, you couldn't accept that you might be gay?"

"I really didn't want to be. I always associated gay with 'sissy'. I'm a dancer. That's as far as I was willing to go. Sure, I had the occasional crush, but I dismissed it as being about 'sex' and I wasn't willing to live like that. And since then, since Ethan was born...I don't want to be a sissy, Kyle. I don't want that for my son."

"Of course not. But something else is different. What do you think you're missing that you're willing to risk so much?"

"How long have you been growing your hair?"

"Fifteen years. I haven't had a haircut since I graduated from high school. Don't change the subject."

"I don't know what you're talking about."

"Kevin."

"Yes?"

"What do you need?" His voice was 'sleepy-sexy' and it made Kevin sink further under his covers.

"What does anyone need?"

"Oh gee whiz..." Kyle chuckled again. "Okay. Tell me something else."

There was another long pause, then the sound of Kevin sighing. "I need to feel safe."

"Okay."

"See! You say, 'okay' like 'okay, yeah, he's really a girl!'" Kevin whined.

"I absolutely did not say it like that, Kevin. I certainly didn't mean it like that. I meant, 'okay, what else?'" Kyle chuckled.

"What do you mean, 'what else?' Isn't that odd enough?"

"What's odd about that?"

"I'm supposed to be 'protector, provider, lover-extraordinaire, Mr. Fix-it, and make it all better'. I don't feel that. Don't get me wrong, I want to be all of those things; but I also want all of those things in another person. A man isn't supposed to feel that way."

"But you are a man. You do feel that way. Your needs aren't 'right' or 'wrong', they just ARE. What else?"

"I want to be loved. I want someone to KNOW me and love me; not the me I'm told to be, but the real person I am on the inside."

"Why don't you think you can have that with your wife?"

"I don't know, doc, you tell me?" Kevin was more nervous than annoyed; but it came out wrong.

"Ouch. I'm sorry. I wasn't trying to make you uncomfortable. I'm just trying to get to know you."

"No, I'm sorry. It's fine. It's more than fine. I like it. I'm just not used to it. I feel all exposed and..."

"And?"

"Free..."

"Mmmm... Free is good, right?"

"I don't know. Free is exciting. But it doesn't feel..."

"...safe?"

"Yeah."

"Well, in order to feel safe, you have to trust."

"That's easy for you to say."

"Why do you assume that?"

"You seem to have a handle on the whole 'walking around in your own skin' thing. Doesn't that require trust?"

"Yes. I trust in God; but I haven't gotten to the good part, yet."

"And what's the good part?"

"Trusting people, just one person enough to let go."

"Yup."

"I really like talking to you. I'm sorry again for getting in your head."

"I really like talking to you, too. There's no need to apologize. This is all really new to me; and, yes, scary, but scary in a good way."

"Me too."

"How so? Did you just wake up yesterday and decide you were gay, too?"

Kyle laughed. "No, I've known most of my life. But most of my life, I've been alone. I haven't trusted much."

"I see. Well, since you're apparently getting as much out of our little session as I am, does that mean you won't be sending me a bill?"

Kyle chuckled. "Actually, yes, the first session is free, but text me your address, please."

Kevin laughed and sent his address while they were still on the phone.

"Seriously, you know what I didn't hear?" Kyle asked.

"What's that?"

"Lust."

"Lust?"

"Yeah, when you talk about your needs, there's no lust."

"Well, I guess physical love is not a 'need' for me, not something I've been missing. Don't get me wrong. I enjoy sex; but that's not the struggle."

"Do you think you're bisexual?"

"No."

"You answered that awfully fast for a married man who figured out he liked men five minutes ago."

"I did, didn't I?" Both chuckled. "Okay, let me think about it...All of my fantasies, my desire, physical, emotional longings, have been centered around masculine qualities. I love women. I think they're beautiful; but if I'm honest, and we're being honest now, right, I've only done what was expected, not what felt natural to me. I love women. But, I LIKE men. Does that make sense?"

"I've never heard it articulated quite so well before."

"You inspire me." Kevin looked at the clock. It was almost four a.m.

"You're kind."

"We've been on the phone for hours. I KNOW I've never done this before. You should get some sleep." Kevin didn't want to hang up, but he knew Kyle had things to do the next day. He could spend his birthday in bed.

"If you insist."

"Wow. Is it like that? I only have to ask?" Kevin hugged his pillow.

"Wouldn't you like to know?"

"Hell, yeah!"

"Good night, Kevin." Kyle chuckled.

"Good night, Kyle."

Kevin finally went to sleep around five o'clock. He was awakened by the sound of Michael pounding on his door around noon. "What?"

Michael opened the door holding a large fruit bouquet, and eating a chocolate covered strawberry on a stem. "Your head's so big you sending yourself fruit flowers now?"

"Huh?" Kevin wanted to go back to sleep. Kyle was there. Michael flung the card at him. It simply read: "Happy Birthday! Enjoy your day! K."

Kevin grinned and pulled the covers over his head.

"Yum-my!" Michael continued munching the strawberry, studied the bouquet to see what he'd try next, and walked away. Kevin jumped out of bed and chased him into the kitchen.

11

THEY DIDN'T KNOW

Kevin dragged himself out of bed and into the shower and thought, "you're really too old for this. The temple needs sleep." Then he smiled, thinking about what had kept him up all night. He'd spent practically every night for the past three months on the phone with Kyle 'til usually three in the morning. Every night they promised, more to themselves than to the other that they'd call it a night early, but never did. They always found a reason to keep the conversation going.

Kyle called Kevin when the weight of being pastor seemed overwhelming. His new friend was full of joy and light. Kevin realized how lonely it must be to have so many people relying on your strength and guidance and he enjoyed being Kyle's escape from all that. Kyle knew how to pray his way through those tough days, but until he met Kevin, he'd forgotten how to laugh and how good it felt to just let go and be silly. Kevin could find humor in anything and made Kyle laugh until his face hurt.

Kevin could have listened to Kyle talk about the weather for hours. Kyle's voice made him…happy. It was just gravy that he was also interesting, intelligent, fun, sweet…They talked about the world, Kyle's ministry and music, Kevin's career. Kevin was opening up as a writer and was excited about the new direction his career was going in, even if it scared him. Kyle encouraged him to explore the feelings writing awakened in him and to journal as much as he wrote for work. Kevin felt whole and happier than he had in years. He even joined MCCNY. Kyle didn't discourage Kevin from visiting Lvolution Church, the church he'd founded; he just encouraged him to stay where he felt like he was being fed. Kyle didn't want him coming to LvC just because he was there.

Their friendship was unlike anything either had experienced before; but they were both very careful that it remained just that, 'friendship'. Kevin was married to Gabby and had no intentions on changing that. They didn't know they were falling in love. Kyle's advice made Kevin a better writer and performer. Gary and Nikki saw the change. They'd believed in his potential from the beginning, but his latest work was as provocative and engaging as it was prolific. So, perhaps it was just fatigue that had Kevin feeling paranoid when he was summoned to Gary's office on his day off.

"Good morning, Sunshine!" Gary greeted Kevin cheerfully. "You look good. I hope I didn't pull you away from anything too exciting. I was trying to catch you before you went to Charlotte."

"I'm not going. EJ's with my parents." Kevin apparently forgot that he still had a wife in North Carolina. Gary remembered, but he was too excited to play 'Are we gay today?' with Kevin. Kevin took a sip of his iced mocha and tried to perk up. "What's up?"

"I have good news and bad news. Which do you want first?"

"The bad; let's end on a high note."

"That's my boy! Okay, the bad news is: we have to delay the opening of 'Church Boys'."

"Well, that's not the worst news I've heard, considering rewriting it is kicking my ass."

"Oh, you're fine. Man-up. It's a lot more challenging than you thought, though, isn't it?

"Yeah, I had no idea how emotionally draining writing could be."

"It only feels that way because it's your first piece and, apparently, it's a little close to home?" Gary tilted his head at Kevin.

Kevin wasn't ready to deal with that yet. "What's the

good news?"

"Oh! When we do open, it's going to be on the 'big stage'! Nikki presented the new script to the Broadway committee, and because of its relevance and new perspective, *Church Boys* will open *on* Broadway, with one condition..."

"Oh, whatever it is, I'll do it, if I get a vote."

"I thought you'd say that. You're directing it, as well."

"Shut up!" Kevin jumped up and hugged Gary.

"Yup, we want this to be your directorial debut."

"Oh my God! Okay, wait...I don't want to write it, direct it and star in it...that's just too much of me for even me!"

"We figured that too. Do you have someone in mind or do you want to open up casting again?"

"Yes, let's do that." Kevin thought for a moment. "Actually...Gary, I've been meaning to ask you something, I mean for years. It's awkward and embarrassing, but I'm only putting it out there now because we're friends, right?

"Of course, Kevin. What is it?"

"What happened with you and Michael... years ago, when I first came in? Did he?"

A wave of red slowly crept up Gary's throat and face like mercury in a thermometer. He took a deep breath. "Wow. No, Kevin, he didn't." Gary took another deep breath and didn't look directly at Kevin. "This is embarrassing. It was so ugly, Kevin; it wasn't all Michael. I shouldn't have even told you that."

"But something must have happened, because he'd told me a similar story himself. What happened?"

"We met at a party. He told me he was an actor...I told him I was with The Company and casting for a new musical. I'd probably had a little too much to drink myself and he looked to be just getting started. Kevin, I don't make a habit of casting from backrooms, you have to know that about me by now..."

"I do, Gary. What happened?"

"...Well, you've seen him, right...Talk about 'crazy beautiful'...I just wanted to keep the conversation going. I meet pretty men every day, but he was just...he is just... different...and it's not about the way he looks. Sure, he's...lovely...hard and soft...a raving lunatic and at the same time sweet as hell... And I could see he was drunk, I just wanted to see what he was like sober. When I told him to stop by the next day, I didn't even realize I hadn't mentioned that the lead needed to dance. I just wanted to see him...I went home and almost forgot he was coming in. He showed up on time and he read... and he sang. He was beautiful... Kevin, I cried. I actually burst into tears right there in the theatre. I brought him back here to talk to him and explain that I couldn't use him for that particular role. I felt like shit. I wanted to rewrite the damn play! And when I told him that he was fabulous, but I needed a dancer...I don't know how to explain what I saw. When he got here, and he was sober, there was this glow; and when he spoke and sang, it was pure joy. But when I said I needed a dancer, the light went out, literally, as if you flipped that switch on the wall. He started talking about you; and I could tell from the way he talked that he loved you, but I didn't realize then that you were brothers. We get confused little gay boys in here all the time. Sure, they aren't always willing to go to the extremes he was suggesting to help out a friend. I just dismissed it as part of his eccentricity. I mean you almost have to be a little screwed up to be that beautiful and that talented, don't you?" A tear streamed down Gary's face. "And I wanted him to touch me... not like that... Kevin, I didn't want him to do that; but I didn't want him to go, either. He was... crazy...I had seen him walk in here as sane and sober as you and I are right now, and then it was like he was someone else! He was dark and sex and childlike all at the same time. And I was as out of control as he was. That beautiful, crazy-as-hell, man was on

94

his knees getting ready to blow me, for you. We were right where you're standing now." Kevin looked to his left and saw his reflection in the full-length mirror and cringed at the thought of what Gary must have seen. "Exactly. I told him to leave, Kevin. I pulled him up. I tried to talk to him before he ran out of here. I wanted to understand what was happening. But I was so ashamed... I still am! You know we've never talked about it? When you suggested him for that part in 'Church Boys', I knew he was perfect, but I couldn't have called him on my own. I'd been trying to pretend I'd never met him! I didn't want to remember that I almost used him and let him debase himself that way. And since he's been here, I've just been trying to keep an eye on him; but it's like it was then, like he's two different people. His darkness breaks my heart, and then his light blows me away. I've never seen anything like him. Some days, this place feels like Hell when he's here, Kevin. I want to be his friend. I'm supposed to be his boss; but I can't look him in the eye. I want to grab him and hold onto him until... I don't know... until it never happened... until we both forget and we can be... something else... anything else; but I can't touch him. It's all I can do to direct him. Do you know I founded 'brother 2 brother', the men's group at church? For years my biggest concern had been 'non-predatory mentorship'! I stepped down because of Michael! I am the thing that I'd been railing against for years! Here was this beautiful young man with all the potential in the world, who clearly needed nothing more than to be nurtured and protected and... I was supposed to help him, Kevin."

"Gary that was eight years ago and nothing actually happened. And you are helping him, now." Kevin knew Gary was a good man. It hurt him to see his friend agonizing over this.

"That it almost happened is bad enough...but...I can't explain it, Kevin. I haven't had a drink since that night. I haven't been alone with him since that day, but Michael haunts me."

"Do you think you have feelings for him?"

Gary was quiet for a long time. "I can't. He's not whole. And when he is, he won't want me. I'm not even sure he's really gay. You think you're confused…My God, someone has done a number on that man!"

"So 'yes', you do." A huge smile slowly crept across Kevin's face…and spread to Gary's.

Gary's smile faded as quickly as it appeared. "You can't say anything, Kevin. I can't do anything about it."

"I understand; but it's nice though. I've never known anyone to love Michael like that before. Not that he's not loveable; it's just that no one else has ever really seen him."

Gary wiped his face. "It is good to acknowledge the feelings, even if nothing can ever come of it."

"You don't know that, Gary." Kevin put his arm around Gary as they headed down the hall. As they continued laughing and talking quietly, they didn't see Michael enter the hallway behind them. They didn't see him stop next to Gary's office door and slide down the wall in a broken, tearful heap. They didn't know that Michael lived every day with the memory of that day in Gary's office feeling worthless. They didn't know that he loved and respected Gary for turning him away, but didn't know how to let him in as a real friend and mentor. They didn't know that, while he loved Kevin, the pain of living in his shadow, of always being just one thing less than 'the great and talented Kevin Rivers' was finally becoming more than he could bear.

12

MOVEMENT

Kevin must have called Gabby a hundred times on his way to Charlotte. She hadn't answered since she called screaming. He could only make out every other word. He understood three things: She was furious; it was his fault, and it wasn't something that could be straightened out over the phone. Halfway there he realized, whatever was going on, he needed to come clean. When he pulled into the driveway, beating his best time by an hour, he said a quick prayer that he could say what he needed to make her understand. When he opened the door, he knew it was not going to be easy. He stepped inside and ducked as a ten-pound vase flew at him and shattered as it hit the wall in the foyer. He remembered and was immediately grateful that EJ was with his parents for the weekend.

"Lying, son of a bitch! How could you?! How could you string me along all those years?"

"Gabby, I'm sorry. I didn't mean to. I didn't know. I didn't want to know."

"What do you mean 'you didn't know'? What did you think it meant when you were running around New York screwing men, Kevin?!"

"I haven't been screwing ANYONE, Gabrielle!" Kevin stopped walking toward her. "Who told you that? Michael?" Kevin had assumed when Gabby sounded so upset and said Michael called her, that he'd told her Kevin was really gay, not that he'd been cheating.

"Oh, no! No. no. no. no. Mike doesn't know what he's talking about?"

"Really? He had a lot to say for someone who doesn't know anything, Kevin. He was ranting and raving about you and Gary. Your director?! God, what a stupid cliché you turned out to be! I told you that would happen! Has that been going on all along?"

"Gabby! No! I AM NOT HAVING, NOR HAVE I EVER HAD SEX WITH A MAN – ANY MAN, and especially not Gary! Gary is my friend. He's been helping me work out some things and Michael has seen us together. You know how irrational Mike can be."

Gabby stared at Kevin. She wanted to believe him. He'd asked her to trust him with harder things than this. She made the decision to believe him now. "He was drunk. But why was he ranting and raving about you living the life my father promised him, and throwing it all away?"

"I don't know. He's been acting kinda wild, wilder than usual lately. I'll find out. I'm sorry this happened like this. I was coming to talk to you when I got your call anyway."

"I don't understand. "Gabby poured a drink while Kevin grabbed a bottle of water out of the refrigerator.

"Wow. This is the most difficult thing I've ever done in my life."

"You're scaring me, Kevin. If you're not screwing around, what's left to say?"

Kevin stared at Gabby, took a deep breath and let it out. "I'm gay, Gabby."

Gabby set her drink down hard and the glass broke into large chunks on the granite countertop. Kevin rushed to clean it up before she cut herself. "Excuse me?" She backed away from Kevin as he moved to clean up the glass.

"I'm gay, Gabrielle. Please don't act so surprised. You know me better than anyone." Gabby still hadn't spoken when she walked into the family room and sat on the sofa. "Surely there were signs." Kevin called out to her as he looked for the broom to get the glass from the vase in the foyer.

"I guess there were; but I dismissed them as 'you're

artistic – metro'."

"Thanks, but I'm afraid it's more than that." Kevin sat down in a chair across from Gabby. "Haven't you ever considered that our life, our relationship is weird?"

"You needed to be in New York; but you wanted our son to have a normal life."

"Yes, that's true; but how much did you miss me while you were in California, and since we got married and you moved down here?"

"We're busy people." Gabby looked at Kevin, searching his face for agreement.

Kevin shook his head. "That's not a real marriage, Gabby. Is that all you want? Don't you want more? I want more."

"It's all my parents have had. I guess it's a little different. They technically live in the same house, but there's no connection. Maybe I did think that was all there was? Okay, fine, I knew better, but how'd you get from 'we're not in love' to, 'you're gay'?" She took a big sip of the drink Kevin poured for her.

"I always have been. I just didn't want to believe it. I wanted our life, Gabby. But it just isn't enough for me anymore. I wanted what everyone told me was the perfect life for someone else. I know who I am, now. I denied it for as long as I could."

"You are the best dancer I've ever seen."

"Okay, that doesn't count. There really are wonderful straight male dancers. I really wish you and Nikki would just accept that." Kevin shook his head.

"Okay, but when we have been together we've had A LOT of sex; and you do things gay men don't do."

"It's just sex. I wanted to please you. I always tried to please you. I did what I thought you'd enjoy. That part was really easy for me, but remember the time I tried to go up your butt?"

"Yeah, spouting some nonsense about 'legroom'."

"Nope, I was practicing. Wasn't sure what for; but I wanted to know what all the fuss was about."

"My ass still hurts just thinking about it. I should punch you in the face. Seriously. Really, KJ? Are you sure?"

"Yes. I'm sorry. I'm sure. I promise you I've never cheated on you. I wouldn't. I couldn't. I love you, Gabby, so much. But, how could you not know?"

Gabby didn't say anything for a long time; instead she closed her eyes and seemed to be searching for the truth inside her self. "Honestly, I think I did. I just didn't want to believe it. I love you, too." She held out her glass and he stood to take it and pour her a refill. "I have questions."

"Of course you do." Kevin answered from the kitchen.

"When did you know?"

"That's hard to say. I realize now I've always known, in the back of my head. I just didn't want to accept it. I wouldn't choose this, Gabby. I wanted our life together."

"Have you ever loved me?"

He answered quickly. That was easy. "Yes. My whole life, as much as I am capable of; but didn't you ever feel something missing?"

"I did." Gabby placed the drink on the coffee table in front of her without drinking it.

"You deserve more than what I can give you. You shouldn't have to spend a single day alone, let alone, weeks at a time. I've been so selfish. Please forgive me." He sat on the sofa next to her and reached for her hand. She didn't pull away.

"If Michael hadn't said anything, would you have? When?"

"I was praying about it. I kept saying I have to. I knew I would have to soon, before..."

"Before you cheated? Kevin, I swear, if...!"

"Gabby, No! I have never been with anyone but you. I

100

can't prove that; but I can prove the more important thing. We can go to get tested tomorrow, together. Have you ever been with anyone else?"

"Not since we got married." Gabby shook her head softly.

"But while you were in college? Fair enough." Kevin thought back to the reunion that produced EJ and realized she'd lied, but didn't think that moment was the time to mention it. "Okay, we can go tomorrow."

"That's not necessary. I've gotten tested annually. You should go, if you still need to." Kevin looked insulted when he realized what she was saying; that in the back of her mind, Gabby expected him to one day bring something other than flowers home. "I told you I always suspected."

"That hurt, Gabby."

"More than the love of your life telling you he doesn't love you? Get over yourself!"

"I'm sorry. But if you knew, why didn't you say something. You call me on my shit more than anyone! Thinking I'm gay, while we're living apart and I'm pretending to be, is some pretty serious shit to keep to yourself, Gabrielle."

Gabby didn't say anything. Kevin tried to be still as a tear ran down her cheek. The words she spoke next assured him he was doing the right thing. "I never imagined there could be anything better. Sure, I knew something was missing. I even knew you weren't in love with me. I'm not stupid, Kevin. But from everything I've seen of love, everything I've been taught, I accepted that this was as good as it could get for us. You ARE a good man. You're a star, for goodness' sake. Being Mrs. Kevin Rivers, at least to the people I could tell, was no real hardship, trust me. You're a good father. I decided those things were more important than what I needed."

Kevin took a deep breath and squeezed her hands and

pressed his lips to her temple. "I'm not the love of your life. You know that. It gets better for you from here; it has to. You deserve true happiness, not this farce of a life we built together."

"What about you? What's going on that you suddenly need to be free?" Kevin was quiet. He didn't want to hurt Gabby. Telling her he was interested in someone would hurt. "Spill it. I do know you, remember. You wouldn't be here if there weren't something more going on - if you didn't have a reason to walk away."

"I want to believe I could 'man-up' just for the sake of doing the right thing."

"Me too; but you hadn't, until now. What is it? Better yet, who is he?"

Kevin got a big goofy grin on his face as the Heather Headley song played in his head. "He is!"

"Oh gee whiz! I haven't seen that look since…"Gabby hopped up and pointed at Kevin. "Oh my God! You had a crush on Sean Mitchell, didn't you?"

Kevin threw a pillow at her. "Guilty."

"Oh wow! I'm an idiot!"

"Don't say that."

"Tell me about him."

"You don't really want to know." Kevin shook his head but couldn't keep from smiling.

"I do." Gabby sat back on the couch and caressed her glass.

"His name is 'Kyle' and he is, wait for it, a pastor."

"No way! Wait. Not your pastor? That would be creepy."

"No, but I did finally join a church; not his, though."

"Wow, Kevin. Now, that I find hard to believe."

"Yeah, it's funny. I heard that when people come out, they run from God. But, when I reconnected, I found myself. I've never felt more at peace."

Gabby took a sip of her drink. "Yeah, yeah. Stop stalling. I want to know, Kevin. I can't remember when I last saw you so happy. I think knowing what's behind it all will make this easier. Help me understand. Are you in love?"

Kevin smiled and closed his eyes, imagining Kyle's smile. "I think I am, Gabby. It's weird. I just get all tingly when I think about him. He's Jamaican and African, so he has this accent... and this voice...He sings... He's smarter than me."

"Everyone is smarter than you, Kevin." Gabby rolled her eyes.

"Hey! ...And better looking."

"Again, who's not?"

"See! If you're gonna be mean, I'm not gonna tell you! Actually, there's not much else to tell. It's just a feeling. I haven't been dating him, Gabby. We went for coffee the night we met, at revival. Coffee lasted about three hours. I haven't seen him since."

"But you've talked to him?"

"Every night for about six weeks?" It had been more like three months. "I'm sorry."

"Stop saying that, Kevin. I think it's okay. How can it not be? I only ever wanted you to be happy. You're happy. You're friggin' glowing, through what must be one of the hardest things you've ever had to do. I see that. I see how hard it is. I believe you. More important than that, I know I've never seen you like this before. I'm happy for you. I really am. Mommy tried to tell me you weren't the one. She'll probably just say, 'I told you so', you know that, right?"

"Yeah, I do, and I love her. I hope she's not too disappointed in me. If I'd had her to talk to, we probably wouldn't have gotten married, huh... since I actually did listen to her."

"Yeah, but Ethan wouldn't be here"

"You're right."

"I'm always right," Gabby laughed.

"Yes, you are! It's kind of annoying, actually... I love you, Gabrielle. Please tell me what you need me to do for you. How can I do right by you?"

"Be my friend."

"Can I still be your best friend?"

"Well, you can't stop now."

"Continue to be the best father in the world to our son."

With that, a tear rolled down Kevin's cheek. "Gabby, how do I tell him?"

"I don't know. I'll help, if you want me to; but you have to tell him, Kevin. You can't start lying to him now. If it means anything, I don't believe you have anything to be ashamed of. I'm as proud of you today as I was yesterday. I may actually love you more, as if that were possible."

He wrapped his arms around her and nestled his head against her breasts. "That means everything. You've been my whole life – well, the part I was living, anyway."

"I'm not sure what we're sitting here crying about. It's really not going to be that different. We just don't have to pretend anymore – to ourselves or to each other. We can't not be in each other's lives. We will share Ethan. You still have to see me. Oh, I am so excited for you – and a little jealous... not of him, but you and your courage. I wish I had the strength to follow my bliss."

"Well, now you can. What does that look like?"

"I have no idea. I think I might be too big a coward to try and find out."

"You're the bravest person I know."

"In what way? I haven't done anything. "

"Are you kidding? Do you realize what it takes to love as deeply and unconditionally as you do? And now, to so gracefully walk away, not knowing what tomorrow will look like?"

Gabrielle chuckled. "Don't get it twisted, honey. I'm giving you a divorce because I don't want someone who doesn't want me. And, because you are the great Kevin Rivers of Broadway, you will pay for my fabulous life until I shrivel up and die!"

Kevin laughed. "You don't need my money! You're loaded!" Gabby sat up to stare at him. "I mean, yes, ma'am. What else?"

"You're gonna get settled and that little man-cub, who looks and acts just like you is going to live with his father – or fathers – or whatever the hell you think you're about to go do... Seriously, I trust you, Kevin. I trust you with our son; but I will kill you, literally – I will end your life – if you abandon him."

"Really? Please don't get me wrong; I want him. I just never imagined you'd let me. I don't understand, Gabby. Why are you so okay?"

Gabby sighed. "I'm not okay, Kevin, I'm terrified. I'm sad. What I AM NOT is surprised, not completely anyway. I wanted so much to believe that we could make it work. I never imagined that I would have to live for JUST ME. But, if I'm really honest, I did see you slipping further and further away; from me, though, not EJ. Over the last few years, I've seen how your participation in our life together requires so much effort. I know you love our son, and he's the reason I see you as often as I do. He loves you. He misses you. He needs you. We'll talk about it; but if he wants to live in New York with you, he can. If you make me regret it, I'll kill you."

"I won't, I promise. Thank you. But, what about you?"

"I'm going to figure out what I'm really supposed to be doing, I guess. When I went to California, I did so because Mommy made me – not because I wanted to be away. I NEVER thought we wouldn't be together. Do you think I didn't stab four people in the back to get assigned to New

York? I've had every day of my life planned since I was 12 years old. I'm not this put together by accident, you know. I have hair and nail appointments scheduled into 2012! I'd predicted Ethan's birth within two weeks, before you'd even proposed to me! I'm insane! How will I live without two other people to plan for, manipulate and schedule around?"

Kevin sat up to stare at her. "Oh my God! You are crazy!" Both laughing

"You didn't know?"

"Uh – uh..." He stared at her shaking his head.

"Shut up."

"No, you shut up."

"Oh!" Gabby jumped up and pointed wildly at Kevin. "Daddy is gonna kill you!"

"Who's gonna tell him?" Kevin said with a straight face.

"You're kidding, right? You don't think the Bishop Robert Nichols isn't going to find out that his Tony Award winning, former son-in-law is gay? Even if you never go public... There are people in and out of the church just waiting to give him some news like that! It's gonna kill him! You're gonna kill my daddy! Okay, I take it all back. You suck! I'm gonna be an orphan, and it's all your fault!"

"Wait a minute. Momma Nichols is still alive. What are you talking about?"

"She always liked you better than me."

"Yeah, that is true." They both laughed. "Shit."

"Um hmm. I wonder if Daddy will be the first bishop to go to prison for killing a Broadway star?"

"Thanks, Gabby. He'll probably get off on some religious technicality."

"Yeah, well, you're the one who wanted to start 'living your truth'. He'll be back from Africa in a month. Live it up, punk! "

"You are enjoying this!" Kevin looked wounded.

"I am!" She threw herself onto his lap and they both

laughed. They laughed even harder at the realization that their break-up was the most fun they'd had together since high school. They continued to reminisce and held each other, sharing final tears and giggles until the sun came up.

Kevin packed some things and made Gabrielle breakfast before heading back to New York. As he left, he pulled her by the hand toward the door. "I'll do whatever you need to make this easy for you, Gabrielle."

"You've done it already, Kevin. You told me the truth. I will always love you for that."

"Thank you." With that, he stood in the doorway to the house that had never felt like his home, and held the only woman he'd ever loved. He felt her let go long before he could pull himself away. He lingered, smelling her hair, touching her face, and kissing her lips for what they both knew would be the last time.

As Kevin drove away, he began to pray for Gabrielle. She'd let him off easy. Tears streamed down his face as he realized her sacrifice. He knew her well enough to know she was holding back a lot of her own pain and anger. Had she always been so generous? Loving? Yes. He made a vow to do whatever she needed. He didn't really believe she would let him have EJ fulltime. That was his first sign that she was holding back. Could she do that? Or was it more about what she needed? Perhaps she'd already started thinking about the life she hadn't been living. Was their life together a shared lie? Either way, he wanted his son; and he was grateful for her trust, graciousness, friendship and love.

He was also filled with an overwhelming sense of relief that he wasn't carrying around the burden of the lie anymore. Nana's words echoed in his head. "Aint no sin worse than the lie you tell yourself." He replayed the conversation in his head. He would always feel guilt over his part in causing Gabby any pain; but there were far worse things he could have done than tell the truth and walk away. He knew he'd never be able to come home to her and Ethan while he'd been out in the world living a 'real' lie. And he knew it was only a matter of time before he would be doing just that, if he'd stayed; even if he never physically cheated. He thought about Kyle more and more every day. He didn't know what could become of their friendship; but he knew it wasn't right to be day-dreaming about another man's voice, his smile, his embrace while he was married. Even if Kyle wasn't the one, Kevin realized he'd never been in love with Gabby. He smiled at the hope that he could fall in love one day with someone else. There was no denying now that he only had those feelings for men. An emotional affair actually seemed worse to him than a real one, and he wasn't willing to subject any of the people he cared for to either. Feeling lighter and lighter the further away he got from his marital home, he wondered out loud, "could this really be the beginning of a real life?"

Then reality and fatigue set in. Signs pointing to the airport inspired him to wait for a flight back to New York. He wouldn't need his car there and could get it when he came back to get the rest of his things in a few weeks. He took the exit and prayed he wouldn't have to wait too long.

13

MY BROTHER'S KEEPER

Kevin stopped the car in the middle of the highway just before he reached the airport. Gabby's words from the night before suddenly echoed in his head... "Why was Michael ranting and raving about you living the life my father promised him?!" Kevin picked up the phone and called Michael. "Mike, it's Kevin, I know what you did. Are you man enough to tell me why you did it? I'm on my way. You'd better be there when I get there. Don't make me come looking for you."

Kevin paid the cab driver and flew up the stairs to his and Michael's apartment, fumbling with keys until he realized the door wasn't locked. He called out to Michael but got no response. He walked down the hall to Michael's bedroom where the door was ajar and the light was dim. Michael appeared to be asleep on the bed and Kevin slapped him in the head to wake him up. When Michael didn't move, Kevin scanned the room and saw the open bottle of sleeping pills on the bed next to him. He listened for breathing and checked Mike's pulse. He was alive. Kevin called 911 and dragged Michael into the shower to try and wake him up as instructed. He was relieved to see that Mike had on clothes for a change. By the time the paramedics arrived, he was semi-conscious. Kevin rode to the hospital with Michael, and when the nurse said only family could go beyond a certain point, he said he was Michael's brother. "Oh, I'm sorry. I do see the resemblance, now. Just wait right here and I'll come and get you as soon as he's settled."

"Thank you." Kevin thought to himself, "That was not a lie. He is my brother."

The same nurse returned almost an hour later. "You can

see him now." Michael looked pale and he wouldn't look at Kevin when he walked into the room.

"See, you know you wrong. I'm supposed to kill you. Mike, what are you doing, man?" Michael turned to look at Kevin. His eyes were red and puffy. Kevin thought, "He looks worse than when they brought him in."

"I'm sorry, Kevin."

"Ya know what, Mike. I forgive you. It's done. I saw Gabby. She's okay. We're okay. You didn't ruin anything."

"She's gonna stay with you?" Michael tried to sit up.

"No. We are getting divorced; but not for the reason you told her we should."

"Look man, I don't know if you noticed, but I just took a whole lotta pills. You're gonna have to start making some sense or I'm going to pass out again."

"Gabby and I are getting divorced because I am gay. But I'm not sleeping with Gary. I don't even know where you would get that. Gary's my friend."

"I thought I was your friend." Michael was too worn out to pretend he was surprised by Kevin's revelation. He'd known their whole lives that Kevin was gay.

"You are my brother. Apparently, you've forgotten. Why did you do that to me Michael? And why was Gabby saying you were doing all that talking about the bishop?"

Michael turned away again, but Kevin wasn't letting him off the hook. "You have to talk to me. You're alive, lying in a hospital bed, because I was too tired to drive home and kill your crazy ass. Michael if I'd driven home or stayed in Charlotte with Gabby, you would be dead! One way or another, you were trying to die today. What the Hell is going on with you?"

"I'm sorry, I can't." Tears streamed down Michael's cheeks. "Please go."

"No. You're talking now, or you're talking later; but either way, I'm not leaving this room."

"You have to. Visiting hours are over. Only family is allowed in here."

"Oh, shut up!" Kevin stepped outside and explained to the nurse that he would be sleeping in the recliner. He was afraid for his brother's safety and wanted to wait with him until his parents could get here in the morning. Then he walked back to Michael's bedside and kissed him on the forehead. "I'll be right over there."

Kevin made himself comfortable in the recliner by the window and tried to stay awake until Michael fell asleep. Even though he was physically exhausted, he couldn't sleep. His mind was racing. What could be going on that Michael would try to kill himself? What did it have to do with him? What could it possibly have to do with Gabby's father? Kevin had been thinking more and more about his childhood and adolescence since coming out. He'd blocked out so much, trying to ignore the truth. Had he blocked out something about Michael too. Kevin believed his friend's life depended on his being able to remember, especially since Michael wasn't talking. Maybe he could recall enough to coax the rest out of him.

Kevin's mind raced back to their childhood in Georgia. From the time they were six years old, Kevin, Gabby and Michael were the best of friends. Michael's mother was the music director at the church that Kevin's family attended and of which Gabby's father was senior pastor. They shared a special bond because they were all only children and, early on, all church kids. Michael had a light similar to Kevin's, but his was for the Word. Gabby and Kevin had never seen a kid so excited about the Bible before. They teased him and said he'd grow up to be a preacher just like Rev. Nichols. Michael thought that would be the best thing in the world. His mother did, too. She spent practically every waking hour in that church rehearsing with the choir, at bible study, women's meetings, basically anything she could do to not take her son home. While she was busy playing 'church mother', her son hung around the church…

Kevin finally drifted off to sleep. In the previous twenty-four hours, he'd driven to Charlotte, stayed up all night with Gabby, hopped a plane back to New York and thwarted his best friend's suicide attempt. He was tired. After an hour or so, he was awakened by the vibrating of his cell phone. He checked to make sure Michael was sleeping and walked outside to return the missed call. Kevin sighed and smiled when he saw that it was Kyle. So much had happened since they last spoke. He didn't know where to begin.

"Hi." Kevin tried to sound 'up'.

"Hey, you! Did I catch you in the middle of rehearsal?"

Kevin's mood lifted the moment he heard Kyle's voice. "No, I'm at the hospital. It's been the longest day of my life. It's really good to hear your voice. Will you tell me about your day?"

"Don't you want to tell me what you're doing at the hospital first?"

"No, not yet. I'm fine. I'm here with a friend. Just tell me something good, please?"

"Mmm. Okay. I think the CD is finished. We laid down the last track today. It's really good. I can't wait for you to hear it."

"That is exciting news. When can I hear it?"

"It should be ready in a week or so."

"Did my favorite song make the cut?"

Kyle smiled into to phone. "Yes, it did. I think it's my favorite now too."

"See. It's beautiful. That's the one, Kyle. It's all good; but that's the one that's gonna change people."

"From your lips…"

Kevin took the phrase completely out of context and bit his lower lip imagining Kyle's. "What else?"

"No, that's all I have… oh, except…" Kyle hesitated.

"What is it?" Kevin braced himself. It really had been a rough day.

"I missed you." Kyle's voice was warm and just a little hesitant, and Kevin instantly wished he were anywhere other than the entrance to Harlem Hospital Center. They'd been trying for months not to 'go there'. The reality was that they were friends and had come to know and understand each other very well. Kyle felt safe telling Kevin the truth, and Kevin was just as tired of pretending.

"Wow. Well, that was the last thing I expected to hear you say. I've missed you, too. You have no idea."

"Well, I hear you're going through something. Are you ready to talk about it?"

"Yeah. I want to; but let me check on Michael, and I'll give you a call on my way home. Give me just about ten minutes, okay?"

"Of course. Take your time."

"No. I'll be right back." Kevin was starting to feel like himself. Talking to Kyle did something to him. He wanted more, and the urgency was evident in his voice.

"Okay."

Kevin returned to Michael's room and found he was still sleeping. He left his number, told the nurse he was going home to shower and change, and asked that she call him if Michael woke before he returned. She was kind and said she'd leave a note just in case she stepped away.

Rejuvenated, Kevin bounced out of the lobby and called Kyle back. He decided to take the long way home, a cab instead of the train, so he wouldn't lose Kyle in a tunnel.

"Is everything okay?" Kyle sounded concerned.

"No. It could certainly be worse; but it is definitely not okay. Remember I mentioned my roommate, Michael?"

"Sure, the one you grew up with?"

"Yeah. He's a pain in the ass, but he's been like a brother to me my whole life."

"I think that's the way it works with real siblings, too."

"He tried to kill himself."

"What do you mean 'tried', Kevin?"

"I mean that if I'd driven back from Charlotte instead of flown, he would no longer be among the living. When I got home, I found him passed out. He'd taken an entire bottle of tranquilizers."

"Where did a perfectly healthy thirty year old man get a whole bottle of tranquilizers?"

"That's a very good question."

"Well, thank God you got there when you did. Do you know why he would do that? Has he been depressed?"

"Not that I noticed; but it's hard to tell with Mike. He's been really off lately. He's always been wild, but in the last year or so, he's just been... off the chain. I was finally able to get him a small role in the show we're working on now. He really is talented; but he's almost always drunk, high, hung over or all of the above. Please pray for him. "

"You know I will; we will pray for him together. And there is no time like the present."

...

"So you went home? That was a quick trip. Did you go to get Ethan?"

"No, he's with my parents for Spring break. Wow, with all of Mike's madness, I forgot. He's the reason I went to Charlotte, actually. That fool called Gabrielle and told her I was having an affair with Gary. She called me hysterical. I've needed to talk to her, so I just got in the car. I left here after we got off the phone yesterday, around six; got there around two, and hopped a flight back here this morning and found Michael around noon."

"That's a lot." Kyle's voice changed. He was less concerned about the suggestion that Kevin was sleeping with Gary than he was that he'd been going through all of that alone.

114

Kevin noticed that tiny change in Kyle's tone. "It was. Kyle, when we hung up yesterday, you said you were on your way to the studio, and after that, you'd be working on your sermon for Sunday. I didn't want to put all my crap in your head. I'm sorry I didn't tell you I was going."

That was all Kyle needed to hear. "It's okay. You don't owe me any explanation at all. It just sounds like a lot to have to deal with alone. I always want to hear from you, Kevin. Are you okay? How is Gabby?"

"Ya know, with everything that's happened with Michael, I'd almost forgotten. Yes, I am okay. Gabby is... good. I told her."

"You told her what?"

Kevin summarized the status of his life and marriage as if he were ordering lunch in a casual dining restaurant: "That I'm gay; that I always have been, that our life was a lie, and I didn't want to lie anymore." And I'd like the dressing on the side, please.

"Well, I hope you didn't say it like that!" Kyle chuckled.

"Of course not!" Kevin chuckled.

"I know. I'm sure you were kind and compassionate and honest. How'd she take it?"

"Well, don't give me too much credit. Remember, I only went there because I had to. Who'd have thought Michael running his mouth would actually be doing me a favor? At first, she was ... hot. She threw things. But once she understood that I hadn't been cheating, we could actually talk. I had to tell her that there was a small amount of truth to Michael's tale, even if the nut didn't know which part."

"Aren't you thankful for 'man-hugs and phone calls' now?" Kyle chuckled.

"No!" Kevin whined as he paid the cab driver. "Fine. I am, but only for her sake."

"So how did you leave things?"

Kevin sat on the stoop. He was in no hurry to go inside

115

and relive the last twelve hours.

"Believe it or not, she let me off the hook. She admitted that she wasn't entirely surprised. You'd have been proud of me. I wisely ignored the obvious insult to my masculinity. We laughed. We cried. She set me free. The divorce is going to cost me a fortune; she's demanding alimony." Kevin laughed at the irony of that. "But when it's all said and done, I will be free to live my life."

"That is the best news I think I've ever heard, Kevin. And I mean that in the most unselfish way, really. I'm so happy for you. How do you want to spend the first day of the rest of your life?"

"Oh, I'm easy. I'd like... a nap... a shower... a cheeseburger... and to see you. Not in that order, of course, but you might like me better if I bathe."

"I'm pretty sure I could stand you; but you probably should rest. Do you want to take a nap and meet me in a few hours for a quick dinner?"

"I would love that."

"Okay, I'm going to be at the church until around six if you need me. Call me when you get up."

"I will."

Kevin felt lighter as he entered the apartment. He immediately went down the hall to Michael's bedroom. The thought of how close his best friend came to dying just a few hours earlier sent a chill through his body. He sat on Michael's bed and prayed for him. He promised God, that he would continue to pray for whatever it was Michael needed until he was able to pray for himself, and after that. He was ashamed of what he hadn't seen. He'd dismissed Michael's behavior as childish, and never considered for a moment that he might really be hurting. He thanked God for the second chance to be a better friend.

Kevin decided to clean Michael's room so he didn't have to when he came home. As he pulled the covers from the bed, a prescription bottle fell on the floor. He picked it up and scanned it for a name as he echoed Kyle's question. "Where does a perfectly healthy thirty year old man get a full bottle of tranquilizers?" Kevin felt nauseous when he saw the name on the bottle, which had been filled at a local pharmacy, just the week before: Robert Nichols. "What the ham sandwich is going on?" He looked around the room and couldn't find anything that made sense. He slipped the bottle into his jacket pocket so he'd have it when he returned to the hospital. He noticed that Michael's room was unusually tidy, changed the linen anyway and closed the door.

As he walked down the hall to his bedroom, Kevin tried to think about something other than Michael for a moment. When he opened the door to his room, he realized he wouldn't be able to do that any time soon. Michael had left a suicide note. Actually it was more like a novella. The handwritten letter dated the day before must have been ten pages long, single-spaced, double-sided. Kevin's head began to throb. He considered for a moment not reading it. Michael was, after all, alive. But he was not well. He remembered his promise to Michael and to God to see his brother through whatever was going on. "Can a Black man get a shower, please?" He answered his own question by tossing the folded pages on the bed and going to take a shower.

The shower wasn't close to what he needed. Kevin struggled to get all thoughts of Michael out of his head, if only for a few moments. He knew he was being selfish; but he didn't want to think about Michael. He wanted to think about Kyle. He wanted to shower so that when he saw Kyle he'd smell good. He wanted to take a nap so that when he saw Kyle, he'd be his beautiful self, not the haggard old man he'd become in the last twenty-four hours. He was still grumbling when he got out of the shower. "Damn drama-queen." Kevin got dressed, grabbed Michael's book and went into the kitchen and poured himself a giant bowl of Cap'n Crunch. He knew he was stalling. It wasn't that he didn't care. He did. He loved Michael. He admitted to himself that he was afraid of what was in that letter. "'I'm sorry; good-bye.' doesn't require a twenty page manifesto, Michael!"

Dear Kevin,

First, I want to say, 'I'm sorry'. I'm sorry you had to be the one who found me. I'm sorry I told Gabby about you and Gary. But, I do have to say, 'you suck.' How could you do that? (Kevin scanned passed Michael's ramblings about Gary.)

Kevin, there are things you need to know. I'll let you decide what you do with what I tell you. I can't bare you not knowing anymore. For most of our lives, since I was six, I've had a different kind of relationship with the Bishop, different from yours, different from Gabby's. I know he always called me 'his son' in front of you both and everyone at church, but it wasn't really like that, Kevin. Maybe it was. I don't know. I never had a real father; but I assume a real father wouldn't do the things to his son that the Bishop did to me, with me. It started the summer you started going to New York. While my mom was at vacation bible school, or with the choir or the women's auxiliary or just hanging out, I would hang out with the Bishop. He told my mom he'd look after me. He said I had 'a real heart for the Word of God and one day I would be a preacher just like him'. One day, I could be associate pastor of the church. He'd teach me everything I needed to know. The first time it happened, he brought me into his office and said we needed to pray before we started. That made sense to me. Bible study always started with prayer. You know I loved that man, Kevin. I never had a dad like yours. So when he sat me on his lap so we could read together, I didn't think there was anything wrong with it. There wouldn't be, right? It didn't bother me to be close to him. I liked it. He smelled good and wore nice clothes every day. Everyone loved him. He was 'my dad'. So I'd sit on his lap and he'd help me read the Bible. I read most of it by myself and he'd help me with the big words and we'd talk about what they meant. We must have done this everyday for a month. When he started to touch me, sure, I thought that was weird. I even asked him why. He said that it was okay because he loved me, and touching me made him feel closer to God. I was a little kid. Who was I to argue with the Bishop? Why would I? He didn't hurt me, and I didn't know it was wrong. I wondered why he told me not to tell, but he said that if anyone knew, we couldn't spend our special time together. Spending time with the Bishop made me feel special. Kevin, I didn't even mind that he kissed me. I didn't mind when he made me kiss him...I loved being with him. I liked having a special secret. I didn't know it was wrong. When you came home and started taking dance classes, I was 'studying' with the Bishop. My mom even asked me once if I wanted to take lessons too. I told her I wanted to study the Word with the Bishop. We started having sex when I was twelve. I didn't like it. It hurt and I said I didn't want to anymore. He said that if I was going to be a leader in the church one day, I needed to learn to do things I didn't like; I would eventually learn to like it. I don't know if I ever liked it, but I loved him, and if he said I should learn to like it, I was going to learn to love it. I must have been pretty good at it, because he started taking me on trips with him and introducing me to everyone as his son. He bought me nice clothes and I got to ride in the limo with him everywhere we went. He told me he loved me and that I was his favorite person in the whole church, that I was more special to him than you, or even Mrs. Nichols. So when we all graduated from high school and you and Gabby talked about going away, I just knew he'd want me to stay; but he didn't. He said I was becoming a man and I needed to go do that. I wanted to stay and learn about the church. Over the years, we studied the Bible less and less. When we went away to seminars and conventions, I didn't go to youth meetings; I stayed in my hotel room and played video games until he was ready for me. I never learned a thing. I wasn't ready to go to college. That's why I asked you to come to New York with me. He said I could go there and be an actor because I was FINE AS HELL and it would be easy for me to find work in the theater. When I said I couldn't, that I was afraid; I'd only been in small parts in school plays, you were the star, he told me I had to – but he would pay my way. He'd see to it that I had everything I needed. And he did. The last trip we took together was to get me setup in this apartment. I've never seen a bill. I don't even know whose name is on the lease. He told me not to worry about it. He came to see me at least once a month while you were at Julliard on campus. He brought me whatever I wanted and gave me money for food and clothes. He even gave me the names of a few people to contact about work. He said he loved me and would always take care of me. He stopped coming to visit after you moved in, except for when he knew you would be away. I knew by then we were wrong and you wouldn't understand but Kevin I wanted you to know. I wanted you to know the Bishop loved me! I don't even know why. I had no real reason to be jealous. You were always good to me. It wasn't your fault you were good at everything and you had two parents and grandparents that loved you. It wasn't your fault that Gabby loved you. I don't know why I thought telling you about my nasty secret with the Bishop would hurt you or even why I would want to hurt you. I love you, Kevin. I've always loved you. You were my brother. But I thought I would die when you married Gabrielle. When we all moved away, I thought that bad part was over and I wouldn't have to feel like the outsider anymore. I still had my special relationship with the Bishop and now YOU were alone! That made me feel good. I could take care of you for a change. That's why I tried to help you get your first gig with The Company. I only wanted to help you. That day you hit me was the first time I wanted to die, Kevin. I wanted to explain, to really tell you why I did it. I didn't see what the big deal was, anyway. I'd been sucking the Bishop's dick for ten years! I thought that was how you got what you wanted out of powerful men – and a lot more than that – If he'd have told me to do more to get my brother the break he deserved, I'd have done THAT, Kevin. And when you looked at me the way you did, like some piece of trash, I wanted to die. I thought you would leave and I'd be alone again. When you stayed, I thought it was because you really did love me. When you married Gabby, I thought you'd leave again. I guess you did, but not really. It wasn't so bad, except to hear the Bishop call YOU son, and talk about what a big star you were and how proud he was that Gabby had married you and given him a grandson. Sure he would still send for me, but he'd talk about you and Ethan, and how he hoped 'his boys' would stop by the church while you were home visiting your parents. He'd go on and on about how you would have made a 'fine preacher' if you hadn't taken the easy way out. When I asked if I could come back, just to become a deacon, he still said NO - that I needed to find my own way the way you and Gabby did. I wanted to, but I didn't know how, Kevin. No one has ever loved me or wanted anything from me except to use me to make them feel good. I don't even blame Gary. I came to him. I practically begged him to let me blow him, and I knew it wouldn't matter. I knew you didn't need that, but I wanted to feel like I was helping you. I don't know how I lived through that day when you hit me and looked at me like I was nothing. And the only day that's been worse since then is when I saw you with him, when he had his arm around you the way the Bishop used to put his arm around me. I know it wasn't the same. You're a grown man, a talented actor and a good friend. Gary had lots of real reasons to want to be with you. You didn't have to get on your knees for him to love you. But you had everything; you've been everything. I've never been anything... but Bishop Robert Nichols whore. I don't know how to live and not be that. I don't want to be that anymore. Please forgive me. I love you.

Your brother, Michael

###

Kevin dropped the tear stained pages, now damp again from his own tears. He barely made it to the bathroom to throw up in the toilet. When the heaving finally subsided, he sat on the floor against the tub. "Oh my God." He tried to compose himself. He needed to get out of there. The hospital still hadn't called, so he called in to check on Michael. He was still sleeping. The nurse explained that along with the tranquilizers he'd consumed, Michael had other drugs in his system. In his delicate condition, they thought it best to give him something to make detox a little more tolerable. He'd be admitted to the psych ward as soon as he was cleared medically. From there, he'd need to get into a treatment facility; but he'd have to go willingly. Kevin didn't know if he could convince Michael to get treatment and didn't know how to reach any of his family. As far as he knew, Michael's mother had remarried and Mike hadn't seen her in years. Kevin didn't even know if she was still alive. He cried for his friend and just kept praying. He couldn't do this by himself. He brushed his teeth, grabbed the letter and his jacket and left the apartment. He called Kyle on the way out.

What felt to Kevin like days since they last spoke had only been a couple of hours. Kyle was still thrilled to hear from Kevin so soon.

"Hi! You ready to see me?"

"I am. I need to. I need your help, Kyle." Kyle could hear that Kevin had been crying.

"Of course. Do you want to come to the church?"

"Yes." Kyle gave Kevin the address to LvC.

"What's going on Kevin? Is Michael worse?"

"He's the same; but I had no idea how bad things were. I can't even tell you. He wrote a suicide note."

"Okay. It's going to be okay, Kevin. He's alive. I need to go and finish something up so I'll be free when you get here. I'll see you in a minute, okay?"

"I'm okay. I'll see you in a minute."

Kevin walked into the church and asked a young woman if she could let Rev. Tye know he was there.

"He's expecting you, just through that door." She pointed. Kevin knocked on the door. When Kyle opened it, Kevin was crying again. Kyle closed the door behind Kevin and reached for his arm and pulled him gently toward him. When Kyle wrapped his arms around Kevin, he let go. Kyle held onto him until the sobbing stopped and Kevin wiped his face with his hands. "I'm sorry."

"What for?" Kyle motioned for Kevin to sit on the couch and sat in a chair across from him.

"This isn't sexy."

"I think you know by now I don't care about that. Talk to me. What's happened?" Kevin pulled the crumpled letter from his jacket pocket and watched Kyle as he read it slowly. As he read, he stood up and began pacing. Kyle didn't have any words. He just kept shaking his head. When he finished, his face was wet and he sat next to Kevin. "Oh my God."

"Yeah, that's the best I could come up with too. I don't know what to do. What do I do, Kyle?"

"You mean after we kill this son of a bitch?" Kevin was only mildly surprised at the reverend's use of profanity in a house of worship. "I'm sorry. I'm searching for better words. I don't have any. Not that what has actually happened isn't bad enough; but this could have been you. This could have been your son. This could still be happening to dozens of other children. He needs to be put down." Kevin just sat quietly and watched Kyle. He felt helpless. Kyle watched Kevin watching him and remembered that his friend was there for his help. "Okay, fine. Let's pray." Kevin smiled and held out his hand. Kyle took it but didn't say anything. Kevin looked at Kyle out the corner of his eye. Kyle looked back as if to say, 'I got nothin' and finally took a deep breath.

"Mother / Father God we come to you right now searching. We will never know why you allow evil to happen to children; but we know that you are a loving God, a wise God. Please help us to see past our hurt for our brother, our fear for his wounded spirit; so that we can help him find the life you have spared him for. We know that he is alive today because your work in him is not done; and we thank You for his life and what You're about to do for him, God! We ask now that you steady our hands and open our hearts and guide us along the path that will lead to healing for Michael and the people who care for him. We ask for your patience as we face this unimaginable (but still all too common) evil and your forgiveness when we stumble. And again we thank you because we know that whatever we ask in your Son's name will be given. Amen."

"Amen."

"Hi." Kyle squeezed Kevin's hand.

"Hi." Kevin sniffled. "Thank you."

"I haven't done anything, yet."

"Yes you have. Actually, two things: I'm here and you said, 'yet'. I don't know what to do. I want to kill him. I don't even know how to look at Michael. I have to. I have to be there when he wakes up."

"Do you want me to go with you? Do you think he'll mind?"

"Oh, well, I don't think his vote counts right now. I mean, I hate to sound harsh, but Michael's gone. I don't know who this is; but Michael apparently left the building about twenty-four years ago." Kevin clutched the letter.

Kyle pried it out of his hands. "I'm just gonna go and make a couple of copies of this for you, okay?"

"Oh yeah, thanks." They made copies of the letter, grabbed a quick bite and went back to the hospital.

By the time they made it back to Michael's room, he was waking up. Kevin went in alone and Kyle waited at the nurses' station and got an update on Michael's condition.

"Hey!" Kevin tried to sound light.

"Have you been here this whole time?"

"No, I've been gone for a few hours, actually. They said you're gonna be pretty sleepy for a few days. When you wake up good, you're gonna feel better than new, though."

"You changed. Have you been home?"

"Yeah, Mike, I have." Kevin tried to hold it together; but he knew that Michael must have finally remembered the letter.

Michael began sobbing again. "Kevin, I'm sorry."

"Please stop saying that, Mike. You haven't done anything wrong. I'm sorry I didn't know; that you didn't feel like you could tell me; that I didn't understand why you did some of the crazy things you did...You ARE my brother. I DO love you. We are going to get through this. You're going to be okay, I promise."

"You don't know that."

"Yes, I do...Mike, I have a friend with me I want you to meet. He's gonna help me help you. Can I bring him in?"

"I got nowhere to be and not an ounce of pride left. Why not?"

"Whatever, man. Hold on." Kevin stepped out of the room and came back in with Kyle. Kyle stood by the side of Michael's bed and smiled at him.

"I always knew Jesus was Black." Kyle chuckled, remembering that Kevin warned him that Michael was silly.

"Mike, I'm really gonna need you to lay off the drugs while you're in here, okay. I told you, you're not dead, dummy." Kevin shook his head.

"Hi, Michael. I'm Kyle."

"Mike, Kyle does a lot of work with victims of abuse."

"I'd like to try and help you put things back together, if you'll let me."

"Why would you do that? You don't even know me." Michael wouldn't look directly at Kyle.

"Kevin knows you. He loves you. I figure you must be

pretty special. You've been friends a long time, right? You really scared him, Michael."

"You don't know who I am, what I've done."

"He read the letter, Mike. And that letter, what's in it, is not 'who you are'." Kevin touched Michael's arm.

"You let him read it?"

"Do you think if you died I would have kept it to myself? I had to tell someone, Michael. I can't tell Gabby. I won't tell Gary. Please let Kyle help you. I don't know what to do. It's all I can do to keep from killing him, Michael." Kevin didn't dare speak his name.

Tears streamed down Michaels cheeks as he looked back and forth slowly between Kevin and Kyle. For the first time in a long time, he actually felt cared for, even if it was just in that moment. "Thank you."

Kyle held Michael's hand and smiled at Kevin then at Michael again. "You're going to be okay." Kevin and Kyle sat with Michael for a little while longer while he tried to eat and then drifted back to sleep. The nurse came in and reminded Kevin, and now Kyle that the next few days would get a lot worse before they got better as all the drugs left his system. Michael wouldn't submit to a chemical detoxification. He was determined to continue punishing himself. The only good news was that, he was being held on a seventy-two hour psych hold. If he left the hospital against doctor's orders, Kevin could have him forcibly committed. But Michael was too tired to run; and he wasn't anxious to go home. He promised them he wouldn't leave and that he'd do whatever they asked. They left and promised that one or both of them would be back in the morning.

They rode in the elevator in silence. Kevin just smiled at Kyle who seemed to be back in reverend mode. "You have to deal with stuff like this all the time, don't you?"

"Unfortunately. I have to say, though, this is a whole new level of sinister. I knew he was evil when I met him, but…damn"

"Yeah, it's pretty bad when a real man of God vacillates between profanity and speechlessness." Kevin shook his head.

"Well, it certainly doesn't happen every day."

"Thank God. And thank you, Kyle. I'm not sure how I'd be getting through this without you."

"I'm glad I could help. I hope I can help. He's going to need a lot of counseling."

"And a place to live." Kevin just remembered the apartment belonged to Satan.

"Oh yeah. Do you need some help with that? I have a friend who may have an available apartment."

"I may need to take you up on that, but let me make some calls in the morning. He's still out of the country. At least we don't have to worry about him showing up."

"What are you going to do when he gets back? "Kyle asked.

"Kill him." There was not a hint of humor on Kevin's face.

"I thought we prayed about that already." Kyle chuckled.

"Oh, yeah. Okay, I'm going to see that he has an accident."

"Oh boy."

On the day the Michael was supposed to get out of the hospital, Kevin went to pick him up. He was actually excited about seeing him. God was so good! Kevin realized while Michael was in the hospital, more than when he talked to Gabby, what Nana had meant by 'the lie destroying everyone around you'. The Bishop's lie, coupled with Kevin's, nearly destroyed Michael. Even if the Bishop never came clean, Michael told one person, and Kevin believed him. He, with Kyle's help, was going to do everything he could to help Michael get his life back.

When he got to the room, Michael was still in bed. "Why

aren't you dressed? Aren't you getting out of here today?"

"Yes, but it's gonna be a little later than they thought. They've got to run some more... tests." Michael wasn't looking at Kevin again.

"What kind of tests, Mike?" Michael didn't answer. "Look, can we not go through this EVERY day, please? I told you, I'm here for you; but you gotta let me know what we're dealing with. Did all those pills cause some damage?" No sooner had he said the words, did Kevin know that was wishful thinking. Michael finally spoke and confirmed Kevin's fear.

"I have AIDS." Michael rolled away from Kevin in his bed. His sobbing shook his body and Kevin reached down to hold him. "No! You can't touch me, not now. Not ever again."

Kevin sat on the bed and pulled Michael so that his head was on his chest. Kevin wrapped his arms around his brother and silently rocked him until the sobbing stopped. When Michael could speak, he looked Kevin squarely in the eye. "Kevin, I swear I've only ever had unprotected sex with one person."

"Who? It was some guy you met in a bar, right? Or some stage ho? Some one-night-stand? A guy who promised you he was a virgin? A woman who promised you she was a virgin? Michael, please tell me you're not telling me you think you contracted HIV from my son's grandfather."

"I really wish I could, Kevin. I guess there's a chance. How's his health?"

"I guess we'll see when he gets back from Africa." Kevin resolved to keep things moving. They'd worry about Michael's status and the Bishop later. He thought it best to focus on one small step at a time. Besides, he figured, hoped, Michael was exaggerating. At worst, and that was bad enough, Mike had HIV. Kevin knew just enough about HIV / AIDS to know that if Michael had full blown AIDS, they'd

131

have talked to him about T-cell counts and risk of infections and pneumonia. All they'd done at this stage is refer him to a counselor and schedule a follow-up visit.

"When are you getting out of here?"

"They said soon, hopefully this afternoon. I'm sorry. I tried to call."

"It's okay. Let's go downstairs and get something to eat." Kevin waited for Michael to put some clothes on. He looked about ten years older than just a few days earlier. Kevin said a silent prayer.

"I need to move us out of that apartment, Mike. I've got a place lined up. I just didn't want to pack your things without telling you first."

"There isn't anything there I want."

"Are you sure?"

"Yes. He paid for everything."

"Your bed? Your clothes?"

"Okay, I guess I need clothes. I guess I earned them."

"Don't do that. It wasn't like that."

"You don't know."

"You were a child, Michael."

"Thank you for being my friend."

"I'm not your friend. I'm your brother."

14

THAT AINT NEWS BOI!

The call came in just as rehearsal was getting started. Kevin almost didn't answer; but it was his mother and she never called when she thought he might be working.

"Hi, Mom. How are you?"

"I'm okay, Sweetie; but I'm calling about your grandfather."

"Papa Bill? What's wrong?"

"He's had another stroke, KJ. It's not good. He's in a coma."

"How is Nana?"

"She's okay. You know this is Dad's second major stroke in six months. She's scared, but she's not surprised."

Kevin grabbed his coat and signaled to Gary that he'd call him. "I'm on my way. Where is he?"

"Presbyterian... Be careful, Baby. Call me after you've seen him. Your dad and I will be there in the morning. I love you."

"I love you, too, Mama."

Kevin prayed as he rushed across town to see his favorite grandfather. He wasn't ready to lose him, yet. He needed his advice, and Kevin knew more than that, his blessing.

Kevin found the room as the nurse was leaving, introduced himself as Bill's grandson and asked for an update. "He's comfortable, but there's been no activity since he arrived this morning. Your grandmother has been here the whole time. We finally accepted that she wasn't going anywhere and have been trying to get her to rest. She's been asleep for an hour or so."

"Thank you for that. Don't let her scare you; she's

harmless, really." Kevin smiled at his grandmother. "She's been no trouble at all. She seems like a fabulous lady. We're all praying for her husband."

"Can he hear me?"

"We think so." The nurse touched Kevin's shoulder as she walked away. "Talk to him. A lot of doctors say it really makes a difference."

"Okay. I will." Kevin took a deep breath and quietly pushed the door open. He put his coat and messenger bag in a chair by the door and kissed his grandmother on the forehead, as she snored softly. Then he turned to Papa Bill's bedside with his back to Nana.

"Hey, Papa Bill. Man, are you in a world of trouble! Mom said Nana missed her scrapbooking club to rush you to the hospital. When you get outta here, she's gonna skin you alive!" Kevin laughed to himself. "I've been missing our summer trips to the theater. Yeah, I know, I'm living and breathing the theater these days; but it's not the same without you. I have to enter through the back, so I don't get to harass the scalpers. The ushers still threaten to throw me out if I forget to take my hat off. Seriously, it's worse than church, Pop."

Kevin pulled up a chair and sat close to Bill's bed. "Did I ever say 'thank you', you know, for all those trips to the theater? I would never be who I am if you hadn't done that. I know, Mom was a performer too... Did you know that she said she never really wanted me to perform? She said that she'd spent twenty years of her life trying to be a star, and she didn't want me to go through that. She said that if it hadn't been for you and Nana dragging me to see The Tap Dance Kid I'd be a doctor. It wouldn't have mattered much that the sight of blood makes me pass out. You know the force of nature Mom is, I'd have graduated from medical school and gone on to be a surgeon. Talk about living a lie!" Kevin squeezed his grandfather's hand and took a deep breath.

"Talk about living a lie." This time it was a whisper. Kevin looked at the monitor attached to his grandfather. He considered for a moment that this was the eighty-five year old man's second stroke in six months. In that time, Kevin had basically resigned himself to accept the truth that he was gay; but he hadn't officially come out to anyone but Gabby, Kyle, and Michael. He didn't want his grandfather to die 'not knowing him.' He knew it was time. Kevin prayed that the doctors and nurses were right and that his grandfather could hear him. He played those early conversations with his grandparents in his head. "Aint nothing worse than a lie, Kevin Jerome."

"Wow. I guess years of having my lines given to me have kind of messed me up. Papa Bill, I need to tell you something and I don't know how. I've spent my whole life trying to be the kind of man you and Nana and Mom and Dad could be proud of. For a long time I've felt like I'd been doing a pretty good job. And I certainly couldn't have asked for a more loving and supportive family, or better role models. You all gave me everything you had – even some things you didn't. If I needed it, I had it. I know I got more than my share of what I wanted. Lately, my prayer is that I'm doing enough with what I've been given, by my family and by God. Am I loving people the right way, the way you and Nana taught me? I've been haunted most of my life by the feeling … that I'm wrong, Pop. I can't remember the last time I felt like a real person and not a character on stage that someone had written. It's like my life is one giant performance. You know acting is just lying, isn't it? And I've known that for a while. But I figured that as long as I could step out of the character, I'd be okay. Right? What if I don't know which is the character and which is the real me? I pray and I pray and I pray and I pray, but I can't shake the feeling that very much of my life has been a lie, and I feel like I'm slowly slipping away. So then I start trying to pick out the parts that are true, because I need something to hold onto. I love God. I love my son. I love my family. I love dance and the theater. I love Gabrielle, because she's all I've ever known..." Kevin paused. "Wow. There it is again. Did you hear that, Pop? You've met my wife, right? She is a beautiful, intelligent, exciting woman! What kind of man has to qualify loving Gabrielle Nichols with a 'because'? She's the mother of my son. She has a smile that can move mountains. She is the kindest, most loving, most understanding woman anyone could...She is my very best friend. She makes me laugh. I wouldn't want anyone but her by my side in a knife fight; yet she is still lovely. She is more wonderful things than any man even knows to ask for." Tears were streaming down Kevin's face. He didn't notice that Nana's snoring had stopped. "Why don't I love her – like that? Why have I never had a dream about anyone remotely resembling her? Why didn't I miss her when we were apart for four solid years? Why has every aspect of my life with her felt scripted? I'm starting to believe she's as good an actor as I am. Maybe better; no one is that damn perfect! Why do I work fourteen hour days, six days a week, three weeks a month, only to drive to a house I keep forgetting how to get to for a week; during which time I do nothing but follow my son around? I know it sounds like I don't like her or that she's the problem. I even hate myself for that. I know it's not Gabby. It's me. I'm gay."

Kevin put his hands over his face. "There. I've said it out loud. See Papa Bill, this is where you wake up and say, 'shut up, boy. Now, you're lying.'" Kevin watched the monitor. "Pop." Tears streamed down Kevin's face. "Why aren't you saying anything?"

"Because he's in a coma, fool; and you didn't tell him anything he hasn't known your whole life."

"Nana? How long have you been listening?"

"How old are you?" She walked over and hugged Kevin.

"I'm sorry, Nana. I just started talking. I don't know what

I was saying. I don't know if any of that is true."

"Yes you do. And yes it is."

"Nana!"

"Don't 'Nana' me, Kevin Jerome."

"Yes, Ma'am, I'm sorry, but, I don't understand. What do you mean, 'he's known my whole life'?"

"I mean what I said, Baby. Your grandfather knows you, has always known you. You didn't tell him anything that he - we haven't known since you were a child."

"Nana!" This time Gladys smacked Kevin in the back of his head.

"Ow-wah!"

"Oh hush! I told you to stop 'Nana-ing' me."

"I just don't understand why you didn't say anything... all that talk about 'living a lie' and the lies destroying everyone I love. If you told me, I could have lived a different life. Why didn't you say anything, Nana?"

"What was I supposed to say, Kevin? 'Don't marry that beautiful girl you've known your whole life'?"

"Um...yes, if you knew I didn't love her..."

"You did love her, didn't you?" Nana sat back down in the rocker and held Kevin's hand.

Kevin considered the question for a moment. "Yes, I did. I do. I just feel differently... on the inside."

"So you weren't lying. Your being... different isn't about Gabrielle or whether or not you do or did love her. It's about you – who you are. Your life, while you were living it wasn't a lie, Baby. You just didn't know. And it wasn't my place to tell you what your truth is. No one can do that for you, but God. Do you love my great-grandson?"

"More than I love myself."

"If you'd realized who you were as a child, he wouldn't be here. Would you change his existence in this world?"

"No!

"Everything happens the way it's supposed to, KJ, even

the bad parts. But your life hasn't been so bad, has it?

"No, ma'am, it certainly has not."

"So, stop all that damn crying; hold your head up, and start living the rest of it. God's got it all worked out."

Kevin just looked lovingly at his Nana. "But you knew?"

"Oh, yes, child!" Nana laughed.

Kevin kissed his grandmother and promised to come back later in the evening. As he stepped off the elevator, he saw Gary. Kevin had called on the way to say he was headed to the hospital. When Gary heard it was Bill, and heard the panic in Kevin's voice, he left the theatre to sit with him immediately. Kevin asked him not to disrupt rehearsals, but Gary wasn't hearing it.

Kevin ordered two cups of coffee and they sat at a table near the window. He was thinking about what Nana had just told him. "What did she mean, 'he's known my whole life'? "Do I give off some gay vibe?"

Gary reached across the table and squeezed Kevin's hand. "How's he doing?"

"There's been no change. I think they're talking to Nana about shutting down life support."

"Wow. That's tough. Does she know his wishes?"

"Yes. And he made it very clear. He's ready to go. If they can't treat him, he doesn't want to lie around in a hospital bed for the rest of his life. I just told my grandparents I'm gay."

That last bit of news caught Gary off guard. "You mean recently?"

"No. I mean just now, upstairs in the room. How's that for 'a deathbed confession?'"

"Yeah... See... I think it's the person who's dying who's supposed to do the confessing." Gary's smile was kind. "How did they take it?" They both giggled at 'they'.

"Well, Pop didn't say much. Actually, it went kinda the way everything always has been with them. Nana did the talking for them, and told me that they already knew, have always known."

"How does that make you feel?"

"A little annoyed, actually. Why couldn't they tell me when they figured it out? And as always, I felt loved. I spent almost as much time with them as I did my mom and dad growing up. They know me; and for them to know that, and love me as much as they do… Wow!"

"You truly are blessed."

"I know."

"Are you sure that you know? You seem uneasy. Are you thinking about your grandfather?" Gary looked Kevin squarely in the face.

"You can tell I'm not, can't you?"

"I don't know. It's just a feeling, something about your expression. I can tell that you're afraid…but it's not so much for him…because you know it's time. Am I close?"

"Keep talking."

"You're afraid of losing him; because he knows you and loves you. You can't possibly think he's the only one."

"No, I know he's not."

"So, what are you afraid of?"

"Living." Gary waited. "If I'm gay, my life, a large part of it has been a lie. Who am I?"

"If?" Gary tilted his head at his friend.

"Fine, Gary. I'm gay and my life has been a lie. How do I face people?"

"You make it sound as though you deliberately tried to deceive people, deceive yourself. Do you think you did?"

"No. I honestly didn't know… for a long time; and when I did, I thought I must be wrong - that the feelings I was having were the lie. I dismissed them as lust, and nothing more. A man can't live his life based on lust, who he's attracted to."

"Well, he certainly shouldn't."

"What do you say to people who say that homosexuality is wrong?"

"Well, first of all, I personally reject labeling myself as such. The unfortunate thing about the word 'homosexual' is that it has the word 'sex' in it, and that is what people choose to focus on. Who a person loves shouldn't be about sex at all. All sex outside of a committed relationship, for instance, is wrong. Loving someone however is never wrong. Some people prefer the term 'same-gender-loving'." Kevin smirked. "Yeah, I know, it's a bit much; but let's test it out. Have you ever had sex with a man before?"

"No."

"Well then what makes you think you're gay? Do you think the fact that you've had thoughts about having sex with men is what makes you gay?"

"No. It's more than that, a lot more. I've had lots of straight sex; but every crush I've ever had has been on a man. The closest I've ever come to being in love… a man, and he hasn't touched me."

"Kyle?" Gary waited.

"Yeah. How'd you know?" Kevin tried to suppress a grin.

"Just a feeling…" Gary was genuinely happy for his friends and he trusted Kevin wouldn't mislead Kyle. Still, he still couldn't help but poke at Kevin. "But you're married – to a woman."

"Technically, and not for long. I told her a few months ago."

"What did you tell her?"

"That I'm gay."

"But, how could you know that if you've never had sex with a man?"

"You actually make a very good point. Would you like to get out of here?" Kevin laughed and hoped Gary knew he was kidding.

Gary smiled back. "Seriously, Kevin. I don't know you like your grandparents, or your soon-to-be-ex wife. Remember, I'm the guy who made you pretend to be gay!

140

When you knew that you needed to be gay to get in with The Company, you insisted you weren't. What's happened since then? Is this my fault? Have you fallen in love with the 'lifestyle'?"

"No, Gary. It's not you. It's not the lifestyle. In fact, that's probably what's been holding me back. I don't need an alternative life; my real one was pretty damn good."

Gary resisted the urge to remind Kevin that he was actually quite miserable. "But."

"Love. Real love. I know this sounds silly; maybe even a little gay, actually; but I really do believe that we each have a soul mate; that one person we are meant to be with. I love Gabby; but I don't believe she's my soul mate. I never have. I've never been in love with her. I just accepted that what we had was as good as it could get."

"Fine. But why do you think that means you're gay?" Gary was really just having fun, now.

"Because the images in my head have always been of a man; a man I had never met before. It's almost as though I felt him calling me, that our hearts were calling each other. My needs, the things I'm attracted to in another person, are for masculine qualities. Not just the physical ones, but yes, those too. Oh, God, I sound like a woman!"

Gary laughed out loud. "Yes, you do, or a really, really gay man. So, now what?"

"I guess I just start living."

"Wise answer, Grasshopper!" Gary smiled and bowed his head slightly at Kevin. Satisfied that his friend was okay, at least for now, he stood to leave. Kevin gave him a hug and thanked him for coming. For the first time in a long time, Kevin was tired and went home early.

15

CHANGE IS GOOD

As soon as Kevin's head hit the pillow, the phone rang. It was Kyle. Suddenly, Kevin wasn't tired anymore. They'd talked on the phone or seen each other every night for months since they met. Kevin knew his life was complicated right now; and he really liked Kyle. He didn't want to bring him in to his early-life crisis. He was just hoping he could get it all worked out before Kyle got tired of him. In the meantime, he let Kyle make all the moves. It wasn't easy; everything about Kyle excited Kevin. And it all started with his voice.

"Good evening." Kyle's subtle African accent still made Kevin all tingly.

"Hi. How are you?" But, Kevin still tried to play it cool.

"I have had a wonderful day. Tell me about yours."

Kevin wanted so much to not be 'heavy' and return some of the light he felt when he heard Kyle's voice, but he couldn't help but be real with him. From the moment they'd met, he hadn't wanted to be anything but completely open and honest with him. It was frustrating to Kevin that his 'simple life' suddenly seemed to be in a constant state of turmoil; but at the same time, it felt so good to let go of all pretenses for a change. "My grandfather had another stroke. He's in a coma." It wasn't sexy, but it was true.

"I'm so sorry to hear that, Kevin. Is there anything I can do for you or your family?"

"Thank you. Pray. My grandparent's pastor has been there with Nana. They're talking about options."

"Hard choices. From what I've heard you say about her, I know she'll make the right ones. What do you need?"

"To hear your voice." The words came out before Kevin had a chance to think.

"Mm. Well it is good to be needed. Are you always this easy?"

"You think this – my real-life dramedy of late is easy?" Kevin's voice was a mixture of disbelief, amusement and relief.

"Well, yeah; what I see is you dealing with life as it comes at you. You don't seem to be creating a whole lot of drama on your own. Life happens; I think you're rolling with things pretty gracefully, actually. There are things you could be doing to make everything that's going on in your life a lot worse. Trust me, I've seen the other side."

"Really; like what?"

"Well, in the case of your coming to terms with your sexual identity, you could have gone on pretending with your wife forever and started living the lie. You could have started cheating and gone into the closet. It happens everyday. You could have turned your back on Michael after he tried to destroy you."

"He didn't try to destroy me, Kyle." Kevin knew Kyle cared about Michael, but he was still very protective of him.

"Actually, he didn't mean to; I believe that he loves you. But, he actually did set out to destroy your marriage and what he perceived as your relationship with her father by exposing you. It's not too far a leap to think that he hoped it would affect your career and your relationship with Gary. And that's what I mean when I say 'you're different'. You only saw your brother in need, not someone who was trying to hurt you."

"Oh, so you think my naiveté is attractive?" Kevin chuckled.

"Ha ha. You know what I'm saying, Kevin. I'm saying that it seems not to be your nature to think of yourself first; and that is incredibly attractive…and rare."

"Funny…" Kevin paused. They'd talked about the ins and outs of his marriage for days when they first met, and Kevin had had enough of it. He was tired of throwing Gabby under the bus.

"What?"

"It's nothing."

"Now, I know that's not true. What is it?"

"Really, it's silly. I said I wasn't going to talk about her. We're moving forward, right?"

"Right. But…"

Kevin chuckled. "I just think it's funny to hear you describe me as someone who doesn't think of themselves in contrast to Gabrielle, who used to tell me I was the most selfish person in the world."

"Perhaps you were, in your relationship with her. That's just not who I see. That is funny, isn't it?"

"Thank God for change." Kevin smiled into the phone.

"Amen!"

"Well, since you mention it, the folks at the office tell me I don't have a whole lot of diva in me. Maybe that's a side of me I need to develop: high-maintenance, demanding, diva-bitch!"

Kyle laughed out loud. "Oh no! What have I done?"

"You mean, 'what have I done, sir?' don't you?"

"Absolutely! Yes, your highness! How may I please you today?"

"The Prince does not think or plan! Amuse me!"

Still chuckling, "… wow, I had no idea you were such a horrible actor. Um…yes, sir, your wish is my command…" Kyle stopped laughing. "…On one condition."

"Anything." And Kevin meant 'ANYTHING'.

"Take a walk with me."

"My block or yours?"

"I'll come to you. Can you meet me outside in thirty minutes?"

"Why so long?" Kevin rolled out of bed.

"I'll hurry."

Kevin took a quick shower, brushed his teeth and threw

on jeans, a sweater and a hat. The autumn air was perfect for a walk and Kevin began to hum with excitement. As he sailed down the stairs, barely touching them, he realized this was the feeling he'd been missing. He'd never once been gleeful about seeing Gabby, even after being apart for years. Not even after they got married and only saw each other once a month. How did he ever think he could live without this feeling? And it really wasn't about sex, even though he'd spent more than a little time imagining what Kyle's lips would taste like and how it would feel to be held. As he sat on his stoop and waited for Kyle, he closed his eyes and smiled.

"You must feel pretty safe out here."

Kyle's voice didn't startle Kevin at all, and he thought to himself, before opening his eyes, "I certainly do now."

"That didn't take too long did it?"

"No, not at all." Kevin stood up and they gave each other the man-hug. That would be the first of many moments when Kevin would have to think about what it looked like to be seen with another man on the street. He didn't like it. He wanted Kyle to greet him with one of those bear hugs he'd seen him give people in church, he wanted to return that hug with a kiss on his cheek, feeling his stubble against his lips. No, he did not like being gay in the middle of Harlem, at nine o'clock, on a Tuesday night at all.

"Which way are we going?"

"How about the Village?"

"Good idea." They hopped on the train and got off at Union Square. Kevin instantly felt more comfortable, but he knew it was a compromise. He didn't appreciate having to go miles away from home just to take a walk and perhaps steal a kiss. He frankly found some of the goings on around him seemly and inappropriate; but he knew here, no one would say anything to them if he stood too close to Kyle, which he knew he was bound to do.

Kyle understood his frustration. "That's why I'm moving back to Canada."

Kevin tried not to panic. "I beg your pardon."

"Just to Toronto. It's actually not as far as you think. Closer, in fact, than the trip you were making. What was it, twice a month? I've been commuting to see if I'd mind the drive. So far, it hasn't been bad at all. It's just across the line, but it is a different world. Gay marriage is not only legal there, it's pretty common."

"What about your ministry?" Kevin still hadn't visited Kyle's church.

"We're starting another church there."

"Wow, I need to come hear you preach again."

Kyle laughed. "It's not about me. People are tired of being treated like second-class citizens. I personally haven't asked anyone to leave; but when people heard I was commuting, they started planning trips to check out the area. One of the deacons heard of an entire congregation that left New York and moved to Charlotte, North Carolina. Now, that doesn't seem like the most practical choice for my congregation, but they figured, just as easy to go north than south. And again, our marriages are legal there in the whole country, not just every tenth state."

"Surely, you see the progress in seven states versus what we had twenty years ago?"

Kyle smiled at Kevin. "Hey! You said, 'we'! Sure, in some form or another; and I'm hopeful that one day, every citizen will feel the same freedom and inclusion. In the meantime…"

"In the meantime, what? Are you giving up on change here?" Kevin didn't like what sounded like defeat in Kyle's voice.

"Of course not." Kyle stopped walking and stood in front of Kevin. "I'm not giving up at all. I'm just positioning myself for another battle. My job is to help build the kingdom as a whole, not just a small church in New York City; a city, by the way, that now has access to dozens of affirming churches locally, and hundreds nationwide. I have to get ready to get the message out of these buildings and into the minds and hearts of all of God's children – the ones who still aren't listening."

"And what message is that?" Kevin knew the answer; he just loved to watch Kyle.

"That God's love is inclusive. It's not as simple as opening up churches. It's more than getting people in the pews. The problem is actually what's going on outside. The problem is the lie people tell themselves, and then run and tell everybody else. I know I'm meant to pastor, but I also know I'm meant to sing. The gospel music industry is both the best and the worst thing to happen to the LGBT faith community. It's wonderful in a sense that there is a broader platform for the anointing for some truly and abundantly gifted individuals. But it's evil in the sense that it actually reinforces the lies that homosexuality is sin and God doesn't love us. It's preposterous when you think about it. Few people are denying that people are born gay or straight. People are born the way God made them. God doesn't make mistakes. God would not pour His gifts into something to be destroyed and mistreated. Do you believe you were born gay, Kevin?"

"It took me a while to get here, but, yes, I do." Kevin wondered when this sermon became about him; but he realized he lit the match.

"Do you believe your talent is of your own doing or a gift from a Loving God?"

"I know that I am blessed."

"Do you have any idea how many beautiful, talented souls would rather die than admit that they love differently? Sure, we've conquered Broadway; maybe even Hollywood. I'm getting ready to pick up my sword and shield and go after the fool that gave the enemy a press pass and a microphone. I'm not giving up and I'm not hiding. I'm going to where I can keep my family safe while I build an army. Does that make any sense?"

"Yeah, except for the 'press pass' part."

"Oh…It's bad enough that we have church leaders, some family members, music, every other member of society telling people that who they are is wrong; but when someone who knows the truth sits by and watches it happen and says nothing? I dated a guy once, well not really dated; there was interest…Anyway, he was a writer and an aspiring journalist, so he started this online publication in which he interviewed recording artists. Now, this is someone who's trying to date me, right?"

"Right."

"So, he knows I'm gay, and it's safe to assume he is too, right?"

"Right."

"Well this nut thought enough of himself to tell me all about his work and how he got to talk to interesting people, and he led me to his website where he has dozens of interviews over the last decade or so. I am a curious guy…"
Kevin stopped and tilted his head at Kyle. "Okay, fine, I'm nosy and a bit of a nerd…so, I started reading the interviews."
Satisfied, Kevin started walking again. "They were well written, thoughtful. And then I found his interview with Sid Stacey; you know the skinny little fellow who feels the need to end all of his songs about victory and deliverance by denouncing homosexuality!"

"Yeah, I'm gonna slap him when I see him; and I don't mean that in a good way."

"Exactly! And I'm thinking, 'okay, this is going to be good. He's gonna git em!' Not a word. Not one word about the damage he was doing to young boys and girls who love God, but don't know why they don't love church. Not one word about his irresponsibility and lack of authority. So, I asked him how it was that, as a gay man, he didn't feel that was relevant to the interview. Do you know what he said?"

"I'm not sure I want to."

"It never came up."

"Na uh."

"Yup, he said he was so excited to be talking to him that he forgot the guy had been on national television talking about how 'the problem isn't the gay choir member, it's the gay choir director.' It never came up. But you're a gay man; and this false prophet is walking around teaching children that who you are, who they may be, goes against God!"

"So you never spoke to him again." Kevin shook his head and started walking backwards in front of Kyle.

"Uh...no. I pray for him, though." Kyle shrugged his shoulders and smiled.

"I really wanna kiss you, right now." Kyle laughed and stopped to oblige him. Kevin was an inch away from the Promised Land when his phone rang. It was his mom. They had turned off Papa Bill's machines and it was all over but the waiting. Kevin should get there as soon as he could.

"Let me ride with you to the hospital. It's not far from where I live."

"I'd like that." When Kyle held out his hand Kevin took it and held onto it until they reached the hospital. He didn't care what it looked like.

16

MANDIGO-JESUS-LION-MAN SAY WHAT?

Gladys Porter heard buzzing behind her. "Oh my, that is a good looking man."

"Which one?"

"You're right. Wow. Is that Bill's grandson?"

"I think so; but who is that with him?"

Gladys turned to address the women behind her. "My husband is being laid to rest. I would appreciate it if you heffas could show a little respect for the dead."

"Yes, ma'am."

"Sorry, Miss Gladys."

Gladys nodded and stared past them to see her grandson and a man she didn't know walking up the aisle of the church. Kevin signaled that he'd sit back there, but she motioned for him to come to her. Kyle took a seat on the aisle near the door.

"I'm so sorry I'm late, Nana."

"It's okay, baby. I told you not to come in all this weather." Kevin had been in Charlotte visiting Ethan and packing up the rest of his things when a snowstorm caused his direct flight to be cancelled. The closest he could get to New York was Philadelphia. Kyle met him at the airport and drove him to his grandfather's funeral in Buffalo.

"Nana, I couldn't have missed Papa Bill's funeral. You know he was my favorite grandparent." Kevin winked at his grandmother and she winked back.

"Yes, I do; and he couldn't have loved you more." With that, Kevin squeezed her hand and held it as the preacher approached the pulpit.

After the service, Kevin found Kyle in the fellowship hall talking to the pastor of his grandparent's church.

"It was a beautiful service, Rev. White."

"Thank you, Kevin. You're grandfather was a good man, a pillar of this community for many, many years, before he moved to the big city. He will be sorely missed."

"In more places than this." Kevin fought back a tear.

"I'm sorry for your loss, son."

"Thank you, Pastor." They continued to talk. Kevin learned that Kyle knew the reverend. The three men stood for a moment and made small talk about how small the world was. Before Kevin could pull Kyle away, his grandmother joined them, looking spry.

"Kevin, Honey, who is this handsome man?"

Kevin seemed startled. He couldn't believe they'd been there for hours and he hadn't introduced Kyle to his grandmother.

"I'm sorry, Nana. This my friend…"

Gladys interrupted. "Kevin Jerome, what did I tell you about lying?"

"Nana!"

"Don't you 'Nana' me, boy." She was still holding Kyle's hand.

"Yes, ma'am. Nana this is Kyle…"

Kyle was glad Kevin had warned him what a pistol his Nana was.

"I'm sorry for your loss, Mrs. Porter; but it is a pleasure to finally meet you. Kevin could talk for hours about you and Mr. Porter. I wish I'd had a chance to meet him."

"Thank you for that, young man. Bill was very proud of this boy. It does my heart good to know the feelings were mutual. Kyle, walk me over to sit with Bill's messy sisters for a moment."

"Yes, ma'am." Kevin winked at Kyle.

"Don't let me stay too long. I have never liked them. Ooh, how they lie!" Kevin shook his head at his grandmother and smiled at Kyle as she whisked him away. He could only laugh at her feeble old lady routine. Everyone had already seen her bouncing around the church.

"Sisters, this is Kyle. He's taken." And with that, she began her complete circle around the fellowship hall with her superstar grandson's handsome man-friend on her arm. Kevin watched them make their rounds and realized in that moment that he was in love, possibly for the first time in his life. Leave it to Nana to be the first to point it out.

When she started to look tired, Kevin walked over to confirm her plans for the rest of the day. "I'm going to go home and sleep, Sweetie. I'll ride back to the city with the sisters." She turned her attention back to Kyle. "It was so nice meeting you, Kyle. Thank you for getting my baby here safely."

"I hope the next time we visit will not be at a funeral, Mrs. Porter."

"You love my grandson, Kyle. You can call me, 'Nana.'" Both of the young men pretended not to notice Nana's presumption; but they were equally, and visibly relieved to have her approval. Kyle looked at Kevin and smiled, then gave Nana a bear hug. She laughed and kissed his cheek. Before she walked away, she looked at her grandson and tapped his cheek.

"I love you, Nana."

"I love you too, baby"

Kyle went to pull the car around while Kevin said his good-byes to the rest of his family. He'd been looking for his parents to introduce them to Kyle, but Nana said they went back to open the house to receive people.

"Do you want me to drive you back to your grandparent's place?"

"No. My parents are staying with her. They're not expecting me."

"When do you need to be back to work?"

"Not until Monday, actually. Gary's got things running

pretty smoothly without me."

Kyle chuckled. "Now, that's a surprise. I figured he'd find it impossible to continue without you."

"What's that about?"

"You do know he's in love with you, don't you?" Kevin knew that was very far from the truth, but explaining why he knew that would betray Gary's confidence. Besides, Kevin found Kyle's tiny, even if just plain wrong, little green monster to be rather adorable.

"What are you talking about? Gary is like my big brother. He introduced us, remember?"

"No. He was in the room when we met; and he couldn't stop it from happening!" Months later, the memory of Kyle's smile that day still gave Kevin butterflies.

"Oh yeah." Kevin reclined in the passenger seat, crossed his legs, and turned to face Kyle. He glanced past Kyle out the driver's side window and noticed that they were going north. "Not that I mind being kidnapped, but you do know that New York City is the other way, don't you?"

"I do." Kyle reached down and rubbed Kevin's leg.

"Oh. Okay." Kevin looked at Kyle's enormous hand on his thigh, tried not to giggle, and flipped through the channels on Kyle's satellite radio to find a classic jazz station. He knew better than to ask where they were going. He didn't even want to. His new friend was full of surprises. Kevin liked surprises; and Kyle had a natural flair for the dramatic. He couldn't possibly have had time to plan anything, or known that Kevin wouldn't want to go home. Kyle just seemed to roll with things in the most graceful way. Kevin thought every moment they spent together was magical; so, he didn't care where they were going or what they would do.

Kevin, who Kyle secretly called 'Sleeping Beauty' had fallen asleep again and was awakened by the beeping of the open car door. "Where are we?"

"Toronto."

"Did you make reservations on the way? ... I do sleep through a lot, don't I?"

"Yeah, you do...This is my home, silly." Kyle popped the trunk. "You coming'?"

"No, I think I'll wait here." Kevin smiled nervously and got out of the SUV.

Kyle's home was a beautiful French Tudor that Kevin was sure must have been a bed and breakfast, not a private residence. Where are all the other people who live here?"

"I live alone. I've been restoring it for a couple of years now. When I bought it, the plan was to open a bed and breakfast, but now that it's finished I think I'll sell it. What do you think?"

"I think it's beautiful. Why on earth would you sell it?"

"Well, it seems way too big to live in by myself. I love to cook and entertain; but I couldn't run a b and b right now. Besides I bought it for a steal and paid cash for it. It's worth a fortune now."

"All the more reason not to sell it... duh..." Kevin walked slowly from room to room taking in the beautifully restored hardwoods and high ceilings. Kyle had kept the original crown molding and repaired the two fireplaces on the first floor to their original working order. The furnishings were exquisite, masculine but not too heavy. It even had a library. "May I ask you a very personal question?"

"Of course."

"How can you afford to live the way you do on a pastor's salary?"

"Oh, well, as a pastor, I don't take a salary at all. I write. I wrote a few books that did pretty well a few years ago, and some of the songs I've written for others have done well."

"Really? What kind of books?"

"Inspirational fiction, nothing too heavy. It's a release, and it pays the bills."

"Still? It's pretty impressive that you're published, and

apparently, successfully. I'd love to read them one day."
Kevin continued to check out the house. He actually gasped
when he saw the kitchen. "Okay. I take it back. You can sell
it."

"Really? That was fast."

"Yup. I'll write you a check. How much do you want for
it?"

Kyle laughed, remembering that Kevin Rivers could
easily write him a check for his restored country house. "Oh
you want it! Well, in that case, I think I'll keep it. You can
visit it. That way I get to see you."

Kevin smiled and thought to himself 'he likes me, he
really likes me!' He walked over to Kyle and put his arms
around him from the back. "Don't get it twisted. I'd come to
see you in a shoebox…on skid row…in the dead of
winter…wearing nothing but a… " Kevin punctuated each
statement with a gentle kiss on the back of Kyle's neck.

Kyle turned around and they held each other for the first
time since they'd met. Kevin studied Kyle's face, his full
sculpted lips, and almond shaped eyes…the cheekbones
inductive of his undiluted African heritage. Kyle took a deep
breath, held it in and closed his eyes. When Kevin leaned in
to kiss him, Kyle held a finger to his lips. "Would you like
some wine?"

Kevin was screaming inside and when Kyle turned his
back, he clawed at the air and silently stomped his feet.
"Wine sounds good. Mind if I freshen up?"

"Of course. I'm sorry I didn't…There's a bathroom to
your right, down that hall."

Kevin returned, having brushed his teeth and changed
from his suit to dance pants and a ballet tee. Kyle sighed
deeply again when he saw him. He handed Kevin a glass of
chardonnay and made a toast. "To Bill Porter."

"To Papa Bill." Kevin took a sip of wine and put it on
the table in front of him. While he was gone, Kyle had lit a

155

fire and slipped into something more comfortable himself. Now in loose fitting shorts and a fitted tee, he sat next to Kevin on the couch, with enough space for three people to sit between them. Kevin had never seen Kyle's hair out of his ponytail and couldn't decide now whether he looked more like Jesus or a lion. He picked up a throw pillow and played with the fringe to keep from reaching for Kyle's locks to play in them. He couldn't remember the last time he'd been more nervous, excited, and aroused. It was only a moment before he was really appreciative of that throw pillow.

"Kevin, I need to tell you something." Kyle's expression was grave and it put a knot in the pit of Kevin's stomach.

"What's wrong?" Kevin feared the worst, and Kyle knew instantly what he was thinking.

"No. I'm not positive, Kevin. I'm celibate."

"Oh!" Kevin was instantly and visibly relieved... and then confused. "Mandigo-Jesus-Lion-Man, say what?!"

Kyle laughed out loud, and it sent shivers through Kevin's body. Kevin laughed back at him and stood up revealing a huge erection. The moment he remembered, he sat back down and grabbed his new best friend, the hand embroidered throw pillow. Kyle's eyes moved quickly back to Kevin's face.

"I don't have sex, Kevin. I know saying this makes me sound like a great big girl, but I'm saving myself for the right man."

That did make Kevin giggle. "No, that's not girly at all," he lied. "But may I ask, 'why'?"

"Of course you can. It's not even something I tell everyone. I'm telling you because..." Kyle struggled to find the right words and came up empty. "You know why I'm telling you, Kevin. I think we're feeling the same thing; and I'm feeling it for the first time."

"I get why you're telling me. I still don't think I understand why you don't have sex." Kevin tried not to pout.

156

"Well, first of all, there's the obvious reason. I'm not willing to put myself at risk for the sake of physical pleasure." He took a deep breath and grabbed a pillow of his own. "The other reason is more spiritual. For most of my life, I prayed the prayer of the gay man…'Lord, if being gay is not Your will for me, please take this from me.' He has not. Without ever having sex with a man, I know I am, and always have been, gay. It isn't about sex at all. It's about my heart, this need I have to love, care for, and be connected to someone masculine and soft, strong and vulnerable. I think women are beautiful; but... And it isn't a result of something that has been done to me. I come from a loving, safe family, just like you. I'd never even met a gay person that I know of, until my twenties. I was born this way. But I also know there is a calling on my life. I have a responsibility to minister to people; and I pray every day that I can do so without hypocrisy. I can't preach to young gay men about the perils of promiscuity, if I am myself promiscuous and an adulterer. I'm going to share that part of myself with a lover I'll spend the rest of my life with, and no one else. God hasn't revealed that person to me, yet…" His last statement was almost a question.

Kevin's expression changed from 'curious' to 'insulted'. "Is it a common practice of yours to speak to men, who you know are interested in you, every day for months and lure them to your lair to seduce them, only to leave them horny and frustrated?"

"Of course not." This time, Kyle was insulted. "Let me try again. Until I met you, God had not revealed him to me. Of course, I'm interested in you, Kevin. You wouldn't be here if I weren't really excited about what's happening between us. But where we are is as far as I've ever gotten before. I don't want to be wrong."

"I understand. It's funny. I've only ever been with Gabrielle. We started early. I think we both thought we'd be together forever. And since I realized... I haven't given a lot of thought to dating men. I hadn't really considered becoming a virgin again."

"It's a more difficult choice than you can imagine, but it's the right one for me." Kyle stretched his long muscular arms and clasped his hands behind his head, his well-defined biceps and triceps flexing subtly.

"Oh, I can imagine just fine; speaking of my imagination, I'm gonna need you not to do that thing you just did with your arms again. Thanks. As a matter of fact, shouldn't you be wearing a robe or something? Or perhaps some kind of veil?" Kevin bit his lip and squirmed in his seat.

Kyle laughed. "I'm not a monk, dummy. I want you too, by the way. I promise."

"Okay. What are the rules? Can you kiss?"

"I think so..."

"Touching?"

"Um. I think we'd better see how the kissing goes." This time Kyle looked nervous. Kevin crawled the long velvet mile across the couch and kissed Kyle softly on the lips. Kyle parted his lips slightly and Kevin licked just inside his upper lip, then tugged softly on the lower. His lips and tongue were sweet and soft.

Kyle put his strong hands on Kevin's chest, careful not to squeeze. "Nope. No kissing. Uh, uh. Can't do that. What was I thinking? Ooh, I think I'm going to leave now. I'll call you tomorrow." He gently shoved Kevin backwards onto the couch and stood to leave.

"This is your house, Kyle. We're in Canada." Kevin felt something wholly unfamiliar. He wasn't sure if it was bliss or agony; but whatever it was, it was intense. He held the pillow over his face and muffled a scream. They both laughed through their desire for one another.

"Oh! Well in that case, are you hungry?" Kyle recovered quickly.

"Duh!" Kevin moved the pillow and looked at Kyle like he'd lost his mind.

"I meant for food, Hotpants."

Kevin considered that for a moment and realized he hadn't eaten since breakfast. He chuckled. "Oh, yes. Yes, I am."

Kyle laughed and held out his hand to help Kevin up.

Kevin glanced at Kyle's hand and then down to his own still semi-erect penis. "I'm gonna need a moment. I'll be right there."

Kyle walked away with a smile on his face, shaking his head, his locks bouncing softly. Kevin pretended again to grab him and fell on the rug between the sofa and the coffee table. As he watched Kyle disappear into the kitchen, he thought to himself, "God's got jokes..."

When Kevin returned to the kitchen, Kyle had changed again and was wearing sweat pants and a long sleeve t-shirt. There was no concealing his broad shoulders and perfectly sculpted torso. He held up his arms for Kevin's approval. "Better?"

"Nope. Not at all, really; but thanks for trying." Kyle kissed Kevin on the cheek. "What smells so good?"

"Shrimp and grits...biscuits. I forgot I needed to go grocery shopping. Is that okay?"

"More than okay. Papa Bill used to do a lot of Low-Country cooking. You're gonna make me cry."

"I hope you like it."

"Where did you learn to cook?"

"My father, actually. My mother did the everyday stuff, mostly Jamaican; but my father's food was my favorite. He traveled a lot and would always come home with a new recipe to try out on us. After spending just a few weeks in Charleston, he cooked nothing but seafood for a month. We got spoiled. My mom gets mad now if you even suggest a seafood restaurant to her. "What I need to go outside fa, when

I got me mon to do dat betta at home?"

Kyle's Jamaican accent was still so thick and natural... As a matter of fact, everything about the man was an assault to Kevin's senses. He hoped to himself that Kyle was kidding about the celibacy thing.

"Nope. Not kidding." Kyle smiled across the table at Kevin.

"I beg your pardon."

"Sorry, I thought I heard you say something. Were you thinking perhaps I was kidding about the celibacy thing?"

"Yes, as a matter of fact I was." Kevin looked suspiciously at Kyle while he watched him eat, wishing for a moment that he were a piece of shrimp. "How could you possibly know that?"

"Lucky guess. Oh, and I was simultaneously asking God to let me off the hook."

"Any luck with that?" Kevin asked anxiously.

"Nope." Kyle smiled and Kevin closed his eyes and sighed deeply remembering their first kiss.

"Well, at least I'm not alone in my agony." Kevin laughed this time.

"Oh, trust me, you are not alone." Kyle did that thing with the sighing and stretching again.

"So you've never had sex before, even with a woman?" They both giggled at the 'even' part.

"No. Weird, huh?"

"Unbelievable is more like it." Kevin sounded slightly annoyed.

"Why? Because I'm a Black gay man and we instinctually copulate like bunnies?" Kyle's face hardened, but Kevin was not concerned.

"No, because you LOOK LIKE SEX – like every fantasy I've ever had – and I mean EVERY one! They've gotten more frequent by the way! It's not YOU I don't believe; it's God! I've been, no pun intended, a pretty straight-laced guy most of my life. I finally come to grips with who I actually am, meet the man of my literal dreams, and you're telling me God says, 'no'?"

"Wow. Are you really that spoiled? Faithless? I don't think God is saying, 'no', Baby; I think God is saying, 'wait'. I've waited all my life for you, too. Do you think this is fun for me?"

Kevin was a little embarrassed. He knew he sounded like a brat, but he was combative by nature. He liked to see how far he could push. "Yes, I do! You prowl around here with your muscles and your lion mane, with your giant hands and feet, and arms and legs like trees; and you think I'm weak because I want to touch you?" They both laugh at Kevin's description of Kyle.

"Oh, and I don't want to touch 'People Magazine's Sexiest Man'?! Shut up, Kevin."

"Shut me up!" Kevin grinned at Kyle across the table.

"Oh! You think I'm a tease and I'm stupid!"

"Fine. Show me the rest of the house?"

"Okay." Kyle got up from the table and held out his hand. This time Kevin accepted it and Kyle effortlessly jerked him out of his chair. Always the dancer, and a bit of a drama queen, Kevin flung himself into Kyle's arms and wrapped a graceful leg around him.

"See. That's not fair. Please behave." Kyle squeezed Kevin's wrists.

"I'll do my best."

"Why don't I believe you? We're going that way." Kyle pointed and gave Kevin a gentle shove towards the door that led to the basement.

The finished basement ran the entire length of the house. Kyle pointed out a wine cellar, media room and professional quality fitness center. "I'm not sure what I'm doing over here, yet." They turned a corner and the basement opened up into a huge open space with hardwood floors and a wall that was mirrored from floor to ceiling. Kevin leapt into the open space like a gazelle. He was a beautiful dancer. Kyle stood and watched in amazement, standing near a baby-grand piano.

When Kevin noticed he had Kyle's attention, he forgot his promise to behave. Perfecting Leroy from *Fame's* audition routine with two decades of training, he danced around Kyle, taunting him. Finally, he ran and threw himself into Kyle's arms. To neither man's surprise, Kyle caught him, but quickly released his grip, and Kevin slid down Kyle's body landing on his knees. As he slid his hand up Kyle's leg, dangerously close to his crotch, Kyle grabbed his wrists, pulled him to his feet and flung him toward the piano. Kyle bent Kevin over the top of the piano holding both of his wrists with one hand. Kevin flashed a wicked grin.

"Is this all you want, Kevin? You want me to tear into you like some wild animal? Look at me!" Kyle looked distraught. Is this what you left your wife and son for, what you're willing to risk your life for? Do you need to hurt me? Is that it? If it is, I can't help you." Kyle walked away. Kevin called out to him as he walked upstairs.

"I need a minute, Kevin. It's my turn."

Kevin respected Kyle's privacy. Not knowing what else to do with himself in the moment, he danced. When he had no strength left, he sat in the middle of the floor and cried. He already knew he loved Kyle, had loved him since before they met... or so he believed. Why was he behaving like a spoiled child... a whore? He thought of worse words, but had never said them out loud before. He realized in that moment that he didn't really know how to pray, not for what he needed right now. But he knew how to sing, so he sat there in the middle of the floor and sang the song that was playing in his head: ♫Lord, make me over. Lord, make me over. Lord, make me over. Make me over again.♫

He repeated the words to Tonex's song over and over

until the song became a prayer. As he sang, he realized that the song had a different meaning than when he'd first heard it years ago. Kevin hoped with his whole heart that the selfishness and disrespect he displayed toward this beautiful man of God could be a distant memory by morning. He hadn't done much that he was ashamed of in his almost thirty years; but when he finally got upstairs, he was feeling a new low.

Still not wanting to disturb Kyle, Kevin busied himself cleaning the kitchen. He looked for his bags in the foyer and couldn't find them. He didn't want to ask, so he quietly looked for a downstairs bedroom. When he found the guestroom, he found his luggage and a note.

"See you in the morning. Sleep well. Kyle"

Kevin smiled and a tear rolled down his cheek. He practically flew up the stairs to Kyle's bedroom. He knocked softly.

"Come in." Kyle was sitting on the floor with his back against the bed, knees up with his hands clasped. It was clear he'd been crying. Kevin, who grabbed a long loose sweater on his way upstairs, sat down on the floor next to Kyle.

"I got your note. I wanted to apologize before you went to sleep. If I learned anything from my parents and my own marriage, it's not to go to bed angry."

Kyle looked at him and nodded. "Good rule. I'm not angry, though."

"You have every right to be. I'm a clown, Kyle. I get paid to entertain people. I am by definition 'a fool'; but I do know better. I feel horrible."

"First of all, I accept your apology. It means a great deal to me. Thank you." Kevin waited. "Can I ask you something?"

"Of course."

"What do you want from me, Kevin, really? Why are you here – I mean aside from the fact that I practically kidnapped you?"

A million things rushed to Kevin's mind at once, but he tried to take his time and gather his thoughts. He moved in front of Kyle and looked him in the eye. Before he spoke, he took Kyle's hands. "You know I've been around men, gay men, my whole life? It wasn't until I met Gary that I felt like I had a role model. None of the boys in the ballet were anything I aspired to be. Sure, I've admired them physically, but I've never been emotionally attracted to another man before. And while you are the most beautiful thing I have ever laid my eyes on, and I'm sure there is a picture of you next to the words 'man' and 'sex' in the dictionary, it's really not about that at all. I've loved you since before we met; when I heard you reveal what a colossal ass my ex-father-in-law is. You represent something I want to be a part of, something good and noble. I know you think my head is full of one-liners and dance counts, but I have been listening… and watching. I know that people are dying 'out there'. Their souls are being ripped out by hatred, hypocrisy, hopelessness and self-loathing – and it's being taught, spread around like poison in other churches, the music they hear, everywhere. I heard your voice and I heard what was missing in the churches I grew up in, that God's love is unconditional. Surprisingly, that's not really news to me; but coming from you, it takes on a different meaning. The moment I saw you, I knew you were living your life alone, and I wondered how that could possibly be when you clearly have so much love to give. I realized the reason someone else isn't loving you is because God made you for me. I know that you are the love God promised me. I can't believe I thought I could live without these feelings! I knew they existed. I've been acting them out on stages most of my life. I know they're real because I've never felt more alive. I'm here because I'm supposed to be, and I want nothing from you except to be everything you need in another person… whatever that is. I understand now that I should probably wait for you to tell me. And again, I ask you to forgive me. I'm in love for the first time in my life. I've never been as certain of anything as I am that we're meant to be together. I promise it's not about sex. It's about my heart. I can't seem to get close enough to you. But, I am a dancer, and I'm used to being able to act my feelings out physically. I don't know how else to share everything I'm feeling with you."

Kyle kissed the inside of Kevin's wrist. "Wow. I think you just did." He stood and pulled Kevin to his feet. "I love you too, by the way. I told you this was harder than it looks. Did I mention that I really, really, want you too? You have to know that. I've been sitting up here thinking that we are only a mile from the finish line. I'm so excited about you, and us; but I have to finish this. Will you help me get there, please?"

"You said, 'we'." Kevin smiled and nodded, and then, careful not to get too close, wiped a tear from Kyle's cheek. Kyle pulled him closer, took a deep breath and softly kissed Kevin on the mouth. Kevin sighed and pulled away slowly.

"Okay, now I am confused."

"Oh, I talked to God. We worked it out."

"Yay!" Kevin squealed. They made out, fully clothed, hands above the waist, and talked for hours about how they could change the world together. Before they knew it, it was morning.

Kevin made breakfast while Kyle worked on his sermon. For the next two days, they played like children and Kevin slept in the guestroom and did behave himself, for the most part. On Sunday morning, they arrived at church bright-eyed and glowing. Kevin was nervous. There were people there who already knew him as Kevin Rivers, the Broadway star. In that space, he just wanted to be Kyle's boyfriend.

The buzz started instantly. Kyle had a casual pastoral style, so interrupting the service to put an end to the mystery was no problem. "Brothers and sisters, I know we're about

165

twenty-five long and boring announcements away from the part of the service where we welcome visitors, but some of you seem to be excited about something other than the Holy Spirit this morning. Honey, stand up, please. Ladies and gentlemen, this is Kevin Rivers – yes, that Kevin Rivers. And, yes, he's my boyfriend." Kyle laughed and Kevin blushed. "You will be seeing more of him – much more, I hope." He turned to the choir stand. "So, please don't scare him off." The sanctuary was sprinkled with laughter and applause and welcome wishes. Kyle winked at Kevin and simultaneously made note of the faces that were not smiling.

17

WHAT'S DONE IN THE DARK

Kyle waited in his truck outside Kevin and Michael's apartment. They'd moved into the basement apartment of Kevin's grandmother's brownstone. It was as much space as they'd had in the other and the price was right. Kevin wanted to be sure he moved Michael into something he'd be able to afford on his own. Nana didn't need the money and she was happy to help Kevin help his friend. Kevin trusted he'd be safe there. Nana had always liked Michael and immediately adopted him. She was fit to be tied when Kevin told her what had been going on. All Kevin could promise his grandmother was that he wouldn't do anything to get himself killed or arrested. She accepted that as the best he could do.

"Let's go. Let's go. Let's go. Good morning, gentlemen!" Michael thought Kyle was way too chipper for five o'clock in the morning. Kevin, of course, thought he was adorable, but kept that to himself. He still didn't have the heart to tell Michael that he and Kyle were dating. It was still really early and Michael's wounds were still too fresh.

"I do love a road trip!" Kevin hopped in the front seat and smiled at Kyle.

"Uh, huh. I'm going back to sleep." Michael crawled into the back seat and stretched out.

"'Night…" Kevin was relieved that Michael would be sleeping. He'd wanted to take this trip to confront the bishop with Kyle alone. He didn't want Michael to see the bishop.

The sound of Michael snoring made Kevin happy. "Finally, we're alone."

"Be nice." Kyle winked at Kevin.

"Thank you for doing this."

"No, this is completely selfish. I want to see his face."

"Remember, my nana said we can't kill him."

"Your nana is not the boss of me."

"You've met her, right?"

As they approached Atlanta, Kevin called his mom.

"Hey baby, how are you?"

"I'm good, Mama. You and Daddy doing alright?"

"We're good. To what do we owe the pleasure?"

"That hurts my feelings, Mama. Do I have to have a reason to call and say, 'hi' to my parents?"

"One would think not, but…"

"I'm sorry. I'll do better from now on, I promise. Mama, do you know where we might find the bishop this afternoon?"

"I think Phyllis said he's coming home today; said something about someone needing to get him from the airport."

"That's perfect. Thanks."

"You're welcome, Kevin Jerome."

"Ma'am?" Kevin knew two names meant she was annoyed. Three meant he was getting a whoopin'. It didn't matter that her tone was always so pleasant. She was a good Christian Southern woman. She didn't need to raise her voice to get her point across.

"Is there something you need to tell me?"

"Oh" Kevin held his breath, but only for a second. He'd decided to go with the 'BandAid approach' to coming out - just spill it. "Yes, ma'am. I'm gay."

"Oh, thank God you finally figured that out. Is that all that's going on?"

"With me? Yes, ma'am. How long have you known?"

"Honey, since you were three. Are you happy, Baby?"

"Yes."

"I love you. Don't have sex."

"I love you, too." Kevin smiled, shook his head and hung up.

"Did you find out where he'll be?" Kyle asked.

"Oh yeah." Kevin flipped through the numbers in his phone for his ex-mother-in-law's.

"Hello Mother Nichols. It's Kevin." Again, he held his breath.

"KJ? How are you, Baby?" The sweetness in her voice surprised him.

Kevin was waiting for some sign that she'd spoken to Gabby. He assumed she would have by now. It had been more than six months since their split. He would've rather waited to talk to her; but this trip wasn't about him. "I'm fine. How are you?"

"Getting old, but I'm not done yet." Kevin thought he was being tortured.

"Mother Nichols, have you talked to Gabrielle recently?"

"Yes, I have KJ. By the way, I'm still just 'Mama' to you." Kevin felt as though the weight of the world had been lifted off his shoulders. Kyle smiled when he saw him physically relax.

"That makes me happy. Thank you, Mama."

"I love you, Kevin. Always have. Always will."

"I love you, too. I can't tell you what it means to me to hear you say that."

"Um hmm. Stop being mushy. Is that why you called?"

"No ma'am." Kevin's expression turned grim again, as he remembered Mama Nichols was the other victim in this mess.

"Mama, I need to talk to the bishop while I'm in town. My other mama said you said something about needing someone to get him from the airport? I'd love to surprise him."

"Oh?" Kevin knew instantly that Mama Nichols knew Kevin was up to no good. She knew darn well he didn't like her husband.

"Yes, ma'am, and then I thought I would stop by and see you. Would that be okay?"

"Of course, Baby. Stop by the church and tell them I sent you. They'll give you the keys and his flight information."

"Thank you."

"Thank you for calling, honey. I hope you make it by."

"I'd love to see you. I'll try to make it." Kevin hung up and looked at Kyle who had a huge grin on his face. If it weren't for Kyle's dimples, Kevin would have cursed him. Instead he was just mildly annoyed.

"I'm just gonna stop telling people. Shit."

Kyle laughed. "Let me guess, she wasn't surprised either?"

"It's not funny. Is it my walk? Do I talk funny?"

Kyle laughed so hard he had to slow the car down. "Well, you do kinda talk funny; but I'm sure it's not any of that. It's you're nature. You're kind and compassionate, loving. Those qualities aren't exclusive to gay men, but they are far less detectable in straight men. You have a sweet spirit. It just makes more sense that you are gay than not. Trust me; most of the time, when I meet someone and my gaydar goes off, it's a good thing."

"Whatever." Kevin pretended to pout. "Oh shut up!" Kyle continued to laugh out loud and Michael stirred in the back seat. "See."

Michael sat up. "Are we there yet?" Kevin rolled his eyes. Michael really was still eight years old.

"We're about an hour away. Are you hungry?" Kyle's kindness and patience made Kevin smile.

"I think I could eat. Did I hear you talking to Mother Nichols, KJ?"

"Yeah. I needed to find out where he was going to be. I told her we might stop by later."

"Um, don't you think we should do that first?" Michael

was wide-awake and sober. Kevin missed his friend. Kevin looked at Kyle, who looked in the rearview mirror at Michael.

"What's the plan, Mike?"

"I need to tell her." Michael stared out the window. He suddenly sounded very small. "I don't want her to hear it from anyone else. And as soon as he realizes people know, he's gonna run."

Kyle looked at Kevin. "He's right."

"Are you sure you're ready for that, Michael?" Kevin turned in the passenger seat to look at Mike.

"Yeah. I'm ready. I have to be."

"What's the address?" As Kevin typed the address into the GPS for Kyle, he glanced back and saw that Michael was crying. He climbed in the back of the SUV and sat next to him. When he reached for Michael's hand, Michael pulled away.

"I'm good, Kev. Time to man-up, right?"

Kevin wiped his own cheeks. "Right."

The men were quiet for the rest of the drive. Kevin and Kyle prayed silently. As they entered the community of palatial homes, Kyle clenched the steering wheel and looked at the time. "We need to get to the church if we're going to get to the airport in time."

"I'll go alone. Just come get me when you get him there."

Michael got out of the SUV and took a deep breath. Kyle looked at Kevin and instinctively knew what he was thinking. "We need to wait." Kyle turned off the engine and looked at the clock. "Ten minutes?"

"Yeah, if she throws him out, it will be in the first five." They waited a full fifteen minutes and when Michael didn't come out they left.

Kevin and Kyle drove to the church and picked up the bishop's car. The church secretary was more than happy to help Kevin and his friend surprise the bishop. They arrived at the airport with time to spare. Kyle even donned the chauffeur's cap for the occasion. He held up the sign with the man's name on it and tossed it in the car once he'd gotten his attention.

"Who are you?" The bishop looked suspiciously at Kyle.

"Back up." Kyle mumbled.

"What's that?"

"Mother Nichols sent me... sir."

"Oh, well I'm in a hurry. I need to get to the church right away." Kyle moved to open the door, using every ounce of self control he could muster not to strike the man. What he did do was slam the door so hard the limo rocked and the old man almost fell inside.

Nichols was very surprised to see Kevin. "Kevin! Ha! This is a nice surprise! How are you doing, son?"

Kevin tried not to throw-up. It took him a long time to speak. "I'm not your son. You don't have any sons."

Nichols was confused. Kevin must have been playing a practical joke on him. "Whatever, boy. Where's my grandson?" He was still smiling. Kyle watched closely through the open partition. He really needed for Kevin not to kill the man. Kevin also needed to stall for time. They were actually running a bit ahead of schedule.

"Have you talked to Gabrielle lately?"

"No, I've been in Africa on a mission trip. You should know that?" The bishop arrogantly assumed that everyone was concerned with his comings and goings. In that instant, Kevin realized that the only reason the bishop was able to get so close to Michael was because no one gave a damn where he was outside of the church. "What's going on, Kevin? Is my daughter okay?"

"She is."

"Good. I wouldn't want to have to put you over my knee." As Kevin clenched his fist, Kyle slammed on the breaks and the limo lurched forward. Seconds later, Kyle opened the door from the passenger side and sat next to Kevin, opposite Nichols.

"What the Hell is going on? Why aren't you driving? What are you doing back here?" Kyle leaned forward so Nichols could see his face. Without the cap, and with his hair pulled back, Nichols recognized Kyle. "You're that faggot from the radio station!" Kyle just watched. He'd been called far worse by far better men. "Kevin, son, I don't know what is going on, but I command you to get me where I need to go, now!"

"We're working on that," Kyle said as he threw the copy of the folded suicide letter in Nichols' lap.

"What is this?"

"That is the last written statement of Michael Anthony Lawson." Kevin didn't bother to mention that Michael was very much alive. They just watched.

"Oh my God, no!" Kevin thought the acting in EJ's second grade production of *The King and I* was better. Kyle nodded at him, indicating that he also saw the relief on the monster's face. "He was a troubled young man…"

"I can't help but notice that you don't seem anxious to read the letter, Bishop. Aren't you curious as to why a healthy, vibrant, thirty year old man would commit suicide in the prime of his life? Are you even surprised?" Kyle was just making conversation.

"Huh! I don't have to read it. It probably says he didn't want to be an abomination anymore! And let me guess, you blame me because some sissified little boy chose to die rather than repent?" Kevin lunged forward, and Kyle pulled him down from behind, holding onto his arms. Nichols noticed that Kyle was holding Kevin and looked at Kyle. "Get your hands off my daughter's husband!" Kyle slowly rubbed Kevin's arms and shoulders to calm him. "What the Hell is going on, Kevin?"

Kevin spoke through clenched teeth. "Read the letter!"

Nichols tried to open the door, but Kyle was holding the remote and kept it locked. "You don't know who you're messing with. I'm calling the police." He fumbled for his phone. When he couldn't find it, Kyle tossed him his.

"Use mine." Nichols caught the phone, but he didn't dial. Instead, he continued to look wildly around the limo.

"Read the letter!"

"Kevin! If you're cheating on my daughter, if you bring that nastiness into my family, son, I'll see to it that you never see Ethan again!"

With that Kyle let Kevin go and said almost to himself, "Hmph... see, I can't help you now..."

Kevin leapt across the limo, grabbed Nichols by his shirt and shoved him down to the floor. He pressed his boot down on the man's chest.

"I told you I'm not your son. I am no longer your son-in-law, I am a gay man and I left your daughter to live a real life! Now that, that thing you just did where you threatened me and spoke my son's name; that was the last time! If I catch you even looking in his direction, I will end you!" Kevin grabbed the letter without removing his foot. "You know what this says, don't you?"

"How the Hell should I know what it says, fool?"

"I always suspected you couldn't read. I'm not going to read it to you. I can't without throwing up. But I'll tell you it outlines every evil thing you did to Michael from the time he was six, you sick twisted bastard!"

"That's a lie!" Kyle noticed the older man was struggling to breath under the weight of Kevin's foot and touched his arm to signal him to lighten up. The last thing they wanted was for him to have a heart attack and die before he could go to prison. Nichols sat up. "I was good to that boy. I treated him like he was my own son! You were just jealous."

"Jealous of being molested and raped by the only person in the world he thought loved him?! How many others were there?"

"None...th-there wasn't even one!" Nichols finally took the letter and began to skim it. "That boy was confused. You'll never be able to prove anything. All you have are the sad ramblings of a dead man who wanted someone to blame for what he turned out to be. You can't even prove I ever had sex with him."

"Can you think of any other reason why he'd know you have an uncircumcised pencil dick and one testicle?" Kevin tried not to chuckle.

"It doesn't say that! When did he say that?" Nichols looked like he'd seen a ghost.

"Don't you worry about that." Kyle looked at his watch and nodded to Kevin. "Here's what's going to happen. You're going to quietly walk inside this building." Kevin pointed out the window. "And you're going to ask for Detective Martinez, she's expecting you. You're going to plead guilty to child molestation and rape. Trust me, you don't want a trial. You're going to quietly go to prison for the rest of your life and you're going to spare your wife and daughter of any more embarrassment..."

"You've lost your mind!"

"...Or you can opt for plan 'B'. You can try to run." Kevin nodded to Kyle who unlocked the limo doors. Nichols crawled out of the limo and tried to straighten his clothes. Kevin and Kyle got out of the car and watched. Nichols looked as if he was heading up the stairs to the municipal building and then suddenly began walking quickly down the sidewalk in the opposite direction. He almost made it to the intersection when two police cars blocked his exit. The old man put his hands above his head and was handcuffed and shoved into the back of a patrol car.

Kevin turned to Kyle who stood with his arms open.

"What, no man-hug?" Kevin teased.

"Come here." Kevin walked into Kyle's arms.

"Oh, would you two get a room, already!" Michael walked from around the limo and stood next to them as they watched the police car circle the building.

"How'd you get here?" Kevin asked, still snuggling Kyle.

"I told Mother Nichols what was going on and she drove me. She said the sight of him being carted away in handcuffs was not something I should miss, considering…"

"Wow." Kevin and Kyle spoke at the same time.

"So she believed you?"

"I guess so. She brought me here."

"Did she make the calls?"

"I think so. I guess we'll know if he makes bail. Can we go home now?" Michael looked exhausted.

"Um, hello, I can't drive all this way and not see my parents. You can take a nap at the house."

"Oh yeah."

18

RENAISSANCE MAN

The men drove to Kevin's parents' house, next door to the Nichols'. They were both home. Kevin was really nervous. He didn't have his keys, and wouldn't have barged in with company if he had, so he rang the doorbell. Tresa opened the door and gave Kevin then Michael each a big hug. She commented that Michael looked thin and that there were leftovers from Sunday's dinner in the oven. Kyle stood quietly off to the side until Kevin got her attention again. "Mama, this is Kyle."

Tresa stood back to inspect Kyle. "It's very nice to meet you, Kyle." He held out his hand and she shooed it away. "Oh, we hug around here, Honey. Wait. Are you Kyle *Tye*?"

"Yes, ma'am." Kyle blushed.

"Mama, you know about Kyle's church in New York?"

Tresa ignored her son. "You are a pastor, aren't you? I forgot I read that. I love your books. I've read all of them. Mm, mm, mm! Wicked!"

"What is she talking about?" Kevin looked at Kyle. He'd completely forgotten his dreamy, musician-pastor, boyfriend was also an award-winning novelist. Michael shrugged his shoulders and headed for the kitchen, as Tresa ran away chattering. She returned with an armload of hardback books and a pen. Kevin picked one up. Kyle was the author of all six of them. "Is there anything you don't do?"

Kyle winked at Kevin as he signed the books. "Yes: dance–well, ski, and fish." Kevin grinned back. His mother still hadn't stopped talking. He was officially no longer worried, that is, until his father emerged from the kitchen chewing and looking grumpy.

"Honey, you told Michael to eat my chicken?"

"Sorry, Pop. My bad. He's done nothing but eat and sleep the whole trip. It's like taking care of a baby. He's up, so he's eatin'. Dad, this is Kyle. Kyle this is my dad, Aaron Rivers."

Aaron held out his hand, "It's AJ. Good to meet you, Kyle. What's this Mike's saying about needing to get someone else to preach on Sunday? I thought the Bishop was back."

"Um, yeah. We need to talk to you about that." Kevin, Kyle and Michael explained everything that had happened, including finally revealing that Michael had been abused by the Bishop from the time he was six. Tresa wept and held Michael. AJ grabbed his coat and keys and headed for the door, mumbling something about an old shotgun in the garage. "Dad! You can't get to him. He's being held in a private cell 'for his own protection.'"

"Well, how the hell did he manage that already?"

"It's okay. It's what we had to accept in order for the police to let us bring him in. Apparently, they'd been investigating him for a while now and were planning to bring him in soon; but if they'd waited until he got home, got settled and then tried to arrest him, he'd lawyer-up and start hiding stuff. Mother Nichols has already been working with her attorney to control the assets she knows about. Michael's charges gave them an excuse to bring him in now, without warning him of the other investigation. He doesn't even know Mike's alive. He's not going anywhere." Tresa excused herself to go next door and check on Phyllis, leaving her husband and the younger men alone.

Kyle found it disturbing that neither of the Rivers' was entirely surprised. He cared about Michael, but wanted to believe that this was an isolated incident. The thought that Nichols could have been molesting other children, and right next door to their family, horrified him. "Mr. Rivers, you don't seem surprised. Do you think what happened to

178

Michael could have been happening to other children in the church?"

"Not that I could prove, Kyle; it's AJ or Aaron, by the way. You're obviously, family. I never saw anything; but I never trusted him. Let's just say, I knew better than to send my grandson over there alone." Tears streamed down Aaron's face as he turned to Michael. "Michael, I'm so sorry I didn't know. You always looked happy. When I asked your mom if you wanted to live with us, she said you said, 'no', I left it at that. I shouldn't have. I don't think I'll ever be able to forgive myself for not seeing, for not protecting you."

"It's not your fault, Pop." Michael looked stronger.

"It's not yours, either; you know that don't you?" Aaron looked Michael squarely in the eyes.

"I'm getting there. Kevin and Kyle have been draggin' me to rehab and counseling and church. I'm feeling better and better every day."

"We have not been dragging you anywhere, and especially not to church. You should hear him, Pop. He sings like he never left."

"Whatever else might have happened, your anointing is still there. Just keep praying and doing the work." Kyle couldn't help but get excited when he thought about Michael returning to the church. Once he'd gotten clean and started coming back, so did his glow.

"Ya know what I just realized?" Michael sat up.

"What's that, son?" AJ looked at Michael.

"For the first time in my life, I'm happy to be alive."

"Amen!" Kyle, Kevin and Aaron said in unison, and with that they turned their attention to the NBA draft Aaron had been watching when they arrived. Kevin and Kyle feigned interest as sufficiently as Kevin had his entire childhood. AJ and Michael were none the wiser, and AJ had a ball with 'his sons'.

19

PASS THE POPCORN

In the eleven months they'd been dating, Kevin had never seen Kyle flustered; but when Kevin arrived at his house so Kevin could meet Kyle's parents, Kyle looked positively unhinged. "What's the matter? Have all your other boyfriends been some sort of doctor too?" Kevin teased as Kyle settled into the driver's seat.

"No, that's just it. They've never met anyone I dated before. I told you, I haven't dated much."

"Well then, they have nothing spectacular to compare me to."

"Oh, baby, I'm sorry. I'm not worried about them liking you; I'm worried about you liking them. They're... different." Kyle touched Kevin's leg, having already relaxed a little.

"Of course they are. They're Ethiopian and Jamaican, and they moved you to Canada to keep you from being killed. They're like no parents I've ever heard of, except perhaps Moses'."

"Just don't say I didn't warn you." Kyle chuckled.

"I'm sure it will be fine." Kevin reclined in the passenger seat and opened the third of Kyle's series of novels about a group of preachers' kids. In the thirty-minute drive to Kyle's parents, he'd laughed out loud, cursed and praised Jesus at least twice. Kyle watched him enjoying his work and decided to go the long way so he could finish the last chapter. When Kevin finished, he closed the book and clapped, "Again! Again! Again!"

"Thank you." Kyle put the SUV in park, leaned over to kiss Kevin slowly, and took a deep breath. "You ready?"

"Oh yeah!" After everything they'd been through, Kevin

knew this would be a breeze. He loved Kyle more than he ever dreamed possible. How could the people who raised him not be fabulous? Kyle rang the doorbell and waited. His mother answered the door and Kevin was suddenly nervous. Naomi Tye was stunning. Kevin thought she looked like one of those African statues his grandparents had all over the house; but real, and not bearing water... and not naked. Kyle had her smile, dimples and build. In her modest heels, she stood eye to eye with Kevin who was just about six feet tall. Her beauty seemed effortless, she wore no makeup, except for lip-gloss and liner (Kevin could always tell) and her thick, graying locks were curled and twisted in a knot that still hung to the middle of her back. Kyle's face lit up when he saw his mom. Even though he lived close, between the church, his music and now, Kevin, he hadn't seen much of her in the last year. At least once a week, he could be heard apologizing for not getting by more often. Her response was always loving and supportive. "Kyle, baby you've been taking care of your mama since you were nine years old. It's time you looked out for yourself, now. Do you hear me, boy?"

"See, boy, I told you, ya mama was fine!" She gave her son a big hug and he lifted her up off the ground.

"You do look good, Mama." Kevin watched quietly and tried not to grin. "Mama, this is Kevin."

Kevin held out his hand, "It's nice to meet you, Mrs. Tye."

"Oh, come 'ere, chile." Naomi opened her arms to give Kevin a hug. "I've been 'earing about you every week for a year! Don't know whether to kiss ya or smack ya on your backside, keeping my baby so busy he can't come home. Got me ready to move to another country again. Starting to think that might be the only way to see him."

"I've been trying to get him to bring me sooner." Kevin laughed and winked at Kyle.

"Mama, is Daddy home?"

"He went to get Grand Mother from the airport. He should be 'ere shortly. Come in 'ere and tell me what's been going on with you before the family gets 'ere and swallows you up."

The boys followed Naomi into the kitchen of the home that looked very much like Kevin's parents', except... tropical. Kevin listened as she talked about their latest vacation and that they were planning to come to New York soon. Kyle's father had recently retired from the hotel business. He still traveled a lot, but now Naomi traveled with him. Kevin followed Naomi around the house as she pointed out pictures of Kyle as a child, his awards and degrees. She clearly could not have been prouder of her son. Kevin was starting to wonder what Kyle was so on edge about. When Kyle's father returned home with his grandmother and aunts, he understood more.

There was only one word to describe Kaleb Tye: 'Regal'. Kevin immediately recognized Kyle in the older man, his stature, his gait and his expression. He was a serious man. He didn't say much. When his father entered the room, Kyle stood and waited to be acknowledged before walking over to greet him. Kevin watched as Kyle suddenly seemed to grow both taller and younger at the same time, straightening his already near-perfect, posture to match his father's, while instinctively relinquishing whatever power he consumed in the room. Kevin had never seen anything like it and thought to himself, "Oh, that's what he's talking about!"

"Father, this is Kevin Rivers."

"It's an honor to meet you, Mr. Tye. I've heard a lot about you." Kevin tried to remember to keep his handshake firm. He'd become very conscious of things like that since coming out.

"Really? What have you heard?" Mr. Tye tilted his head slightly as if summing Kevin up and finding him lacking.

Kevin stuttered. "W well..."Mr. Tye began to chuckle

and released his grip on Kevin's hand.

"Oh, don't look so serious, boy! I'm retired. I don't get to have much fun anymore. It's very nice to meet you, too, Kevin. I hear you've made quite an impression on my son. I do hope you're not keeping him from his work. Kyle, have you written anything lately?"

"Actually, I have, Father. Music mostly, and Kevin and I are writing a play together, a musical."

Kaleb's face suddenly turned to stone again. "Of for goodness' sake! Is that what I worked all those years for, for you to run off to New York and waste your time writing silly musicals? What happened to all that talk about preaching and writing music that ministered to people? You think you're in love so now you don't care about God anymore?"

Kyle was offended, but he was not intimidated. "There is more than one way to minister to people, Father. My work, our work, has the power to reach more people than ever before. I have not forgotten my calling; in fact, more and more, I believe I've realized it. It's clearer."

"Oh really? And to what do you attribute this revelation?" Kevin sat very still and watched the two men go at it. If he weren't terrified of the older one, he'd have liked some popcorn.

Kyle knew that last question was trap. "God, Father. God is solely responsible for my realization that, to reach people, I need to be where they are, rather than standing behind a pulpit waiting on them to come in so I can point to the cross. If you're asking how much Kevin has to do with my new direction, the answer is 'a great deal'. I find his work and passion for people as inspiring as any sermon I've ever heard or preached." Kevin blushed and hoped Mr. Tye would just ignore him. He had no such luck.

"But, aren't you a dancer?"

"Yes, sir I am; a choreographer actually, and a writer, actor and singer. It actually works nicely. I think about what I enjoyed about church, the music, and we just build on it. People like to be entertained. There's no sin in sending a message of hope and love in any of the different ways people can receive it, is there? Sometimes a dance can tell a story much more clearly than words can."

"Well, I tink your partnership is beautiful; and I'm very excited about seeing the work that comes from it." Naomi was tired of her husband's bullying; besides, he was losing, and as much as she was enjoying that, she didn't want to have to hear about it later. The Tyes actually reminded Kevin of his grandparents. They apparently never agreed; the lady was always right, and they made you think. Kevin smiled across the room at Kyle who winked back. Kyle's grandmother and one of his aunties joined them for dinner and the conversation changed to what was going on in Jamaica. After several hours of fantastic food and conversation that Kevin only understood half of, Kyle and Kevin excused themselves to the back deck. Once outside, Kyle seemed to relax, but not so much he was comfortable touching Kevin in his father's house.

"See, I told you it would be fine." Kevin held Kyle's hand anyway.

"You think that was 'fine'? Kyle squinted at Kevin.

"Honey, you had me thinking the man was gonna eat me!" Kyle chucked and pulled Kevin close. He really couldn't resist him.

"I'm sorry. He just sucks all the fun out of every room he walks into."

"I actually like your dad, very much. He is fun …in his own stoic, dictatorial, alpha-male kinda way."

"I guess he's not bad. My mom looks really good, doesn't she – happy?"

"Are you kidding, she's positively beautiful; and I know beautiful, I live in New York."

"Mom says he's really been different since he retired. They spend a lot more time together, but he still has his moments. I guess it's hard being home every day when you've spent thirty years on the road. My mom was so lonely, though Kevin. I know his work, literally, made my life possible, but when I think about how lonely she was…I really resent him."

"That's not fair, Kyle. From everything you tell me, it sounds like they made all of the big decisions together. Maybe she thought being able to raise you in a safe, nurturing environment was worth any sacrifice she had to make. It certainly looks like she's happy, now. Just pray that they have another thirty years to enjoy each other."

"You're right. Thirty years, huh? They've already been together for thirty-five. You ever heard of a couple staying together for sixty-five years?" Kevin had his arms wrapped around Kyle's waist and was nuzzling his favorite spot on his neck. Kyle hummed softly.

"Well it is rare…But I'd like to give it a shot." Kevin slowly pulled away, still holding both of Kyle's hands. He stood still looking at Kyle until he opened his eyes. "Will you marry me?"

"What?" Kyle smiled, but looked just a little confused.

"I said, Kyle Tsegaye Tye, will you do me the honor of spending the rest of your life with me?"

"I love you…" Just as Kyle was about to answer, his father walked outside. He did not speak and instead fixed his laser like gaze on Kyle's face and slowly let it drop down to their clasped hands. Kyle released Kevin's hands slowly.

"Your grandmother is ready to go. Would you take her to her hotel on your way home?"

"Of course." Kyle nodded to his father who immediately turned away; then he followed quickly behind him. Kevin was on his heels. They said, 'good-bye' to Kyle's mother and quietly put the ladies in the truck and drove away. Kyle didn't speak except to exchange pleasantries with the women. They even made the short trip back to Kyle's house in silence.

Kevin's proposal surprised Kyle for two reasons. That he assumed he would be the one proposing was only the second reason.

"I really want to say, 'yes'."

"Yet, you have not."

"I love you."

"I know that. Forgive me if this sounds arrogant, but more importantly, I know I love you! I want to spend the rest of my life with you. I don't understand, Baby."

Kyle pulled Kevin close and pressed his lips to Kevin's forehead. Kevin reached for Kyle's hair and held his breath.

"I don't know that I could be a good husband, Kevin. This is the only serious relationship I've ever had."

"Are you waiting for something better to come along?"

"Don't be stupid. There is *nothing* better than you. I work all the time. Between the music and the church, I'm afraid I don't have enough left to give you. And Ethan! I want to be a real father to him; but I'm selfish. I go inside my own head and I stay there for days.

"I know. I've been there; it's nice." Kevin wrapped his arms around Kyle and nuzzled his cheek.

"I want to be a better husband and father to you and Ethan than my father was to my mother and me. He was never there. You met him. He's cold. I'm a lot like him."

"You are nothing like that man. Don't get me wrong, I clearly see him in you; your presence, your intelligence, your sense of responsibility. But you are the kindest, most loving person I've ever known. You're fun. You're sexy. You are the opposite of cold. Did I mention 'sexy'?"

"I'm serious, Baby. I don't want you to be lonely living with me.

"I'm serious, too. Don't you think I know you by now? I see you. I love it all. Do you think I want to change you? It would break my heart if you stopped being the man I fell in love with because of me. Haven't you noticed that I basically haven't left Canada, except to work myself? We spend plenty of time together. We'll make it work. Everyone is going to get what they need." Kevin held Kyle's hand to his heart. "Do you feel that?" Kyle felt Kevin's heart beating. He could almost hear it. "It's time for you to let someone take care of you. I don't care if you're a good husband. I know that you're a good man. Please let me love you."

Kyle stared into Kevin's eyes for a long moment then closed his own and took a deep breath. They stood still for what felt to Kevin like forever, while Kyle said a silent prayer of 'Thanks'. When Kyle finally opened his eyes, his worried expression was replaced with a smile. "Yes."

"Yes?" Kevin smiled back.

"Yes."

Kevin kissed Kyle and began bouncing around the room before he pulled his lips away. "Doves! I want white doves, and no attendants except for EJ, Gary and Michael! Is that okay? You don't have any cousins you promised could be bridesmaids or anything, do you? What are we going to wear? Armani, of course! Too cliché? No! Classic! Oh my God! All of that in a tux! The ceremony is gonna need to be ba-reef! We can honeymoon in Paris!

Kyle interrupted. "We can finally have sex."

"We can finally have sex!" Kevin stopped bouncing and started pulling at Kyle's shirt. "Please tell me you mean 'we can finally have sex, now'!" They were both giggling when Kevin started tugging on Kyle's belt.

"We've come this far, Baby what's another six months?" Kyle wrestled control of Kevin's arms and held them firmly at his sides.

"One month." Kevin was stronger than he looked and broke Kyle's grip, slipping his hands under Kyle's shirt, caressing his stomach and chest.

"Okay, three months." Kyle closed his eyes, momentarily surrendering to Kevin's touch.

"Fine, three." Kevin let his hand slip down to Kyle's crotch and felt him growing.

Kyle breathed with intent, in what looked like a cross between a Lamaze and Tantric exercise. "Okay. Can you plan a wedding in six weeks?"

"Can you preach a word and sing 'til ushers start rolling their eyes at you?" Kevin rubbed Kyle ever so slightly through his pants.

"Mmmmm. Baby, that's not fair. You promised. Hey, speaking of promises, where's my ring?" Kyle was joking.

Kevin was still kissing Kyle but stopped touching him to reach into his own pocket and pull out a gorgeous platinum and diamond band. When he had it in his hand, he stopped kissing Kyle and took his right hand. "I'm going to make you the happiest man in the world."

"You already have." Kyle closed his eyes and kissed Kevin. Kevin slid his hand down Kyle's chest and tried to squeeze his hand inside his pants without taking the belt off. "But you gotta go!"

Kevin whined. "I wanna play with it!"

"Yeah, that sounds like fun; not gonna happen. I love you. You don't have to go home, but you have to get the hell, and I mean 'Hell', away from me."

"Fine, I'll go work on some things downstairs."

"I'll walk you down."

"See, you're a tease! You know what happens when I get you down there."

"C'mon." Kyle took a deep breath and tried to think of funerals and road kill. When they made it to the basement door he stopped. "After you."

Kevin bounced down the stairs expecting Kyle to come after him; which was silly, since Kyle hadn't slipped once in the eleven months they'd been together, despite Kevin's best efforts. Instead, Kyle flipped the switch to light the stairwell, slammed the basement door shut and locked it, all the time laughing and cussing Kevin out in French. After he'd taken a very long, very cold shower, he released his prisoner to watch movies with him.

"You suck!" Kevin swung half-heartedly at Kyle when he got out of the basement.

"You wish." Kyle blocked the punch and gently and effortlessly twisted Kevin's arm behind his back.

"Hey! Award-winning dancer and choreographer here; I need to not get broken!"

"Yeah? Celibate pastor here! I need to not be tested *every* time we're alone together."

"Good point."

"Ya think?"

"I'm sorry."

"No, you're not. Seriously, Baby, you're killin' me. I am barely holding on. Please help me get through this last six weeks."

"Okay...I'm gonna need a distraction." Kevin turned away from Kyle as if looking for something to do with himself.

"How about you...help me write a musical, plan our wedding, tell your son you're getting re-married...to a man; you know, stuff like that?"

"Oh yeah."

Kevin 'sobered up' and immediately started making the calls. His parents were thrilled and even asked if they could help in any way. His mom mused at having won the beauty and talent lottery, and only regretted that they could not biologically produce another grandchild. His father's only concern was that he was happy and would still be home for Thanksgiving, now that the in-laws weren't next door.

Kevin went to Charlotte the next day and told Gabrielle and Ethan in person. EJ asked if he would get to wear a tuxedo in the wedding and if Kyle could teach him Tae Kwon do. Gabby was still just sincerely happy that Kevin was happy. She really did love him more than she needed to be with him. So, rather than pretend to be bitter, she took advantage of the opportunity to call and congratulate Kyle and offer her PR services.

20

ABOMINATION!

Kyle hung up the phone and returned to the piano. He and Kevin had been in their basement studio when Kyle's mom called. Kevin knew instantly Kyle was holding something in. "What's wrong?"

"It's nothing."

"That's not true. When you went upstairs, you were whistling; now you look like your cat died."

"I can't stand cats."

"See! You love everything and everyone! Please tell me what's wrong. Was that your mother?"

"Yes. She said my father isn't coming to the wedding." Kyle returned his attention to the melody he'd been working.

"Oh. Baby, I'm so sorry. Did he say why?" Kevin sat straddling the piano bench, facing Kyle.

"No, and it doesn't matter." Kevin heard the words, but he could tell it did matter. Kyle pleaded with Kevin to keep the ceremony simple and the guest list short; but by the time they'd invited all of the people they loved, who loved them…between their two church families, their immediate families, Kevin's theater family and Kyle's friends in the music industry, their union was becoming a full-scale, star-studded event. But Kevin knew that it wouldn't matter if there were a thousand people in the room if both of Kyle's parents weren't there. Kyle would never admit that to Kevin. He didn't have to.

"Mmm." Kyle kissed Kevin and squeezed his hand, and Kevin forgot what they'd been talking about. When he opened his eyes, the sadness on Kyle's face reminded him.

"Maybe he needs more time to get used to the idea. Do you want to push the wedding back a few months?"

"Uh, no! Are you kidding?" Kyle pulled Kevin closer, sliding him across the short bench. "I've been waiting for you my whole life. It's time. In six days..." Kyle looked at his watch. "...And approximately three hours, we will be united as one, before God and everyone else we care about. Am I disappointed that he won't be there? Of course I am! But our union isn't about him. Please don't worry. I'm fine. I just need to shake it off."

"The sting?" Kevin stroked a spot on Kyle's arm with the back of his index finger.

"Yeah. That's it."

"I might be able to help with that." Kevin kissed Kyle sweetly and lingered a moment before getting up.

"Oh boy..."Kyle prepared to run.

"No. I'm not gonna try anything. You're not the only one who can see the finish line." Kevin actually had been on his very best behavior during their brief engagement. Of course, he'd been abstinent for the entire year, but he'd also been deliberately consecrating himself in other ways. He'd given up meat, and sweets; and more importantly, he stopped taunting Kyle. "I can do anything for six weeks." Kevin got up from the bench and stood behind Kyle and massaged his neck, back and shoulders.

"Mmm. That's really nice, Baby. Thank you."

"You're very welcome." Kevin tugged on Kyle's ponytail and kissed his forehead.

"Is that it?" Kyle whined.

"Uh, yeah! You told me to be good."

"Since when do you listen to me?" Kyle pulled Kevin onto his lap and kissed him deeply.

"That's not fair." Kevin protested but didn't get up.

"Payback's a bitch, aint it?" Kyle bit Kevin's lip gently and ran his hands down his back. The tables had turned and he'd been having way too much fun torturing Kevin.

"You're a reverend. Remember your vow?"

"I'm a man." Kyle took Kevin's hand and moved it to his own thigh where, about six inches above his knee, Kevin found...Kyle's manhood.

Kevin thought, "Oh shit, oh shit, oh shit..." but said simply, "Baby, please..."

"Please what?" Kyle squeezed Kevin's hand against his third leg and kissed his throat.

"Please... don't... stop..."

"But what about your vow?"

"I'm a dancer... besides, what's six days?"

Kyle laughed out loud and kissed Kevin's collarbone. "Back to work."

"What?" Kevin had been leaning back against the piano and suddenly sat straight up.

"You heard me. We need to work on the refrain. What we have right now isn't working for me."

"I should cut you." Kevin sat on the bench pouting. Kyle just laughed. "No. I am gonna cut you." Kevin moved as if he were going to the kitchen and Kyle pulled him back by the back of his jeans. "Let me go. I don't like you."

"You love me."

"Nope. You're mean...and funny lookin'...

"What's the matter?" Kyle asked innocently. Kevin stood up and stared at Kyle whose eyes moved immediately to Kevin's erection.

"Oh that? I see. You want me to do something about that? I know all about that. Let me tell you my secret." Kyle pulled Kevin close so he could whisper in his ear. "Prayer."

"'Prayer'? Ya know what? I really am gonna cut you!" Kevin tried to pull away, but Kyle had his wrists in a vice grip.

"Okay. Okay." Kyle glanced down and could see a small dark spot had formed on Kevin's jeans. "We're beyond that point. I feel your pain. I mean literally, I've been feeling your pain for almost a year now. There were days when I literally wanted to pound a hole in you. Do you know how I kept from fornicating us into coma that first night you were here?" Kyle was getting on Kevin's nerves now so the pressure was slightly less intense, until that last part.

"Do tell."

"Showers. Long, cold, just let the water run… don't touch it, 'cause that's cheatin'…showers. This house has five of them. Have fun."

"I am not marrying you." Kevin walked slowly toward the stairs.

Kyle shouted after him. "Yes, you are! Can we go get something to eat when you're done? I'm hungry! Can we have steak? Oh, wait; you can't have steak. Maybe a burger? Oh wait; you can't have a burger. That's okay. I'll just have a salad and dessert. How's that sound? You want salad and dessert? I'm sorry. You can't have dessert. Maybe we should just stay in. Yes, let's do that. Let's stay in and have steak, chocolate cake and sex!"

By the time Kevin made it up the stairs, he was laughing so hard his hardness was almost gone. He took a shower and changed anyway. When he came down, they went to Kyle's favorite vegetarian restaurant.

The next day, while Kyle went to the church, Kevin stayed in Toronto. He told Kyle it was to handle some wedding business. What he actually did was go and see Kyle's parents. Naomi greeted him at the door with a big hug. "Hello, my angel! Are you excited?"

Kevin gave her a kiss on the cheek. "I am. I'm nervous, though. I just want everything to be right."

"I'm sure it will be, regardless of who's there, Kevin." She touched his cheek.

Kevin sighed deeply. "I know. But, I have to try. Is he still here?"

"He is. He's on the patio. Go on in."

Kevin walked through the house to the back patio and

found Mr. Tye reading a newspaper. Always the gentleman, he stood to shake Kevin's hand. "Hello, Kevin. Naomi said you'd be stopping by. To what do we owe the pleasure?" Kevin resisted the urge to tell the man he was full of crap, and that he knew full well why he was there.

"I came to ask you if you would reconsider coming to our ceremony."

"Well, what do you need me there for? You will have half of New York City and all of Toronto here to witness your *holy union.*"

"I know the guest list looks like a lot of people, but it's really a little more than one hundred, very small by normal wedding standards."

"But there's nothing normal about this wedding, is there? I have no role in the ceremony. There is no bride to be walked down the aisle. You haven't come to ask my son's hand in marriage, have you?"

Kevin was caught off guard. He assumed Kyle's father's aversion to the ceremony was that they were both men, not that he wasn't included. "Mr. Tye, we just assumed that since it is a 'holy union' ceremony and not a traditional wedding, that we would do many things differently. We were trying to be respectful of our families and not cause them any embarrassment by asking them to participate. It would mean so much to Kyle, and to me, if you were there."

Kaleb would not be won over that easily. "Is that it, Kevin? Do you think you can just walk in here and say, 'we're getting married' and expect that we'll jump for joy?"

Kevin thought to himself, "Oh geez, now what?" "I'm sorry. You're right. I didn't ask how you felt about it; but Kyle's a thirty-one year old man. Even if he were a woman, I'd think you'd trust him to make a decision like this on his own. I don't understand what you're asking of me."

Kaleb could feel the sincerity coming from Kevin. "Kevin, do you love my son?"

Kevin tried to stop a tear that threatened to run down his cheek. "More than I ever imagined possible. Yes."

"Do you believe in him, his calling, his work?"

"I do, so much so that it's become my passion, too."

"Does he know you're here?"

"Of course not. And I know I have no right to ask anything of you, but please don't tell him. Really, Mr. Tye, he was so hurt that you weren't coming. I had to try; but he would be very upset if he knew I did this, especially if you don't come."

"Well, in that case, we won't tell him. My son is very special to me, Kevin. I don't ever want to see him hurt, or disappointed, or taken advantage of, or mistreated...I know that he looks like a giant, and he is strong; but if you break his heart...and Kevin, you could break his heart..."

Kevin interrupted. "No. I couldn't. I won't." There was no stopping the tears, but Kevin tried to control his voice. "I wish I could make you understand..." Kaleb watched Kevin who sat with his eyes closed. "Okay. I'm a dancer, right?"

"Yes, and a gifted one, I'm told."

Kevin took a deep breath and placed both of his hands on his right thigh. "I would gladly give up this leg before I'd hurt Kyle. If sparing him an ounce of pain meant I'd never dance again, I'd choose him."

"That's foolish, and a pretty powerful statement, except that it will never be tested. Life-marriage doesn't work like that. You don't get to pick. Things happen and the choices you make can change your lives forever." Kaleb looked past Kevin as if reflecting on his own life.

"I love your son, Mr. Tye...as much as you do...as much as you love your wife. You're not going to intimidate me or make me feel so small that I run away from him. There isn't anything I can say to prove to you that I want to spend the rest of my life with him; but I'm here because he loves you and he wants you to be there when he makes the same promise to me. Doesn't that tell you anything?"

"It does."

"Thank you."

"Thank you, Kevin" Kaleb got up and poured them a each a drink. "So, what would you like as a wedding gift?"

"Isn't that obvious?" Kevin chuckled.

"No, that's for Kyle. What do you want?"

"I'd be more than happy with the shared gift of your presence, but if you want to do something for me..."

The night before their wedding, Kyle came home to a candlelit dinner. "Wow! What's this?"

"Well, it's our last night together before the rest of our lives together. I wanted it to be special."

"Shouldn't you be at your bachelorette party or something?" Kyle set his bag down and pulled Kevin close.

"Ha! You are fun-knee! Actually, Michael said something like that, but can you imagine what that would be like? I'm not sure who those things are for, but it aint me. I've got no oats left to sew, and I don't need some half-neked-ho shaking his junk in my face." Kevin did a raunchy butterfly, and ended by cocking his leg up in the air.

"Ew!" Kyle chuckled and made a smelly face.

"Exactly. This is where I want to be." He pulled Kyle back toward him and wrapped his arms around his waist. "But if you'd rather spend the night alone...?"

"No! Absolutely not! I think this is perfect." Kyle shook his head and smiled.

"What?"

"I didn't want to be away from you for even one night. How did you know?"

"Because I felt the same way, Silly. Besides, bachelor parties, spending the night apart; they wouldn't be the first traditions we've broken." Kevin let his hands rest on Kyle's chest.

"I think we've left enough to look forward to, don't you?" Kyle nibbled on Kevin's ear lobe.

"Uh huh, but if you want to make it to the church tomorrow, you might not want to do that anymore."

"Twenty-four hours huh?"

"Actually, twenty-eight hours, twenty five minutes and a fourteen-hour flight."

They had dinner. Kevin made up a tale about how he spent the week, filling in the part he spent with Kyle's father with 'a last minute trip to the florist'. They kissed and cuddled for the last time as an unmarried couple. They'd made an art of teasing each other. They'd even gone as far as establishing a 'safe word' so each knew when the other was reaching his point of no return. So as they played on the big comfy couch, fully clothed and hands above the waist (that was the only rule), Kevin slipped his hand under Kyle's shirt and squeezed his left nipple. Kyle bolted upright and shouted "Abomination!" Kevin fell to the floor laughing and immediately got up and did his victory dance.

"In yo' face! I won! I wa-un! La-ooooza!" Kyle stuck out his leg and tripped Kevin. When he landed on the couch Kyle casually reached for Kevin's hand and stuck his finger in his mouth, biting the tip gently before sucking the whole finger.

"You got nothing! I'm…fine. See…"

"Mm huh" Kyle nodded still nibbling and sucking on Kevin's finger. Then he held up his free hand and counted down, five, four, three…

"Sh… no…" Kevin jerked his hand away. "I refuse."

"Cheater." Kyle lay back on the couch laughing.

"You're a cheater!" Kevin whined. "I already won. After you say it, you can't play anymore!"

Kyle laughed. "Fine, you won. So what does that make the final score: 36-1?"

"Shut up!" Kevin returned to his spot on top of Kyle on

the couch.

"You should get some sleep, Baby." Kyle looked at the clock. It was four am.

"I don't want to go to bed." Kevin whined and sunk further into Kyle.

"I know. Hold on." Kyle got up, blew out the candles, turned off the music, and returned to the couch. He took Kevin's hand and they prayed together for their special day and their new lives together. They slept on the couch in each other's arms. Their groomsmen, Michael and Gary, along with EJ arrived at noon with breakfast and their clothes.

21

SO AMAZING

The ceremony was held in Lvolution Church, Toronto, and officiated by Elder Tracy Nation, Kevin's pastor from MCC, New York. Kyle and Kevin waited outside the sanctuary doors as the music began to play and Michael, Gary and EJ processed in, followed by the minister. Kyle stared at Kevin as *Never Felt This Way* ended and their song began. Kevin looked at Kyle and was already beginning to cry. He mouthed the words "how did you?" As they entered the sanctuary, escorted by their mothers, Kevin searched for the source of the music. Michael was singing *So Amazing*, accompanied by Gary. As their mothers were seated and the groomsmen returned to their places, Elder Nation spoke.

"It is such an honor to be with you this evening. ...

"...Kyle, Kevin has asked someone special to read your favorite scripture today." Kyle stared at Kevin. By the time he looked away, both of their fathers were standing in front of the church. Kevin had no idea Kaleb had asked his father to participate in the reading with him.

Kaleb spoke first. "When Kyle was eight, all of the students in his bible study class were given the assignment of studying scripture to recite at the end of the term. Even though they were given months to prepare, most still chose something simple like John 11:35 or John 3:16; but not my son. He spent hours a day, reading, and eventually writing so he could fully understand what he'd be saying when the day finally came. When I learned that he was going to recite all of 1 Corinthians 13, I asked why the whole chapter." Kaleb looked at Kyle and Kevin. "Kevin, he said it was 'because he needed people to understand that we have to do more than just know what love is. Love is all of those wonderful things listed in verses four through eight. What people don't seem to understand is that not only is love wonderful, but it is our duty, honor and responsibility to learn how to love. It is a gift that we are incomplete without and must learn how to receive'." As Kevin's father began to read the scripture, Elder Nation stepped back and Kyle reached for Kevin's hand. Tears streamed down their faces as Kyle softly spoke the words as Aaron read them out loud.

1 Corinthians 13 - The Excellence of Love
If I speak with the tongues of men and of angels, but do not have love, I have become a noisy gong or a clanging cymbal.

If I have the gift of prophecy, and know all mysteries and all knowledge; and if I have all faith, so as to remove mountains, but do not have love, I am nothing.

And if I give all my possessions to feed the poor, and if I surrender my body to be burned, but do not have love, it profits me nothing.

Love is patient, love is kind and is not jealous; love does not brag and is not arrogant,

does not act unbecomingly; it does not seek its own, is not provoked, does not take into account a wrong suffered,

does not rejoice in unrighteousness, but rejoices with the truth;

bears all things, believes all things, hopes all things, endures all things.

Love never fails; but if there are gifts of prophecy, they will be done away; if there are tongues, they will cease; if there is knowledge, it will be done away.

For we know in part and we prophesy in part;

but when the perfect comes, the partial will be done away.

When I was a child, I used to speak like a child, think like a child, reason like a child; when I became a man, I did away with childish things.

For now we see in a mirror dimly, but then face to face; now I know in part, but then I will know fully just as I also have been fully known.

But now faith, hope, love, abide these three; but the greatest of these is love."

The dads remained standing as Elder Nation spoke again. "I've never done this before. Kevin and Kyle, well mostly Kevin, I understand, have spent a lot of time preparing their vows; but I don't think they knew about this part of the ceremony?" They shook their heads. "I always say that by the time a couple comes to me to be united, the work is already done in their hearts; all that's left for me to do is offer their love up to God to be blessed. I believe their fathers have done that pretty sufficiently, and I dare say they are more than qualified to do so. Would you agree?" Still holding hands and crying, they each nodded slowly. "Is there anything else either of you needs to say?" They shook their heads softly.

"Do you Kyle take Kevin ..."

"I do."

"Do you Kevin take Kyle..."

"I do."

Then by the power vested in me by the Providence of Toronto, I pronounce you holy united!

Without waiting for instruction, the couple kissed and embraced for a long while, as the sanctuary erupted in applause. They spent a quiet moment together in Kyle's office, while the wedding party exited. Kyle finally stepped outside to see if their parents were around. Michael and Gary were standing guard outside the door. Michael knew instantly who Kyle was looking for and pointed to the men standing together at the end of the hall. Kaleb spotted Kyle before he could get to him and met him halfway.

"Thank you." Kyle stood very still in front of his father.

"What for?" Kaleb smiled at his son.

"For loving me."

"Thank you, son."

"What for?"

"Showing me how to love." Kaleb held out his harms and embraced his son. Kevin stood nearby, along with their groomsmen and his father and watched. That moment was the wedding gift he'd asked for. When he finally walked over to get Kyle, Kaleb rubbed his head, gave him a big hug and then shooed them away. They could only spend an hour or so at the reception, which was another surprise, before they had to leave for the airport.

The simple but elegant after party was moved, at the last minute, from a nearby hotel to Kyle's parent's home. Both sets of parents wanted to do more for the couple to show their love and support; so they shared the expense of moving the party. Kyle's dad turned out to be a surprisingly gracious, and fun, host.

Out of care for Michael, no alcohol was served, and there was way too much food. When it was time for the Best Men to make their toasts, Gary had Michael pried away from the buffet and asked everyone to raise their glasses of sparkling cider. Michael spoke first:

"Wow! I never thought I'd live to see this day!" The handful of people in the room who knew how true that statement was stared lovingly at Michael. Some fought back tears. "Kyle, I've known Kevin most of my life; and I have never seen him happier. Everyone always said he was special, that he had this glow around him. I must admit, I didn't see it. Sure I loved him; and yes, he is a lot of wonderful things. But to me, he was just my knuckle-headed little brother. But with you, I can see the glow - this smile – a real – deep down, so happy on the inside – smile that lights up everything around him. Seeing the two of you together, seeing my brother truly happy, and finally really living his life, makes me so hopeful... about life, about love, about my own life, and about God and what God can do, and wants to do for me. I know that you both know that you have the love and prayers of everyone in this room. I know that this union is blessed by God, has been from the beginning and will continue to be, as long as you continue to cherish each other. What I want to say is 'thank you'...for having the courage to love...and allowing all of us to see it and experience just a small part of it with you. It truly is a beautiful thing."

Gary stared at Michael for a long time and holding his glass before clearing his throat, he turned to Kevin and Kyle. "See, Kevin, I told you I needed to go first...Michael that toast was a beautiful thing..." Deep breath. "For those of you who don't know Michael or me personally, you might not know that we each have the privilege and honor of serving as 'best man' to both of Kevin and Kyle. Kevin and I have been friends for nearly ten years; Kyle and I for, well, let's just say, 'a lot longer than that.' We went to seminary together; and, not that he's lost anything, but, if you think the Rev. Dr. Tye is magnetic now, you should have seen him...many moons ago." Gary turned to Michael. "But like Kevin, Mike, he seemed to be living...just a little less than. I asked him once why that was. He told me he was waiting on God. So for years, I've watched him wait. And I was there the night they met. It was at revival at MCCNY, and as Kevin and I were getting ready to leave, Kyle bounced up to me. Yes, he actually bounced! It was the first time I'd ever seen it, but I've seen it quite often since then...Anyway, he bounced up to me and said, 'Do you remember what God told me about love - that I'd know him when I saw him?' Kevin, he turned to you and said, 'That's him.'" Laughter and amen's sprinkled the room. Kyle squeezed Kevin's hand as they smiled at their friend. Gary paused, trying to hold it together. "And I have to say, I have been more excited about God since then. Because I feel like I actually witnessed the manifestation of God's promise in watching Kyle wait, seeing you meet and fall in love; and now today, experiencing your...amazing-love-in-abundance – holy union. The patience it must have taken to get to this day! The love that has stayed around you! The people your love has brought together!" Gary winked at Gabrielle. "Funny, I always thought weddings were all about the people getting married. But watching your parents and your friends and families interact, I think this celebration will go on long after you've boarded your plane, enjoyed your honeymoon, come back and started your lives together. I thank God for the blessing that the two of you together are in all of our lives. May you be as happy for the rest of your lives as you were the day you met, on this day; and may this day, for the rest of us, always be a reminder of God's promises and enduring love." Gary lifted his glass as he and Michael said together, "to Kevin and Kyle!"

22

TEN DAYS IN PARIS

"I hate to fly." Kevin confessed.

"Did you think we would drive to France?"

"You just assumed I meant Paris, France. I was actually thinking Paris, Texas. I hear they've got the best barbeque in the world."

"You really are cute. You lie, but you're cute."

Kevin laughed. "How do you know I'm lying?"

"I can hear your thoughts, remember?" Kyle squeezed the hand he'd been holding since they boarded.

"Oh, yeah..." Kevin kissed Kyle before reclining his seat. "Do you mind if I sleep through the takeoff?"

"I'll wake you if your services are needed." Kevin erupted in his cheesiest fake laugh, snatched the pillow Kyle was holding for him and made himself comfortable on Kyle's shoulder. He awoke an hour into the fourteen-hour flight. "What did I miss?"

"The pilot mistook your snoring for engine trouble and has turned the plane around." The flight attendant chuckled as he approached with the beverage cart. "May I get you something to drink, Mr. Rivers-Tye?"

"Just water, please. Thank you. I do not snore."

"How do you know?"

"Good point."

"You sure are gullible, though. No, baby, you don't snore. You slept like an angel." Kyle kissed Kevin's temple.

"What are you reading?" Kevin glanced at the brochure Kyle was holding.

"I had this travel guide mailed to me and I'm planning our itinerary. I thought we'd start with a late afternoon stroll down the Rue St. Croix de la Bretonnerie. Apparently, it's the gay thing to do. And it's near our hotel. We can drop off our luggage and see some sights before dinner."

"You're kidding, right?" Kevin was mortified.

"Of course, I am." Kyle breathed into Kevin's ear and then began to hum.

"Mmm... What's that?"

He sang softly so that only Kevin could hear...

♫Love has truly been good to me
Not even one sad day or minute
have I had since you've come my way
I hope you know I'd gladly
go anywhere you take me.
It's so amazing to be loved.
I'd follow you to the moon in the sky above...♫

Kevin sighed and rested his head on Kyle's shoulder and went back to sleep.

It was mid afternoon when they finally arrived in Paris. Kyle hailed a taxi and gave the driver the address in what sounded to Kevin like perfect French. He asked something else when they stopped, and tipped the driver in Euros.

They checked in and entered the elevator on their way to the thirty-fifth floor. They were alone except for the bellman. They stood facing each other on opposite sides of the small glass box. Their eyes locked and it appeared that each was holding his breath. The bellman asked a question in French, and Kyle pretended not to understand. When the man turned his attention back to the elevator door, Kyle pressed his finger to his lips. Kevin winked back, as they entered their private world. The elevator ride seemed to take days. Once inside, Kyle asked the bellman a question, in French, tipped him and bolted the door behind him.

Kevin was behind him before he could turn around. They were still... silent. Kevin slid his hands down Kyle's arms to find his hands and positioned them on the door in front of him. Kevin gently tugged on Kyle's locks, exposing

207

his graceful neck to kiss him. He was sweet and salty. Kyle purred and turned slowly around.

Their kisses were slow and deep. Kyle pulled at Kevin's belt and pulled his shirt over his head. Kevin pulled Kyle further into the suite, looking for the shower. Once in the bathroom, Kyle turned on the shower and closed the door, allowing the steam to fill the room. Kevin reached into the small carryon bag, directed Kyle into the shower and left the bathroom. He quickly lit candles, threw the remaining luggage in the closet and returned with Kyle's favorite shower gel. He paused for a moment to admire his husband before joining him. Kyle waited, standing directly below one of six showerheads. His expression, loving. Every muscle in his body was illuminated by the light and water. Seeing Kyle for the first time, Kevin thought to himself, "He looks like a friggin' super hero; and what the hell am I supposed to do with THAT?"

Kyle stared at Kevin, interrupting his thoughts. "Get your ass in here."

Kevin obeyed Kyle's voice in his head and entered the shower facing Kyle under another stream of water. They stood toe-to-toe, completely still except for their breathing. With their hands at their sides, each examined the other...

...A virgin no more, Kyle released a moan that startled Kevin. It was low and guttural and didn't sound like Kyle at all. Kevin spoke the first words in hours. "Should I stop?"

Kyle's response was a low whisper. "Only if you want to *die* in Paris."

"Oh yeah?" Kevin continued.

"Yes." Kyle's reply was muffled but intense.

"Tell me when."

"Just... don't... stop."

"Baby..." Many moments later, Kyle's warning was barely a whisper, but Kevin understood. "Five." The countdown was silent, as each held his breath and braced for impact. Four, three two, one...Kevin finally collapsed next to Kyle on the bed. Kyle, breathless, patted his chest. "Come here."

"I can't move." Kyle reached for Kevin and found his wrist. Seemingly effortlessly, he tugged on his arm and rolled Kevin onto him. Kevin rested his head where he landed on Kyle's still pounding chest. "Damn, and I thought dancers were graceful." They laughed and fell asleep.

Kevin woke to the sound of running water. Kyle had drawn a bath and was ordering room service. A few moments later, the phone rang.

The concierge asked if they'd like the package that just arrived sent up with their brunch.

Kyle replied, "Oiu, merci"

Kevin slowly rose from the bed and stretched. "What's up?"

"Not sure. Apparently, we have a package from the US."

Kevin jumped up and down, clapping his hands. "I love a package from the US!"

"You are so cute." Kyle walked over and buried his face in the crook of his swanlike neck. "You know the elevator ride up here is going to take an hour."

"You were just horny, Sweetie. It was actually more like two minutes." As soon as Kevin got the words out, there was a knock on the door.

"Room service!"

Kyle opened the door, stepped out of the way as the cart was being wheeled in, and tipped the attendant.

Kevin returned from the bathroom just as the door closed. "What's in the box? What's in the box?"

"Are you sure you don't want to eat first?" Kyle already knew the answer; he just liked watching Kevin.

Kevin pouted and whined. "Yes, I'm sure. What's in the box? What's in the box?"

Kyle laughed out loud. "Oh my goodness! You're a giant girl!"

Kevin batted his long lashes, "Only for you, my love."

"Better be."

"Open the booooox!"

Kyle found a letter opener in the desk and opened the box. There was no name in the return address, just a New York address that he didn't recognize.

Kevin tore into the box like a five-year-old on Christmas

morning, revealing more condoms than either had ever seen before and dozens of plastic bottles and tubes. They were both puzzled until Kyle noticed the card on top of the pink packing paper. The note simply read, "Congratulations Kevin and Kyle! Enjoy your honeymoon! Love, Gary!"

Kevin laughed out loud. "That nut got us a year's supply of lube as a wedding gift! Oh! Wait... not just any lube - Astroglide! Halleluiah! Praise Jehovah!" Kevin pulled out a tiny white bottle labeled 'Booty Ease' and began to do what looked like a cross between a Holy Ghost dance and the cabbage patch.

Kyle laughed so hard he bounced from the bed to the floor; and before he could get up, Kevin was pulling at his pants. Kevin hadn't anticipated the possibility of being with a man more well endowed than he was himself. He'd been looking at his new husband for two days wondering, "what the hell does he think he's going to do with that?" And for two days he'd been keeping him distracted and, he hoped satisfied, enough that he hadn't noticed he'd been designated the bottom in their relationship.

Kyle read Kevin's thoughts. "Oh, I noticed." Kevin lifted his head and released his grip on Kyle.

"How are you doing that?"

"Doing what?"

"Hearing my thoughts? And don't tell me I said it out loud, because I know I didn't. I was raised not to speak with my mouth full!"

Kyle threw his head back and laughed. "I don't know. I'm sure I only do it with you. I figured it was because we are so connected. Does it bother you? I don't know how I would stop, if you wanted me to."

"No! I like it. It's weird, but it's cool at the same time; kinda sexy, actually. You really are a super hero!"

Kyle chuckled and gently guided Kevin back to his 'distraction drill'. "Mmmm" He let Kevin continue until just before he reached his point of no return, and motioned for him to stop. Kevin was defiant. Kyle bucked and broke Kevin's grip. "Now."

"What?"

Kyle got up and flung Kevin on the bed face down. Kevin giggled through his protest. "No… Stop… wait…"

"If that's how you want it…" Kyle flipped him back over so he could see his face.

Kevin bit his lip, clawed at Kyle's chest, smiled, moaned and screamed. His sounds were distinctly feminine, and finally he let out a sound that seemed to shake the walls. He pulled Kyle's hair and their screams were indistinguishable as each released a lifetime of desire.

Kyle moaned in his sleep, awakened by a distinct and loud slurping sound. He thought he must have been having his favorite dream. As he had for years, he opened his eyes – he was always awakened right here. But this time, he was not alone. To his absolute pleasure he woke to see the top of Kevin's bald head bobbing up and down. He reached out to touch Kevin, but found he could barely lift his arms. He hadn't been dreaming. Kevin had indeed discovered a bottle of 'Great Head' in Gary's box of goodies, and had set out to suck Kyle dry, completely and repeatedly. He'd been at it for an hour. Kyle looked over and spotted the tube on the bedside table and picked it up. His laugh startled Kevin, but not enough that he came up for air. Instead he just reached up and caught a fist full of Kyle's hair, wrapped the locks around his wrist and let his hand rest on Kyle's chest, pulling his hair and squeezing his nipple at the same time. When Kevin realized Kyle was fully awake, he slowly released his grip and crawled up the bed and straddled him.

"Good morning, sleepy-head." Kevin kissed Kyle's throat as he positioned himself.

Kyle moaned as his hands slid down Kevin's back. "Mmm. Hi? You stopped. Baby, we talked about the stopping... please."

Kevin guided Kyle's arms back behind his head. "Relax. I'm not done..." He was, in fact just getting started.

"Oh shit! Baby... what are you d...?" Kyle put his hands around Kevin's waist. Kevin screamed and dug his nails into Kyle's arms...

His work complete, Kevin finally collapsed on Kyle's chest, reaching up to rub his face against Kyle's beard. "Was that worth waiting for?" He asked when he could finally speak.

Kyle looked down at Kevin. "You're kidding, right? You're just making conversation...pillow talk?"

"I think I really want to know." Kevin's hand was still

213

on Kyle's chest. Kyle held it in his for a moment, then kissed his palm and took a deep breath.

"You, all of you, not just this part, are more than I've ever dreamed of. I don't think I have the words to tell you how much I love you. Was it worth waiting for? If by "it" you mean these mind blowing, out of this world, 'I pray we make it out of this room alive', wicked things you've been doing and making me do to you..."

"Hey!" Kevin sat up. Kyle chuckled and pulled him back down.

"...Yes, but only because I know that when we leave here, it will be to spend every day of the rest of our lives, and beyond together. I want you." Kyle slid Kevin's hand down to his recovered penis. "I have always wanted you, from the moment we met, in a million different ways; and in a way I have never wanted anyone else...ever. I never imagined I would need to... hear your voice... kiss your lips... see your smile...I dreamed of what love would feel like; but I didn't know. I didn't know I could care so much about another person's day! But I do. I never dreamed I would be a father; but you share your son with me! You have given me so many more wonderful reasons to be thankful... I was lonely. I had no idea how lonely I was, or how happy I could be. You are the love God promised me. Do I think the thirty years I waited for you was worth it? I'd wait another thirty years just to hear you laugh... or for this... you in my arms. I'd wait a lifetime, if I knew it would end with one night with you. I have songs to sing and sermons to preach. I've got a testimony about God's love that I didn't have before I met you...and waited."

Kevin lifted his head and kissed a tear running down Kyle's cheek. "See, you're glad I asked, aren't you?"

Kyle chuckled. "Yeah. I am. Wow."

It was Kevin who finally noticed the view of the Eiffel Tower outside their window. They'd been locked away in that suite for three days and seen nothing but each other. Kevin twirled around the corner suite pulling the heavy drapes open to reveal their panoramic view of Paris.

"Baby, we have to get down there!"

Kyle lay in bed with a smile on his face watching Kevin.

"Okay, but first I need you to cut my hair."

"I beg your pardon?"

"It's time to let it go."

"But I love your dreads. Besides, we just got married; they're mine now!"

"I know, baby; that's part of it. I feel like a new man. My hair is heavy. I feel light, new; but that's not what I see when I look in the mirror. It's time."

"Fine! But why do I have to do it?"

"Because I trust you, and I don't want to share this experience with anyone else."

Kevin took a deep breath. "Okay. Let's do it." He slowly walked to where Kyle was sitting on the bed and reached into the thick locks and wrapped them around his wrists and hands. He sighed deeply and closed his eyes.

"It's okay, Baby. I am not my hair. Please do this for me." Kevin kissed Kyle's full lips and smiled, pulling him up from the bed and leading him to a chair he'd pulled from the writing desk. He hummed while he walked away to find his clippers and shaving kit. Kyle closed his eyes and began to pray. As each rope was snipped a tear rolled down his cheek. Kevin watched Kyle's reflection in the mirror and noticed the tears. When he realized they were tears of joy, he laughed and cried along with him. Neither man said a word. When the last lock was gone, Kyle opened his eyes and ran his hands over what was left of his hair.

"Wow." Kevin starred at Kyle and tugged at his short

nappy hair.

Kyle closed his eyes, reveling in Kevin's touch. "More."

"Yes, your majesty." Kyle chucked. Kevin grabbed the clippers and a comb and lovingly transformed the remains of Kyle's regal mane into a low, dark Caesar cut. He shaved and trimmed the full beard that had appeared since they'd been in France; and when he was finished, he laughed out loud. "Warrior – Prince."

Kyle laughed nervously. "Does that mean you like it?"

"I would never have thought it possible; but I like it more. Damn, you fine!"

Kyle grabbed Kevin and kissed him. "Thank you."

"You're welcome. Thank you for trusting me."

For the next seven days, they enjoyed the history, culture and food of Paris. Kyle took pictures of everything. Later, he would paint. Kevin shopped like a drunken heiress, more for Kyle and Ethan and their friends and family at home than for himself. They had thoroughly enjoyed their honeymoon, but by the tenth day, they were ready to get home and begin their lives together.

23

MA MAISON EST VOTRE MAISON

To their amusement, they had the same male flight attendant they'd had on the last leg of the flight to France. He did a double-take when he saw Kyle. "Did you gentlemen enjoy Paris?"

Kevin opened his eyes and examined the chiseled, stylish-even in a poly knit-man smiling at his husband, and not so subtly reached for Kyle's hand. "Yes, we did, thank you." He thought out loud, "I don't want to have to beat an air-ho down today." He ordered coffee and resolved to stay awake for as long as he could.

Kyle shook his head and chuckled. "You're silly."

"Whatever." He leaned toward Kyle and kissed his cheek. As he shifted in his seat he said, "Gary didn't mention how much my bottom – shoot, my whole body – was gonna hurt."

Kyle giggled to himself, "Did he just say 'bottom'?" Then, "perhaps that's not such a problem for Gary." The only thing he actually did say out loud was, "I'm sorry."

"Oh, trust me, it was worth it." Kevin reached over and ran his nails down the inside of Kyle's forearm. Kyle closed his eyes, breathed deeply and held Kevin's hand tightly.

Once they were in the car and on their way home, Kyle made a phone call. Kevin had been staring out the window enjoying the scenic views of his new home and turned to him, "What's up?'"

"Just checking on the house." Kyle tried to conceal a grin.

When they arrived home, Kyle paused in front of the door and looked at Kevin, kissing him softly with his hand on the door. As he pushed it open, he said, "Welcome home." Kyle led Kevin into their home by the hand. When they saw what had been done, Kyle was as thrilled as Kevin, who stood standing in the middle of the living room with his mouth open. The contents of Kevin's apartment had been brought to Toronto and lovingly unpacked and put away. Awards, photographs, and pieces from his art collection were thoughtfully placed on once bare walls and empty surfaces, dispersed among Kyle's things. He couldn't find one item he'd have placed differently.

"Who? When?"

"Our moms and Michael, actually. When I called to say we'd be staying a few extra days, they volunteered to move your things in. I think they did an amazing job, don't you?"

"I think it's almost the best wedding gift ever!"

"I'm so glad you're pleased." Kyle squeezed Kevin, kissed him, and then sent him to check out the basement.

Kevin met Kyle on the main level, oblivious to the fact that he'd been sent away as a distraction, and reported that even their wedding gifts were neatly stacked in the den downstairs. Then he kissed Kyle sweetly. "Thank you."

Kyle sighed. "You're welcome. Tell me what I did, so I can do it again and again, please."

"Well, all of this, really; but the kiss was for downstairs. Did you instruct them to turn that empty space into a studio for me, and make the media room into a game room? EJ is going to flip."

"I'm so glad you like it. But you don't need to thank me. This is our home. I just wanted to surprise you."

"You do surprise me. Actually, you take my breath away...repeatedly." They stood making out in the living room near the stairs.

"Oh!" Kyle remembered what he was doing before Kevin came back upstairs. "There is one more thing." He grabbed Kevin's hand and led him upstairs. Kevin assumed Kyle was leading him to the master bedroom, so when Kyle turned right at the top of the stairs instead of left, he was curious. Kyle opened the double doors to what Kevin thought had been an empty bonus room. Kevin gasped when he saw the luxurious master suite, complete with fireplace, a palace compared to the sparse mission-style bedroom Kyle slept in before the wedding. He was speechless, until he found the master bath with its enormous claw-foot tub, drawn bath and lit candles. "How do you manage to think of everything?"

"I don't. I actually forgot something." Kyle pulled Kevin close and led him in a dance in the center of the room, humming their song against Kevin's cheek. Kevin whispered back:

♫Bye-bye sadness. Hello mellow.

What a wonderful day! It's so amazing to be loved.

I'd follow you to the moon in the sky above. ♫

Then Kevin started to chuckle, stopped dancing and pointed at Kyle. "Liar!"

"I beg your pardon?" Kyle tilted his head quizzically.

"You said you don't dance!"

Kyle chuckled. "No, baby, I said I don't dance...well..."And to prove it, he attempted to dip Kevin and dropped him onto the man-sized chaise that had once been Kevin's only piece of living room furniture.

24

BACK TO LIFE, BACK TO REALITY

Ethan ran toward Kevin and Kyle and gave them each a big hug. "Pop, you cut your dreads!"

"It was time. Do you like it?"

"Yeah. Before you looked like Jesus. Now you look like a movie star." Kevin chuckled and Kyle blushed. Ethan ran back down the hall to wait for Gabrielle who was talking to someone at the elevator.

"Why does everyone keep saying that?" Kyle frowned.

"Oh, like you didn't know you looked like Jesus? I kept trying to tell you."

"I seriously thought you were just taking the Lord's name in vain. You know you mumble."

"Whatever." Kyle pouted and Kevin wrapped his arms around his waist and kissed him tugging on the lip he had stuck out.

"Are y'all sure you don't need a wife?" Gabby stood and watched the newlyweds, biting the tip of her index finger. "Kevin, you look...rested." She winked and gave him a long hug.

"Rev. Dr. Tye, you look...hotttt." She hugged Kyle.

"That's 'Rev. Dr. *Rivers*-Tye', thank you very much." Kevin made a clawing gesture at Gabby then flicked his wrist to wave his wedding ring at her. She released Kyle and pretended to straighten her clothes.

"Oh shut up. I was there, remember? Kyle, tell me this fool didn't rip your hair out. I know you were really, really excited about the honeymoon and all, Kevin, but damn." Gabby rolled her eyes at Kevin.

"Oh my." Kyle pretended to fan himself, still blushing.

"I love it. The locks were beautiful; but now you look...

ready for the world stage. I'd been trying to figure out how to get you to cut them. There's an hour-long conversation I don't have to bill you for." Gabrielle had taken on Kyle and Kevin as PR clients and had been working with them to get Kyle's latest music played. He refused to deny he was gay, and Black gospel stations weren't willing to risk losing advertising revenues by making waves. Still, she believed in both their music and ministry and was determined that Kyle could break through without compromising his principles.

"Tom is ready for you all." The receptionist pointed to the conference room just behind her and the four of them filed in.

The attorney greeted them all warmly. "Congratulations again, gentlemen. The ceremony was beautiful. How was Paris?"

Gabby mumbled, "A blur."

Kevin giggled; Kyle blushed but managed to answer with a straight face. "It was…spectacular." Kevin knew he wasn't talking about France.

"Well, then, let's make this family official, shall we? I first need to confirm for the record why we're here. Gabby, Kevin, have you agreed that it is your desire to enter into a third-parent adoption of your son, Ethan Jerome Rivers, sharing all parental rights and responsibilities with Kyle Rivers-Tye?"

"We have." Both nodded.

"Ethan, do you understand and agree to this?"

"Yes, sir."

"Can you tell me who you're going to live with?"

"I'm gonna live with my dads in Canada, while I go to school; and then I'll spend summers and holidays with my mom." Gabby squeezed her son's hand.

"Well, in that case, all that's left is the signing."

The new family celebrated with lunch at Ethan's favorite restaurant, a sushi bar and Japanese steakhouse. The adults were grateful for EJ's mature palette. After they ordered,

Gabrielle began eyeing the newlyweds again, staring back and forth between them.

"Okay, really, Gabby. Now, you're just creepin' me out." Kevin squinted at her.

"What?" She asked innocently.

"Why do you keep looking at us like that?"

"How am I looking at you?"

"Like you expect us to just start making out right here in the restaurant..." Kevin whispered so that only Gabby and Kyle could hear while Ethan watched lunch being prepared.

"Oh get over yourself; I have. I'm wondering why neither of you has said anything about my wedding gift."

Kevin looked at Kyle. They had finally opened all the gifts just the night before. Neither could recall one from Gabby, but there were a couple that they couldn't associate with anyone.

"Oh! Was it the three-pot crock-pot? I was getting ready to order that one just before the wedding! Thank you! I can't wait to use it." Kyle was sincerely excited about his new small appliances.

"I didn't give you a crock-pot, man; although I'd love to see what you do with it. I've never cooked anything other than rice in mine. My package was flatter..."

The men stared at each other again. Gabby started grinning. "Okay, I can't take it anymore!" She reached into her briefcase and pulled out a thin package wrapped in traditional wedding paper and handed it to Kyle. "Congratulations!"

Kyle assumed it was something relating to the adoption of EJ and tried not to get teary. Whatever it was, it was in a heavy frame. Kyle was taking too long so finally, Kevin ripped the last of the paper away. It was not their certificate of adoption. They quickly skimmed the document. Kyle saw it first and laughed out loud. "Wow!" Kevin applauded wildly. Kyle was being nominated for an American Music

Award for 'Contemporary Inspirational – Favorite Artist'. "How is that possible? Gospel stations haven't been playing my stuff."

"Not yet, but Contemporary Christian stations have! How do you not know that?"

Kevin answered for him. "Oh, he doesn't listen to the radio…" They all chuckled.

"Thank you, Gabby. I'm sure I couldn't have done this without you."

"You could have, but that's my job. You just continue to make the music. It is going to cross-over, Kyle. This nomination alone is going to help with that. The show is in two months, and for the first time ever, the vote is open to the public. America needs to see the man behind the music. Can I start booking some spots?"

"How many are we talking about?" Kyle looked nervous. Of course, performing was no big deal, and neither was interviewing. He just wasn't prepared for the spotlight. He was not looking forward to that.

"About half a dozen: 'Ronnie Reynolds', the major morning shows and late nights. It's standard for the nominees to perform live in the weeks before the ceremony."

Kyle looked at Kevin. "You can do this, Baby. It's part of the process. This is how you're going to reach the people."

Kyle closed his eyes and breathed deeply. "Let's do it."

Gabby, Kevin and Ethan started clapping wildly.

"Yay! You have 'Wake Up America!' and 'Now' on Monday?" Gabby looked sheepishly at Kyle.

"Gabrielle!" Kevin glared at her.

"What? He said 'yes'."

"But you didn't know he would." Kevin thought back to what Gabby said when he came out about needing someone to manage and manipulate. At the time he didn't know what she was talking about.

"Honey, it's fine. We haven't exactly been accessible the

last few weeks. In the future I'll need more notice though, Gabby. I'm preaching here Sunday. We'll just stay in New York?" Kyle looked at Kevin, referring to his Manhattan apartment. Kevin realized he hadn't seen it. The few nights they'd spent together were spent in Toronto. When they were both in New York, they thought it was safer for Kevin to go to his and Michael's apartment than to try and share a bed in Kyle's.

"Sure. I need to get back to work, anyway." Kevin had been working on their play from home, fine-tuning the music with Kyle and the choreography alone, while Kyle was out. Now that it was written and scored, it was time to start casting. This would be Kevin's directorial debut.

"Okay, then it's all set. I'll meet you at five a.m. at ABC."

"Can I come?" Ethan interjected. He wasn't moving to Canada until after Christmas break, but he was excited about hanging out with both of his dads. He loved to hear Kyle sing and preach. He loved both of his new churches. They were a lot more fun than the one his granddad used to preach in.

"This is a pretty big deal. I could use the support." Kyle looked at Gabby and winked at EJ.

"Sure, we'll stay until Monday night, but then you need to get back to school."

"Yes, ma'am."

25

THESE GIFTS AREN'T MINE...

Kyle woke at three a.m. on the morning of his first live television interview, without the help of his alarm clock, and jumped in the shower. He tried to move quietly so not to wake Kevin, but it was his absence from their bed that woke him. Kevin found Kyle in the bathroom and watched as he showered and sang softly with his back to the glass door.

"Join me?" Kyle sensed Kevin's presence and called out to him without turning around. Kevin hesitated for a moment. He understood Kyle's morning routine. This wasn't entirely different than any Sunday morning. Sure, he was getting ready to be interviewed on national television and performing for a live studio audience, but to Kyle, it was just another opportunity to minister to people. It wasn't about him. Kevin knew Kyle was preparing for service, and wanted to be careful not to disturb that. He entered the shower, grabbed a sponge and soaped and scrubbed Kyle's back. Kyle turned to rinse and greeted him warmly with a kiss. As he turned around so Kyle could return the favor, Kevin congratulated himself that he read properly, understood and anticipated his husband's needs. Kyle just wanted him close.

Kyle continued to hum and sing, but spoke very little as they got dressed and left for the studio. Once inside the car Gabby sent for them, he held Kevin's hand and pulled him closer so Kevin could rest his head on his chest, but still didn't speak.

Gabby met them at the studio. Kyle greeted her briefly and excused himself to the men's room. "Good morning. Where's Ethan?" Kevin asked.

"He's in one of the greenrooms lying down. Kyle doesn't go on for another couple of hours. I promised him we'd come and get him before anything fun happened. "How is he?" Gabby asked referring to Kyle. Gabby and Kyle had become fast friends. Each instantly recognized what it was Kevin loved about the other, and Gabby could see that Kevin was an entirely different person and father to EJ with Kyle than he was with her. She honestly liked him better 'this way'. Whatever selfishness she saw in him had faded away. She could appreciate that his marriage to her had been out of obligation and he'd gotten very little out of it himself. It was clear that Kyle truly loved and respected him, and that made it easy to see them together. It wasn't as strange as people insisted it should be that they were all so close. Kevin and Gabby had been together because Ethan was supposed to be in the world; beyond that, they were only meant to be friends.

"He's good...ready. Gabby, this can't become a circus." Kevin was still annoyed at Gabby for scheduling the shows without consulting Kyle first.

"I know, KJ. I get it, he's a minister first and a performer second. He won't get lost. I promise.

"Okay. I do trust you. I know you're good at what you do, but he's ..."

Gabby squeezed his hand. "I get it, Kevin."

Kyle returned from the men's room with a spring in his step and his twinkle back, smelling minty fresh. "I'm ready."

Gabby whisked Kyle away, chattering as they walked, signaling to Kevin to keep up. Kevin vowed he was going to keep his mouth shut and just stay close. He had done all of this himself; the morning shows, backstage interviews, the cameras. It was just another sign that you'd truly arrived to any stage performer; but to someone who never envisioned themselves as a performer, like Kyle, it was stressful. Kevin prayed that Kyle's nerves wouldn't get in the way and that only God's light would shine through.

Kevin woke EJ just before seven as a production assistant came to take Kyle to makeup. Kevin winked at Kyle who cringed. Kevin wasn't worried. Kyle had flawless skin, the color of Hershey's dark chocolate. The most they would do is ensure he didn't look shiny. It only sounded to Kyle like something unnatural was about to happen to him. Kyle sat in the chair and tried to ignore the people fussing over him as he prayed. "… These gifts aren't mine, they're yours to use as only God you would…Thank you, Lord for this open door and for this moment…"

When Kyle arrived earlier that morning and met the show's hosts for the first time, there was still some confusion as to who would be leading the interview, Nicole Meyers, the show's senior anchor or, Rico Williams, the young newcomer from a sister station in Canada. Kyle's appearance had been booked in the same manner as any other 'filler' piece, unassigned and researched at the last minute. But when they read his bio, everyone wanted it. Kyle was well-educated, talented, published, gorgeous, and 'controversial'. He was about to make every Internet search engines top-ten list. Who wouldn't want to be seen firing questions at him when thousands watched the interview again on *Youtube*? Rico won by being the only person on the team who'd actually known who Kyle was before the interview.

"Our next guest is nominated for an American Music Award for 'Favorite Contemporary Inspirational Artist', and is my personal pick for Best New Artist. He's not new to Canadians, at all; and you'll find his latest single on any of the contemporary Christian stations here in the US. Music critics say he is poised to cross-over into pop and gospel airplay any minute. Please welcome, Kyle Rivers Tye!

The camera cut to Kyle who was already sitting at the piano in the studio. As he began to play the intro to Kevin's favorite song, Kevin closed his eyes. The sound of Kyle's voice filled the studio and, through the speakers installed for listeners outside, flooded the street just outside the building.

♫...So, guide me Lord please show me, I'm ready to begin
This life is but a vessel. Please pour your blessings in
These gifts aren't mine, they're yours to use,
as only God, You would
Thank God you know
So glad you made me
My God, you love
Like nobody ever could ♫

The studio was still as Kyle sung his final perfect falsetto note, and remained still until he stood and the studio audience erupted in cheers and applause. As he walked over to the anchor desk, Kyle could see Kevin, Gabby and EJ. Gabby applauded wildly, EJ jumped up and down and Kevin stood smiling with his hands clasped and stared at his husband. The song was beautiful, and it was important, but it had always been the least of their concerns.

"Wow, Kyle that was beautiful. It's so nice to have you here. This single is the first release from your second CD, is that right?"

"It is. I released my debut, self-titled album about four years ago."

"And it's still available in stores..." Nicole Meyers interjected and Kyle nodded and chuckled. Rico continued.

"But I understand CD sales are of little concern to you?"

"Yes and no. I pay attention to them, because the sales are an indication that my music is being listened to. Then again, I try not to sweat them, because what's most important is that the music is actually being listened to – the message is being heard." Kyle smiled. He was very comfortable.

"It's more about the ministry?" Rico understood.

"It really is." Kyle nodded.

"Because you are also pastor of a thriving church?"

"Two actually, one here, and another in Canada. The

Toronto church is newer."

The segment was already running long, but the producers signaled to keep it going. The camera, the audience and the crew all loved Kyle. They could record the 'cute kid who juggled' to air later in the week.

"My goodness you're busy... The two churches, the music, six books and I understand you're with us today just back from your honeymoon!" Nicole stepped in.

Kyle grinned while the co-hosts Kerry, and Lara swooned from their positions at the semicircular desk. "Yes I am. That's my sleepy family right over there." The camera cut to Kevin, EJ and Gabby. EJ waved and Kyle waved back.

"What a beautiful family! Who do we have here?" Kerry asked for clarity.

"We have my son, Ethan, my husband, Kevin; and that gorgeous woman with them is my publicist, Gabrielle." The professional team didn't miss a beat. Kyle was not the first gay man they'd interviewed. But Rico knew what was going on, and brought the interview back to the real reason Kyle was there.

"Do you think your being openly gay is keeping your music from being accepted?"

"No, I think the gospel music industry's inability to accept that I'm gay and Christian, and their influence over the broadcasting industry, or vice versa, is what's keeping my music off of gospel airways." Kyle shifted in his seat. It felt really good to say that out loud.

"But you are on contemporary Christian stations?"

"I am; and I'm grateful, don't get me wrong. It's just not enough for me." Kyle smiled.

"Why is that?"

"Because the gospel industry, in particular, is at odds with the LGBT community. Some of the music is, quite frankly, abusive and offensive to the spirit of gay, lesbian and transgender people, myself included, who believe God loves

229

us as much as any straight person. And then there's the hypocrisy…"

"What hypocrisy is that?"

"The fact that gifted musicians, singers and choir directors who want to serve God are encouraged to work in the industry but discouraged from being honest about who we are and who we love."

"And where do you think that's coming from?"

"Wow. That's a really tough question, Rico, and one that I'd rather not answer. I don't want to point fingers. I can't say for sure what the true source of the problem is, but I know the solution lies in what's being taught in churches."

"Is it a simple solution?"

"It is. God's love is inclusive. Whatever we sing about God should speak of God's goodness, not what one person or group defines as wrong."

"Well, it sounds simple enough to me. I wish we had more time. Maybe you can come back after you win! Thank you so much for taking time to come and talk with us this morning. Good luck with your music. And may I add on a personal note, God bless your ministry. Kyle Rivers-Tye everyone…"

The show went to commercial and a production assistant came over to remove Kyle's microphone. "Great piece, Mr. Tye".

"Thank you."

"You know you just got your name put on the top of that 'secret' Black conservative church watch list, don't you?" Rico smiled at Kyle.

"I do. Unfortunately, sometimes you have to start a fight to win a war."

"Amen, brother. Thank you, Kyle."

"Thank you, Rico." They hugged and Kyle walked off the set toward his silently cheering family.

Kevin got to him first, greeting him with the 'Michelle to Barack double fist bump' followed by the kiss he'd been saving all morning.

Gabby was practically gushing. "Oh wow! Kyle, that was awesome. The camera loved you. The audience loved you. You sound phenomenal! ...One down, seven to go..." Gabby whispered, hoping Kyle and especially Kevin didn't notice. Kevin did.

"Gabrielle! Kyle, move, Honey! I'm gonna cut her!"

"Kyle, I'm sorry! I just got the calls late yesterday. Your story is interesting!" Gabby was speed-walking circles around Kyle and EJ, as Kevin pretended to chase her.

"Just send me the dates, please; and thank you, Gabby, really. You're doing exactly what we asked you to do." Kyle looked at Kevin and then at Gabby again. "But no more after these eight?"

"No more. I promise. Okay, we just need to walk across the lot to the *"Now!"* set and you'll be free for two weeks."

They hitched a ride on a golf cart to the next set. That show went as well as the first one. Kyle was a natural. The questions were similar. Again, Kyle resisted the prompting to point a finger directly at the Black church. He didn't even need to attack the gospel music industry. His music spoke for him. It was rich, soulful, spiritual and relevant. The message, although universal, was also in direct contrast to what was being said on and off recordings by many artists. What saddened Kyle most was that the 'attacks' came from younger performers, men and women who know personally who they are harming. Kyle didn't start this war; but the more he prayed, and the more he spoke out loud about his music and what was happening, the more he realized he was where he was supposed to be. As he and his family prepared to leave the lot, he got further confirmation of that.

A guard approached them as they were waiting for their cars. "Rev. Tye, will you come with me please? The producers have asked me to escort you back in." Kevin, Gabby and Kyle just looked at each other.

"Sure." Kyle turned away from the car and followed the guard back to the offices adjacent to the WUA set. They were met by the show's executive producer, Linda Willis, Rico Williams and a production assistant. Linda introduced herself. "Kyle, thank you for coming back in. I'm sorry for the hold-up, I know you guys must be exhausted. It was a great interview, by the way. We've gotten more response from your segment than we have on anything since the presidential elections." Gabby clapped silently. Linda continued. "That's the good news; but I'm afraid the news isn't all good." Kyle looked around the room to see where Ethan was. The production assistant had taken him to a corner of the room and was entertaining him with a weather program that looked like a video game.

"What is it?" Kevin spoke as soon as he realized EJ was being intentionally distracted.

"You're getting death threats."

"Wow. Already?" Gabby only sounded surprised that it was happening so quickly, not concerned that it was happening at all.

Linda saw Kevin's concern and tried to explain. "It's not unusual at all, and they're probably nothing to be concerned about, but it would be irresponsible of us not to tell you. We've received an overwhelming response to your interview, and the vast majority of it has been favorable, or predictable: "that faggots going to hell" stuff like that. But when people start talking about wanting to harm you, your family or churches, we have to take it seriously, and that's what's happened." Linda handed Kyle three pieces of paper clipped together and he flipped through them with Kevin and Gabby reading over his shoulders.

Gabby was the first to speak. "Kyle, I'm so sorry. I knew you would ruffle some feathers, but I had no idea people took this stuff so seriously."

Kevin was furious. "Gabrielle, 'this stuff' as you put it, is

232

his life, his music, his ministry, who he loves, the need to rescue people from this…We're not talking about album sales. Is that what you thought this was about?"

"Kevin, stop. Baby, I know you're upset, but this isn't Gabby's fault. I asked her to help us. I knew the risk." Kevin's anger was triggered by Gabby's choice of words. Reducing the situation to 'this stuff' was an example of the smallness he sometimes saw in her. But it was his idea to have her work with Kyle. He'd kick himself, and pinch her, later. He could clearly see that Kyle needed him to reel it in.

Gabby bounced back quickly. "Actually, Kyle I am somewhat prepared. I can have personal security here in an hour."

"Good. Have them meet you here and take you and Ethan to your hotel and then to the airport, please." Kyle glanced over to see that EJ was still oblivious to what was happening.

"But, we have…" Gabby tried to remain professional. She wasn't afraid of anything, and she wanted to stay and go over the schedule.

"No, Kyle's right, Gabby. We need you and our son out of New York. Now, please."

"Do you want me to cancel the other spots?" Kevin and Gabby stared at Kyle.

"Absolutely not."

"Good." They said in unison. Gabby pulled her phone from her purse and stepped away with Linda to make calls.

Kevin and Kyle turned their attention to their son. Kyle squatted down so he was almost eye-level with Ethan. "Did you have a good time, Peanut?"

"I did! That thing is so cool! You gotta see it." EJ tugged on Kyle, trying to pull him toward the weather show control panel and gave up when he didn't budge. "Your part was good too. I want to come to all of them!"

"We discussed that already though, didn't we, Son? You've got to go home with your mom and go back to school."

Gabby interrupted. "But I think we can arrange it so that you can come back for the AMA's.

"That would be AWESOME!" Kyle nodded and stood up, satisfied that EJ was happy.

"Are they here?" Kevin asked of the security detail.

"Yes."

"Okay. Don't let him see them, okay?" Kevin spoke quietly to Gabby.

"I've got this, Kevin." Gabby said sharply. She was still stinging from Kevin's chastising.

"I know. I'm sorry. You're an awesome mother and an even better publicist." Kevin gave Gabby a hug.

"Thank you." She hugged him back. "Kyle, call me as soon as you get back to Toronto? I should have the rest of the numbers from the morning shows in about an hour or so."

"Will do. Thank you, again, Gabrielle...for everything.

Gabby winked at him and left the studio with Ethan.

Kyle and Kevin left the studio again. Their original car and driver was still waiting for them. The driver had already been given instructions to drive them to Toronto. Kevin closed the partition and pulled off his sport coat while Kyle loosened his tie. "Four hours in the back of a limo with all this!" Kevin kissed Kyle who just chuckled.

"Baby, you aren't remotely concerned that some nuts just threatened to kill me?"

"Uh, no...You're doing the Lord's work. Are you concerned?" Kevin stopped rubbing Kyle long enough for him to answer.

"Actually, no, not at all. I mean, we did just get married; so of course, I'd rather not die. And I don't want to scare Ethan, but this is what I asked for. I believe I'm doing what God wants me to do."

"Have I mentioned today how proud I am of you?" Kevin reclined and pulled Kyle toward him so that Kyle's back rested on his chest.

"Not in so many words, but I can feel it, so 'yes'. Mmm. That's nice." Kyle closed his eyes as Kevin massaged his arms, chest and shoulders. Kyle fell asleep before they made it out of the city.

They arrived home to peace and quiet, but overflowing voicemail and email. Kyle called Gabby as soon as they settled in.

"How's Ethan?"

"Oblivious, Kyle, really." Kyle reserved any hint of concern for Gabby, rather than upset Kevin any further. "We're all fine. Don't get distracted. It's working."

"What do you mean?"

"I forwarded you a copy of a message I received from a Joy Records representative who basically stated that 'the reason you haven't made it to gospel radio is because your music isn't 'gospel enough'."

Kyle chuckled and did a quick two-step. He immediately recognized that as the challenge it was. Kevin was doing his Holy Ghost / cabbage patch in the background. "Oh no he di'int."

"Yes, he did. The next show is in two weeks. How many people should I tell Ronnie's people to prepare for?"

"Just thirty... oh and the band... so, forty..."

"And the praise dancers..." Kevin shouted.

"Hammer don't hurt 'em!" Gabby laughed out loud.

"Is it your professional advice that I should ignore this blatant challenge?"

"Uh, no. As your publicist, I'm sayin' 'bring it!' Oh, I just wish Manolo made sneakers. It's just plain unladylike, not to mention unprofessional, to be kicking off my stilettos to shout anywhere other than in church. They have no idea what they just did!"

"Okay, I need to make some calls. Is there anything else?" Kyle wanted to call Michael. He'd been trying him out as the choir director for the New York church, and this would be his national debut.

"Nope. Except from those initial postings, all of the response has been positive. I'll call you if anything changes."

"K. Thanks, G." Kyle pressed the button to release the call and turned to Kevin. He was dancing and humming the refrain to the full gospel version of the song Kyle performed earlier.

"That's beautiful, Baby; but who do you think you can get to do that, *like that* in two weeks?"

Kevin bowed and then held his hands together.

"Oh, you wanna do it?" Kyle wasn't sure why Kevin had suddenly gone into mime mode, but he sure was cute. "Please and thank you." Kyle tugged on Kevin's arm the same way he had their first night together, and Kevin wrapped himself around Kyle, just as he did that first night. Kyle moaned and looked quickly around the kitchen for a safe spot to lay Kevin down. When he didn't find one, he pinned him to the wall in the hallway between the kitchen and dining room.

"Is this what you wanted me to do?" Kyle asked as Kevin wrapped his legs around Kyle's waist and kissed him as Kyle unzipped his own pants with his free hand.

Kevin released a high-pitched moan and dug his nails into Kyle's shoulders. He released his legs and slid slowly down the wall landing on his knees in front of Kyle. They took turns pleasing each other, over and over until Kevin finally spoke. "Yes."

"What's that, Baby?" Kyle asked, breathing heavy.

"Yes, that is what I wanted that night." Kevin let his hand rest on Kyle's thigh.

Kyle chuckled. "Oh, well you could have had that.

"Liar!"

26

THE RONNIE REYNOLDS SHOW

The Ronnie Reynolds Show was the hottest thing to hit late night since, *Saturday Night Live*. In his first year on the air, Ronnie had hosted more controversial, inspiring and groundbreaking guests than any of the big three late-night shows combined. The competition attributed the show's success to 'timing', but fans and producers knew it was all about their star. Ronnie was funny, intelligent, down-to-earth and honest. He didn't care if you liked him or whether his guests' views aligned with yours. It was about more than entertainment. *TRRS* was a show with a mission.

Ronnie didn't need to explain that mission to Kyle, he was just happy to share the stage. He found him backstage moments before the show went live. "How's the saying go? 'If people are trying to kill you, you know you're doing something right.'" Ronnie shook Kyle's hand. "It is such an honor to meet you, Rev. Rivers-Tye. I'm a big, big fan. And as excited as I am to have you here, you know you don't have to do this, right? You can leave this studio and go back to your quiet life in Canada."

"Actually, Ronnie, I do have to do this. I have to do this so that my son will never be afraid to live his whole life, whoever he is, wherever he chooses to live it. Half of my life is right here in New York. Kevin's work is here. We have a home here. I'm not just gay in Canada. I'm gay wherever I go. My life and my family are in North Carolina, Atlanta, Jamaica, New York and Toronto. And, God help me, through the music, my ministry will be worldwide."

"Well, in that case, thank you." Ronnie nodded knowingly at Kyle.

Kyle shook his head at the man standing in front of him.

"You're welcome? What have I done?"

"Thank you for standing. Thank you for your life and your work, for the books, the music and now this. People like you make my life possible."

"Oh, you're gay." Kyle felt silly not picking up on that.

"No…I was born a woman, Kyle."

"Wow." Kyle tried not to stare. "I've met lots of trans men and women before, but I had no clue. Congratulations."

Ronnie blushed. "So you can see why I'm so excited about your work? I want to help however I can. Is there anything I can do?"

"Well, are you out?"

"No. I meant professionally. I'm new, but I have contacts, both here in the US and in Canada."

"That's great, Ronnie, but the single biggest thing you can do to help the LGBT community is to come out. It's that simple. People need to know people like you. I know it sounds like an impossible thing to ask. I imagine you've dedicated a large part of your life to making sure people only see you as a man, right? Did you know any transgender men when you realized who you are?" Ronnie shook his head. "If your story could help one child feel less alone and scared, wouldn't you want to help them? Can you imagine how different your life might have been had you seen someone like yourself on television? Would that have made it easier for you, or for your family and friends to understand you?"

"Of course, but…"

"You don't have to do it now, Ronnie, or at all, for that matter; but you asked what you can do to help. Just pray about it." Kyle smiled and patted Ronnie on the back as he walked onto the set.

"Three weeks ago, when the American Music Awards announced their 2009 nominees, my next guest was virtually unknown to anyone outside of New York or Canada. A week later, his single "I'm Yours" hit number one on the contemporary Christian charts. Here to perform that hit and his newest release, "Love, Unconditional" is Kyle Rivers-Tye!

♫Love sustaining, Love remaining, Love everlasting,
 In spite of what they say
 Your love is unconditional
 When I'm frightened, And when I falter,
 When they hurt me, And walk away
 Your love is unconditional♫

The studio audience remained standing as Kyle played the intro to his hit single.

♫I don't know why you help me
When I fail, and fail again
How you pick me up and tell me
The race is mine to win
I wanna be all I can be, all that you said I would
Oh Lord, you know me, like nobody ever could.♫

As Kyle sang the last line of the second verse, the curtain opened to reveal the choir, small by gospel standards, but powerful. Michael directed as they sang the refrain with everyone in the studio audience on their feet.

♫I'm Yours (God)!
(I am) I'm good!
You made me, as only you could!
I am!
I will go!
(I am) Your child, Lord!
That's all I need to know!)♫

Kevin danced his heart out. Kyle sang with his eyes closed. He knew better than to watch him. When they returned from the commercial break, Kevin joined Kyle on the guest couch.

Ronnie Reynolds was still dancing as Kyle and Kevin settled in. "Man, we haven't had chuch like that since... well, okay, we've never had chuch like that! Where did you come from?"

Kyle smiled. "Canada...by way of Jamaica."

"So, after your stops on the morning shows, I understand you had some problems with the 'gospel' folks."

"No, no, no. Not the people, 'the machine'. I love the people." Kyle wanted to be very clear.

"Okay, you said 'the machine' wasn't playing your music because you're gay."

"That's my theory, yes. No one seemed to be able to give me a better reason."

"Until after the shows? And then what did they tell you?"

Kyle smiled. "That my music wasn't 'gospel enough' for gospel radio."

Kevin and Ronnie laughed out loud. "Oh. Okay. Well, I'm gonna just put it out there. I listen to gospel radio. I have nieces and nephews and I and their parents don't allow them to listen to anything else unsupervised. Yeah, I know... And I wanna hear you when I'm stuck in my truck with 'my kids'. Did I say 'stuck'? I love my kids... We've been wearing this CD out." He held up Kyle's newest release. So say, you're right, Kyle. Let's say that the powers that be have determined that there is no place in gospel music for an openly gay man, and his dancing husband, his fabulous choir, and his happy choir director. What's wrong with that?"

"I think you already answered the question. Your kids listen to gospel music and they listen to my music. You know who I am. You don't let them listen to anything other than gospel radio unsupervised, because you don't want them exposed, right? Our son doesn't listen to regular radio for the same reason. But he can't listen to most gospel stations unsupervised, either, because we don't want anyone teaching him to judge people. We don't want him to hear from someone else that they think who his parents are, who he might be, is wrong. No singer has the authority to do that. Any 'gospel singer' should know better. My brothers and sisters are being assaulted, on morning shows, at the end of songs they dance to and sing and know all the words to. I want to contribute music that builds people up and encourages them to seek God. My gift isn't at the business end of music; I can't control what gets played. My hope is that someone will hear the difference and 'the machine' will stop being afraid of 'who I am' and 'who I love' and allow people to hear 'what I'm saying', what I believe God is saying through me. My prayer is that I can offer something that gives people the strength to stand up and say to the next person who tries to tell them they need to be delivered from who they are and who they love, 'You can't say that to me!'"

"Preach."

"See, I can't go on a regular morning radio show and start talking about God; because not everyone wants to hear all about why I sing and how I get through every day with people telling me I'm wrong. That's too heavy for pop music. So I think, 'fine, I'll go tell the people of God'. But then they tell me, 'you can talk about God, as long as you lie about who you are.' I'm not willing to do that; but I keep singing, because I am more than a gay man and I do have a testimony about God's love. But I can't talk to other 'believers' about the God who saved me from the world by sending His Son, because when I tell that I have to tell about the other things God did for me."

"What did He do, Kyle?" Ronnie asked.

"God made me different. God gave me a heart for people and a love for words and song. God put me in the most dangerous place in the world for a gay, bible-thumping, piano-playing, church-kid. That same God, my God, gave me to Kaleb and Naomi and told them to get me out of Jamaica. So, my mother left her whole family and moved with me, and my father, who worked like a slave in a suit to keep us safe and happy, to Toronto Canada, because they knew me. They could have said, 'don't be that, Kyle; that's wrong'. They could have pretended not to notice and waited for me to be abused and destroyed like every other little gay boi in Jamaica. But My God gave me to Kaleb and Naomi because My God loves me, and knew that they would love me, too. You can't tell me that God doesn't love me! You can't tell me that God didn't make me this way...unless you're ready to *stop* singing 'God is in control'! I'm not a surprise to the God who made the mountains, and the birds, and the seas! My God is the reason I speak five languages and could read music before most children could read books. My God gave me to parents who love and protected me. My God gave me gifts that until recently, I didn't know what to do with, because I had almost let some fool on the radio convince me that God couldn't use me 'like this'. But the devil is a liar! And when I said, 'Use me, Lord. Take my heart, my hands, my voice... use ALL OF ME, LORD for Your Glory, guess what My God did, Ronnie..."

"What'd He do, Kyle?" Ronnie was standing up pointing at Kyle.

"He sent me love." Kyle turned and pointed to Kevin who wanted to do his little dance so bad he could pee. Instead, he just waved and walked around the couch.

"Tell it." Ronnie was sitting again and rocking back and forth in his seat.

Kyle continued. "My God sent me my heart's desire and more kindness, and joy, and laughter, and patience, and passion, more love, than I ever imagined possible, in that man...yes, that beautiful man over there dancing for Jesus with the band... My God sent me this Amazing Love...but there are people who claim to know God and love God who would have me believe that God wouldn't do that, that God wouldn't put love for a man in another man. And I don't expect everyone to understand. I am sure that you have gifts I don't have or understand. But what I know is that this love, and who I am, and who he is to me…" Kyle pointed again to Kevin. "…is a gift from the same kind and loving God who made you, Ronnie…and the folks on the radio!

Ronnie was laughing and crying at the same time.

Kyle was fired up. "I'm sorry. I don't remember what the question was."

Ronnie answered through his laughter, "What are you going to do if you can't get your music on gospel radio, Kyle Rivers-Tye?"

"Oh. I'm just gonna keep singing…"

"Amen! Man, go sing your song! Is the choir still here? Just go sing! We're just gonna have church tonight. I'm gonna get fired tomorrow; but I am happy right now!"

Kyle, Kevin, Michael, the choir and the band returned to the stage and they had church right there on the set of the 'Ronnie Reynolds Show'. To Kyle's surprise, but no one else's, no one left and no one remained seated. The Holy Ghost party ended a full hour after the live show stopped.

As they were all leaving, Ronnie stopped Kyle and Kevin. "Whatever happens with the AMA's, whether they ever play your music on 104.9, that was the best show I've ever had and the best gospel concert I've ever been to. God bless you, my brothas."

Gabby called on their way home. "Oh…my…God…! Kyle!…" Gabby was screaming into the phone but still hadn't said a complete sentence.

Kevin took the phone from Kyle and set it down in the limo. "She's gonna be doing that for a minute."

"…Okay, my professional opinion?"

"Absolutely." Kyle fumbled to pick up the phone.

"You don't need to do another interview. I don't want you

to get over-exposed and you will not top what you just did on the 'Ronnie Reynolds Show'! If that doesn't get you airplay, you won't be getting it. They'll be watching that interview and that concert on *Youtube* for weeks. Just go home and rest... and write."

"So you're canceling the other shows?" Kyle couldn't contain the relief in his voice.

"Yes, if that's okay with you."

"Yes! Thank you!"

"Get some rest. I'll call tomorrow with the official numbers. Love you guys."

"We love you, too." They said together.

For the next month before the American Music Awards, Kyle followed Gabby's advice and laid low. He went back to focusing on church business and writing with Kevin, and he didn't leave Toronto. He tried to skip the ceremony altogether, but neither Kevin nor Gabby was having that. Kyle couldn't care less about winning an AMA, particularly when he still wasn't being heard on Black gospel stations; but Gabby reminded him that the old adage was true: it truly was an honor to be nominated. He needed to be in the audience when his name was called and his song was played along with other artists.

27

AND THE AWARD GOES TO...

Kyle's category was announced off air, near the beginning of the show. He did not win; but he agreed with Gabby that it felt good to hear the nomination. They all knew he was a long shot. In an effort to teach Ethan a lesson in sportsmanship, they stayed for the entire program. EJ had a blast seeing the live performances and all the stars. He jumped up and down when Riyonica crossed the stage to announce the Breakthrough Artist Award nominees. Kyle could have killed Gabby when his name was called in the same category as Lady Gaga, Keri Hilson, Gloriana, and Kid Cudi.

"And the award goes to..." Riyonica's face lit up. "...Kyle Rivers-Tye!"

Kyle kissed Gabby on the cheek; "I'll get you later." and brought Kevin and EJ with him to the stage.

"Wow. I know people always say they're surprised by these things... but I honestly had no idea I was even nominated for this." "... Okay, be brief, Kyle." He closed his eyes in a private moment of 'Thanks'. "To my parents, and my new family, thank you for loving me. To my church family, thank you for your patience. We did this! Gabby, okay, some secrets you can keep. Kevin and Ethan" He turned to look at them. "God and my parents gave me life; you make my life worth living ... and so much fun. To everyone who voted... wow... really? I don't have the words to tell you what this means. This is for the 'church kids'! Don't ever let anyone judge your experience or tell you about the God in you! Thank you!" He walked away from the podium, handed EJ the trophy and held Kevin's hand, holding it up in the air as they walked away.

That award would be one of the last of the night and no

one wanted to pretend they were interested anymore. Kevin had planned a surprise after-party at their apartment if they won. Gabby sent EJ to their suite with a sitter and followed the guys home in her own car. Kevin and Kyle opened the door to cheers and champagne. Their parents, Gary, Michael, Nikki, Gabby and new friends Ronnie and Rico toasted Kyle and teased him for not knowing about the second nomination.

"You really do need to pay attention to secular radio and TV, man. I didn't even believe them when they said you didn't know you were nominated." Ronnie shook his head.

"Well from now on, I'm doing whatever this lady tells me to do." Kyle put his arm around Gabby.

"Told ya." Gabby stuck her tongue out at Kevin.

"Oh shut up."

"No, you shut up!" Gabby winked at Kevin and relieved him of the champagne he seemed to be nursing.

Nikki walked over with Gary. "Hi, I'm Nikki. I was meaning to introduce myself at the wedding. Men are just rude."

"Tell me about it, especially these two." She waved her glass at Kevin and Gary. "I'm Gabrielle – Gabby."

"Nice to meet you Gabby. So, how did you land the Rev. Dr. Tye as a client? Reps in New York have been trying to sign him for years."

"I guess it's a family thing...I'm his baby-mama."

"You are not. Kyle Tye does not have a lovechild!" They both giggled at the thought.

"Hey! It could happen!" Gabby pretended to be insulted. "Actually, I was married to Kevin. My son is Kyle's stepson."

"You…" Nikki stepped back to look at Gabby. Gary and Kevin realized what was happening and tried to sneak away. Nikki caught them out of the corner of her eye. "Freeze…You were married to Kevin Rivers?"

"Yup, for almost eight years."

"So you got married in… "

"2001… but we'd been together forever before that. We'd been neighbors since we were six."

"Wow. Will you excuse me please, Gabby?"

"Sure…" Gabby polished off her champagne.

Nikki found Gary whispering to Kevin while Kyle watched them and chuckled. "You're fired; and you owe me a car!"

"Whatever…"Kevin wrapped his arms around Kyle. Nikki no longer had the power to fire him; and even if she had it, he wouldn't have cared.

"Okay, fine, you're not fired; but you", she pointed at Gary; "still owe me a car!"

"Why? He clearly *is* gay!"

"Actually, Nik, he is quite gay; I can vouch for him." Kyle kissed Kevin to demonstrate.

"He wasn't gay when you hired him! That…" Nikki pointed rudely at Gabby. "…is the opposite of a man!"

Michael had been watching the excitement while munching cheese and crackers and bounced over to help. "He really has been very, very gay for as long as I've known him."

"Oh, shut up, Mike! I can still fire you!" Michael laughed and took his snacks and water back to his chaise.

"I didn't know, Nikki." Kevin missed the whole 'not knowing is not relevant' conversation.

"He was confused; but he clearly meets The Company's criteria now." Gary was splitting hairs.

"Confused, my ass. He married a woman and had sex with her after you made me hire him! I want my Mercedes… in Navy, tomorrow!" Nikki was practically shrieking.

"Hey, you said if she found out you'd have to buy her a Prius!" Kevin wasn't helping at all.

"Actually, you did say that, Nikki." Gary prepared to surrender. His ears were ringing.

"That's because Mercedes didn't make the S Class in a hybrid in 2000. You promised me 'the new S Class' if he was straight. He was straight. I want the new Mercedes Benz S Class, hybrid, in navy blue… tomorrow."

"Ooh, that's nice… I have one." Gabby came over to see what all the fuss was about. "It's black though, not blue…wanna see it?"

"Thanks, no. Gary is going to buy me one tomorrow. Wanna come with?"

"Sure… can I bring my kid?"

"No!" Kyle and Kevin answered in unison. They didn't know what unholy mess was going on between Gabby and Nikki, but it scared them and they didn't want EJ anywhere near it. Kyle tried to clean it up. "We're taking him shopping."

"Well if I have to go car shopping, 'Twinkle-Toes' has to come, too. I told you, you spill, you split the cost."

Kevin looked at Kyle. "Don't look at me. I told you that little lie was gonna bite you in the butt. It sounds to me like you and Gary owe the lady a car."

"She's no 'lady'." Gary rolled his eyes.

"Fine, I'll pay, but I won't be seen in public with her." Kevin walked away and returned with a blank check, folded it and stuck it in Nikki's cleavage. "Go away."

"Oh, stop acting like you don't love me." Nikki put her arm around Kevin.

"I don't. You're mean… and funny looking!"

Kyle, Kevin and Ethan set out on their shopping expedition early the next morning. Ethan was still buzzing from the night before. He was used to seeing Broadway stars, but not people he'd heard on the radio and saw on television. "Dad, can we listen to something else, please?" He was also tired of the classic jazz and satellite news stations that were always on in Kyle's truck. Kyle was humming and not listening to the radio anyway and just shrugged at Kevin. Kevin shrugged back. Kyle thought they would try and endure one of the local hip-hop stations for EJ's sake; it was a short enough trip. He changed from satellite to the radio and pressed the 'seek' button. Kevin stabbed at the 'set' button the moment he heard Kyle's name:

"Last night's big AMA surprise was 'gospel newcomer' Kyle Rivers-Tye. I saw him on the *Ronnie* show a few weeks ago and could not believe we haven't been playing his stuff. Here he is with 'I'm Yours!'"

Kyle pointed upward and Kevin screamed as his favorite song filled the SUV. The three of them sang together and listened as if hearing it for the first time. When the song was over, Kevin shushed them as the station broke for a commercial. "That was Kyle Rivers-Tye with 'I'm Yours!' and you are listening to Joy Gospel 104.9!"

Read on for an excerpt from the next book by T. Randall Jones

Just Walk

Chapter Six
Gabrielle Nichols crazy, mixed up, mostly wonderful life...

"You're in room 2214, Mr. Reynolds. Will you be needing anything else this evening?" Ronnie shook his head but didn't look directly at the clerk. He just leaned against the counter and stared into the bar. He couldn't take his eyes off of her. Was she alone? If she were, it was surely by choice. She was in the darkest possible corner in an exclusive hotel. "She wants to be alone." Ronnie smiled to himself and turned toward the elevator. Gabrielle watched him walk across the lobby and into the elevator. His heart skipped a beat as their eyes finally met and the elevator doors closed.

Inside his room, he hung his garment bag in the closet and tossed his briefcase aside, forgetting for a moment that his laptop was also in there. He also forgot the urgent message to call his producer as soon as he checked in. Instead he brushed his teeth, washed his face and left the room. He breathed deeply as the elevator descended the twenty-two floors to the lobby. "Maybe she's gone." His heart raced as he realized she was still there. He noticed instantly that she'd removed her jacket, revealing her delicately sculpted shoulders. Ronnie shivered a little as he approached the table. "What'd she do that for? Like those legs aren't distracting enough?"

"May I join you?"

She didn't look up. "I can't talk about the trial." Not exactly a 'yes', but he sat anyway.

"Why on earth would I want to talk about that?" He smiled innocently at her.

"You seemed pretty adamant earlier." She turned her head slightly in his direction.

"I was doing my job, Ms. Nichols. As far as I'm concerned, you're as much a victim as the accusers in this case. Besides, I've been wanting to formally introduce myself since Kyle's AMA party."

"Oh yeah, I forgot..."

"Thanks." Ronnie held his left hand to his wounded heart. She watched him. He had nice hands, long, slender fingers, manicured nails and no jewelry.

"I'm sorry, there was a lot going on that night. Of course I remember you, Ronnie Reynolds. I meant I forgot that we'd already met prior to your shoving a microphone in my face today."

"Again, please forgive me. I'm paid to get the big story."

"I'm not the story. There is no story. I wish everyone would just leave us alone. It's just family stuff."

"You may not think so; but your support of your father is courageous. Where does that come from?"

"I told you, I can't talk about the trial."

"I'm not talking about the trial. I'm talking about you. How are you doing it?"

Gabby rolled her eyes and held up her glass. "I drink a lot."

Ronnie chuckled and stood to leave. She was clearly in no mood for company. "Okay, that's my cue. Enjoy your evening, Ms. Nichols."

"It's Gabby." Her smile stopped him in his tracks and took his breath away, but he kept his cool. He smiled back and held out his hand.

"It's a pleasure to make your acquaintance...again, Gabby." He sat back down and signaled for the waiter to bring two more of whatever she was having.

"Are you following me?"

Ronnie chuckled again. "Not intentionally, I promise. The network made my reservation. Are you staying here?"

"Yes."

"I thought you lived here in Atlanta?"

"You know I do, and apparently so does every other reporter in the Southeast. I can barely get down my street, let alone inside my house."

"I'm really sorry about that."

"Please don't tell anyone I'm here."

"Scouts honor." Ronnie held up three fingers and Gabby chuckled.

"What?"

"How could you possibly have figured out I was a Girl Scout already; and what possible relevance could that have to my father's trial?"

"Uh... none, I didn't." Ronnie's face grew hot. He watched Gabby sip her drink and stare passed him into the lobby. She wasn't thinking about his silly hand gesture, just wondering what was happening to her life. Ronnie stared at her face. She was lovely, with Barbie-doll features carved in Hershey's milk chocolate and natural curls pulled back into a loose twist at the nape of her swan-like neck. No one that beautiful should be so sad. Ronnie knew something about sad.

"Whatever." She seemed to be retreating into that dark place again. Ronnie didn't want her to go. He remembered their original meeting and his conversation with her ex-husband's new husband, his hero, Kyle Rivers-Tye.

"Well, a Girl Scout never forgets," he said. Gabrielle turned her gaze slowly back to Ronnie.

"I'm listening." After the year she'd had, nothing surprised her anymore. Ronnie searched her face and immediately saw the sadness in her pretty eyes turn to softness. She was a friend.

"Where should I start?"

"How long were you a scout?" They both giggled.

"Daisy to Junior, two years each, so six years."

"Ha! I was an Ambassador! I'd still be a Girl Scout if I'd had a daughter." She continued to giggle as she reflected briefly on her childhood. Then she was quiet again.

"What is it?"

"I am surrounded by... otherness..." She took a long sip of her drink. "I'm sorry...it's just that I'm starting to feel like Alice."

"In Wonderland?

"Yeah."

"You're just magnetic, that's all. Special people are drawn to you. I think that makes you pretty special, too."

"Whatever." She stared into her empty glass.

"Why so bitter?"

"Wouldn't you be if..."

"If what?" Ronnie listened intently while he watched a reporter from a competing network enter the lobby.

"If the only people you'd ever been attracted to were gay, and you weren't?"

"Oh. Yeah, that might bring me down a bit, I guess." Ronnie signaled for a waiter and paid for their drinks. "May I escort you to your room?"

"No thanks. I already know great sex is no indication of one's actual sexual preference."

"Wow. Um, I just thought that you might want to get out of here before the lights and the microphones start coming out..." Ronnie gestured to the blond checking in at the desk.

Gabby blushed. Even in her altered state she knew she'd stuck her foot in her mouth. "Oh. Thank you." She took his hand and he walked her quickly across the lobby and into the elevator.

"What floor?"

"Yours."

"Um...I would love to; but if she saw you with me, she'll have no trouble finding you in my room. There's a scandal neither of us need."

"Ooh. You're smart, too." Gabby twirled toward Ronnie, released his hand and wrapped her arms around his neck. Ronnie felt another familiar rush and breathed deeply. For the first time ever he was grateful for his...*otherness*. A million feelings washed over him as the most beautiful creature he'd ever seen pressed her body against him; ironically, most of them not sexual.

"What floor, Gabby?"

"Oh, yeah..." She still didn't say as she reached in her bag for her keycard and slipped it in his shirt pocket, letting her hand rest there.

He breathed deeply. "Gabrielle. Where are we going, sweetie?"

"Don't call me that! My son's father calls me that when he's mad at me. Shit. So does my actual father. Don't call me that. Are you mad at me?"

"No. Of course not; but we've been standing in this elevator for five minutes now. I can't get you to your room if I don't know what floor you're on."

"Oh. That's easy. The penthouse, silly."

"Of course...but why in the world were you down in the lobby?"

"I didn't want to be alone up there. I'm lucky you showed up, huh?"

"No, I'm the lucky one." Ronnie used Gabby's keycard to press the button to the penthouse.

Gabby continued to cling to Ronnie during the express, yet still excruciatingly slow ride to the top floor. The doors finally opened and Gabby stumbled slightly into the palatial suite. She seemed completely unfamiliar with her surroundings but managed to find the phone and called down for a bottle of champagne. Ronnie just watched her. He just wanted to be sure she was safe, and then he was leaving. He didn't want to take advantage of her or let her do anything she'd regret. He was relieved that she was hiding out and wouldn't be calling anyone else for company. He was even more relieved when she kicked off her stilettos and climbed into bed with most of her clothes still on. He walked to her bedside and pulled the covers over her shoulders.

She reached up to him. "Don't go. You're nice."

He held her hands and smiled down at her, pointing to the couch at the far end of the room. "I'll be right over there." Before he made himself comfortable, he called back down to cancel her bottle of champagne. "That's the last thing she needs."

Ronnie sat for a long time watching Gabby before falling to sleep himself. Completely plastered, or as his brother would say, 'toe-up from the flo-up', she even slept like an angel. No snoring, no drool, no tossing; just the occasional whimper. After several of those puppy-like sounds, he considered lying next to her, even stood to go to her; but then he thought better of it. Wide-awake, she was more than a little amorous. No telling what she would do if she stirred and found him in bed with her. And while variations of this moment had played in his head since the moment he first laid eyes on her, he knew this was not *the* moment. He wanted her, in a million different ways, but drunk and likely to press charges in the morning was not one of them. Besides, he knew it was the bourbon talking, not Gabrielle Nichols. As he became aware of his protective instincts kicking in and overriding his urges, Ronnie felt more masculine in that moment than he had in any of his way too many sexual encounters. Was this the moment his therapist eluded to, when he would 'stop acting like a man and just be one'? His mind wandered and he slowly drifted off to sleep.

Gabby woke in the middle of the night. Still a little tipsy, she looked around and tried not to panic. She watched Ronnie Reynolds sleeping on the couch, recalled the hours before she fell asleep and instantly checked to make sure she had clothes on. She was still wearing her dress and panties. She didn't remember anything happening. If she'd had a blackout, it would be her first. She relaxed a little as she watched him, feeling like a girl again. The only thought she could articulate was "he's so damn cute." Not 'fine' or 'sexy' like Kevin. Ronnie had a quality Gabby could not put her finger on, even as she lay across the bed watching him sleep. In his, classically handsome, face there was softness, something sweet. The voice was perfect, strong, more alto than tenor, but still, masculine, sultry. And those hands! Gabby closed her eyes for a moment and remembered Ronnie's touch. She let her mind and her hands wander down her own body as she imagined his hands. She sighed as she reached her hemline, which had drifted from just below her knees to the top of her thighs. As soft as it was, the sound she made woke him and he silently bolted upright.

"I didn't mean to wake you." She pulled the covers back over her hips hoping he hadn't noticed where her hands had been.

"I didn't mean to fall asleep." He stood, stretched and walked toward her. Gabby squeezed her thighs together. "I should go." She realized she should see him out and tried to get out of bed and stand without looking like complete trash. She tried to ignore the heat...

She finally made it to the door, and wondered for a moment why he was leaving. Then she wondered why she cared. He was one of them. "Thank you."

If Gabby weren't perfection, Ronnie didn't have a clue. "What for?"

"For keeping me company and for not...for everything."

"It was my pleasure, really..." He paused before turning to the door. "Would you like to have dinner with me tomorrow?"

"Well, the trial is just getting started. I don't want..."

"I understand. I'm sorry I asked. Good night."

"No. Wait. I want to, Ronnie." She touched his bare forearm. Bliss.

"Then meet me-here, somewhere else. I don't care. Just tell me when and where." His sudden burst of enthusiasm startled them both, but only for a moment. He smiled down at her and held out his hand. She stared at it for a long time before taking it, and he pulled her toward him, and kissed her slowly. In the second before it happened, she thought "no! I haven't brushed! Yuck!" But as their lips met, the world went away along with her protest. She reached for his face; it was baby-smooth. He caressed her curls and stepped back slowly until his back found the door, pulling her closer to him. She inhaled his scent and sighed deeply. She pulled away slowly. "I'm sorry, I shouldn't have."

"But you did. How did you?" She wasn't angry. She was confused.

Ronnie stared at her. "I don't understand."

"Aren't you gay? How can you kiss me like that, if you don't *love* women?"

"I never said I was gay, Gabby; and I assure you, I adore women." He reached for her arm and pulled her in again. A little more sober now and a lot more confused, she kissed him back, reluctantly this time. Ronnie thought it would really be okay if the world ended in that instant and resolved not to move from that spot on the wall. That moment, that kiss was enough. When Gabby reached for his hands and guided them to her waist and let go, so did he. "I'll see you tomorrow? Eight o'clock?"

Gabby opened her eyes and sighed. But without his touch, the spell was instantly broken, and she returned to the real world. "I can't promise; but I'll try. My brother's supposed to testify tomorrow. I expect it's going to be a very bad day."

Ronnie nodded slowly. "I can imagine. Let me keep you company. I'll even bring dinner. Call me and let me know what you're in the mood for."

"You're very sweet. Why? How do you even have time for all of this? Shouldn't you be working?"

"I do have things to do. They'll get done. I'm taking a break from the show, though, and just freelancing mostly. I've got access to a crew, but there's no pressure..." Ronnie closed his eyes for a moment. No pressure, just his whole world: the woman of his dreams; a trial that could change his career, and a decision to make.

"What?"

He opened his eyes and smiled at her. "That's all. I'll see you tomorrow." He touched her hair and backed into the waiting elevator.

About the Author

Tia Randall Jones is a writer-activist, occasional poet and accidental songwriter. She writes to uplift, inspire and celebrate gay, lesbian, bisexual and transgender people of faith, and to affect positive change by telling their stories. She lives in North Carolina with her family, and is currently, and always, working on her next novel.

www.TRandallJones.com